"Lena, wait."

"Find someone else to believe your bullshit," I called back.

I made it through the restricted door and back into the long white hallway leading out to the top floor of the mall before he caught up.

"Lena, let me explain. Please, I'm not lying." Arthur grabbed my forearm. I stopped running as soon as I passed the door. I never thought he would hurt me in any way, but I did not need another weirdo in my life. I halted in his hold, hoping no extra attention would be drawn toward us if someone walked by.

"You must have mistaken my grandmother and me for some other family. We are not witches. We have no powers."

"Tell that to the mole on the side of your eyebrow. You may be avoiding your birthright, but you can't deny you feel it in your skin, your bones, your heart." His pointer finger touched my sweater over my heart.

"Oh my God, it's a mole. A small bundle of tissue that gets irritated every time I wax. That does not mean I'm a witch. I feel nothing in my heart other than your finger intruding into my personal space."

He scoffed, dropping his hand down to his side. "You were a witch at some point. Maybe a hundred years ago, or a thousand years ago."

Praise for Melanie Hoffer

Reviews of Falling for Two
"Falling for Two is a steamy tribute to throuple positivity. I absolutely loved this book."

"Holy Guacamole! Five red hot exploding sticks of dynamite! This review is over because I have to go take a cold shower!"

"Couldn't put it down since I picked it up! Hope to see more!"

Reviews of Spritz Cookie Showdown
"This was a cute little read!"

"Oh the sexy tension!"

"Short and sweet. A cute and fun Christmas read!"

No Witch Here

by

Melanie Hoffer

A Witchy Duet Book

This is a work of fiction. Names, characters, places, and incidents are either the product of the author's imagination or are used fictitiously, and any resemblance to actual persons living or dead, business establishments, events, or locales, is entirely coincidental.

No Witch Here

Cover Art by *Diana Carlile*

The Wild Rose Press, Inc.
PO Box 708
Adams Basin, NY 14410-0708
Visit us at www.thewildrosepress.com

Publishing History
First Edition, 2023
Trade Paperback ISBN 978-1-5092-4926-8
Digital ISBN 978-1-5092-4927-5

A Witchy Duet Book
Published in the United States of America

Dedication

This book is dedicated to my grandmothers. I love you both so much. Thank you for teaching me to dream big!

Prologue

The air prickled around me like static off a balloon. I stopped scrubbing the dirty plate in my hand. The last of Grandmother's bridge club left ten minutes ago. No one should be mourning in my living room. Respect had been paid in full.

"Are we too late?"

A voice boomed through the small hallway toward the kitchen. The spray of lukewarm water, tolerable a moment ago, singed my skin. I yanked my hand away, the plate clattering into the sink. Pain seared through the tops of my fingers, leading around to my wrist. The small soft patch of skin pulsing from my heartbeat ached the most.

"Hello? Anyone alive in here?"

Grandma's ashes rested on the small table in front of the poster board of photos from her life. I hated the latecomers already. The words *too soon* bounced in my head.

"Yes, I'll be there in a minute," I shouted.

I rubbed my sore hand and rounded the corner toward the living room. I almost tripped on the dog-eared corner of my carpet runner because at least twenty people of all ages huddled around my grandmother's urn. Dressed all in black, each person displayed a different stage of grief. Women, wearing heavy lace dresses, cried into handkerchiefs. One man wailed his tears into the shoulder of another man standing next to him.

"Lena?" My name floated up from the strangers.

The pungent odor of extinguished flames filled the room. All the candles I lit had been blown out.

"Do you have a leader?" I scanned the first row of mourners. Their brows knitted together, and trapped tears rested on their bottom eyelids. My grandmother had been a popular woman. For all I knew, these people were from her yoga class or the cult she accidentally joined a few years back.

"We're not aliens, dear. There is no leader, but I keep track of the members," the speaker answered. As if the queen arrived, the others parted, and an older gray-haired woman stepped forward. "Your grandmother was very important to us. I am so sorry for your loss. How kind of you to allow people in your home for a memorial."

"I didn't want the undertaker rushing us out of the funeral home." I blurted out the truth.

"Smart thinking, dear. Your grandmother would be proud of you."

Her hand beat against her chest, covering her heart. She kept the patting at a steady pace distracting me from another person's sorrowful sentiment. One by one, the other members expressed their condolences, lifting their fists and patting their own hearts. By the time each one spoke, their pounding fists created a low, irritating hum.

An overwhelming sense of confusion forced a curt smile on my face. No one revealed any clues as to whom they were to my grandmother. "I just cleaned up, but can I get anyone a cookie or coffee?"

"That won't be necessary," the leader remarked. "We should be on our way."

With their heads bowed down and hands clasped in front of them, as quick as they appeared, one by one, the odd crowd shuffled out my front door. The leader stayed back. She blessed herself in a Christian way over my grandmother's urn. Before the "Amen" left her ruby lips, her knees gave out, tumbling her to the floor.

"Ma'am!" I rushed over to the woman. Each exhale of her panting breath grew louder, almost panicked, when she tried lifting her head off the carpet. Her shaky palms slipped as if her body became a dense metal anchor weighing her down.

My fingertips brushed against the back of her black lace dress. Static shock pierced down my right hand, bothering the same area I scalded with the hot water. I reached out again, but the woman inched away from my touch.

"Babushka, we need to leave," a young man said. He stood outside, right before the threshold. His palm smacked the weatherworn molding decorating my doorway. His dark gaze tainted a handsome face with an angular jawline models lusted over. He said something else in a language I couldn't place. His annoyance was apparent in English and the other.

"Coming."

I stared at the man long enough that the woman stood up and walked around me. Her flustered breathing slowed back to normal, and she waved before she reached the front door.

"Who are you?" I asked.

"Oh, we're your grandmother's coven. Goodbye, Lena."

Babushka walked out the door, past the man who scolded her. He nodded his head with an expressionless

3

face, and his long arm reached into the foyer, slamming my front door shut. I rose from my crouched position and ran after them.

I threw open the front door. No one stood on the long path leading to my garage, lined with this season's dying, orange cosmos. No cars remained parked by the curb, either. I never heard them arrive, and I missed their exit.

My grandmother's coven? Who the fuck were they?

Chapter One

The training video I designed loaded onto my computer screen. People already logged in, and a few more names popped up on the shared viewing platform. There should be five more participants, but at three in the morning my time, I barely kept my eyes opened as I pressed the start button. Luckily, the German company learning about their new remote communication system only saw the pre-recorded video and not my current state.

Twenty minutes of video, then thirty minutes for questions. I muted the microphone and worked on my second job. Ten special arrangements organized and primped for my best friend Kim's gift basket business. A candle, a package of gourmet cookies or nuts, a pouch of gemstones, and a piece of jewelry personally picked by her with the recipient's tastes in mind. I twirled a small bee pendant on a copper chain around the small tube of gift-wrapping paper. Kim barely curled ribbon well, but her business boomed thanks to me and my ex, Kim's brother, Ray, who snored from my couch.

A long yawn shook my body all over. My heavy eyelids blinked closed too long, and my head thudded back against my desk chair. The annoying alarm signaling the training video had five minutes left jarred me awake.

"Is the call over?" Ray called from the living room.

"No, go back to sleep."

The old couch groaned as Ray sat up from his sleeping position. He took a swig from the beer leaving a dirty ring on my coffee table. When we broke up two years ago, for a long time, we stayed apart. I did better than him bouncing back into the world. Overdosing on gummy bears and wine helped me crawl up from break-up hell. But, due to Kim, many nights I watched him sleep, waiting for my finishing touches on his sister's gift baskets. I put aside a lot of the emotional triggers and the remaining fringes of desire for him.

One thing had me almost losing the battle each time he slept over. Drowsy looked sexy as fuck on him. After he took off his shirt, removed his trucker hat, and slipped off his thick-rimmed glasses, the memories rushed back of our quality time snuggle sessions ending in us fucking at least twice on the couch.

I ignored his shuffling zombie walk to the bathroom. My traitorous side gaze caught him lifting his undershirt, granting me a peak at the fine trail of dark hair leading down toward his dick.

"You're going to catch a fly in your mouth if you keep ogling me," Ray accused.

"You wish," I threw back.

My second alarm shrilled over his response. I imagined him saying 'yes, I do.' We had been down that road before. I avoided it ever since he kissed me on the mouth by accident.

"Thank you so much for watching. Please stay tuned for the Q and A portion of the demo," the pre-recorded script stated. One more yawn forced its way out of my mouth. I hated the middle-of-the-night demos.

The manager, an American transplant, thanked me for hosting them and waking up at the ungodly hour.

After Ray flushed the loudest toilet known to man, I cranked the volume of the microphone up.

"You're welcome. Did everyone get a chance to preview the program before the call?" I asked.

Sure enough, the second the sensitive microphone picked up any stray sound from my kitchen, Ray farted like a bulldog after a full meal. The man in the bubble on the far right smiled, then laughed behind his palm. I threw a bag of caramelized nuts at Ray. He caught it and opened his mouth wide, grinding the tops of the teeth together. I flashed him the middle finger, then pointed toward the stairs. He tip-toed away, tearing open the pretentious bag of nuts.

I missed the first person talking in my fury. At least, the people on the call were ignorant to the tussle of two exes, bound together every Wednesday night. I caught up quickly, answering the few questions in record time. I ended the call and resumed my product arranging. Three baskets remained undone. Ray ate the nuts for the last one, so I improvised from last month's special gift items. *Hopefully, Kim won't notice.*

My fingers hurt from curling all that damn ribbon and twisting the perfect bows, but I completed all ten baskets. Ray always snuck out of my house early, lugging two baskets at a time to his truck. One tucked under his arm and the other swinging from his hand, disrupting the meticulous placement I worked hard on. Once they left here, it was Kim's problem.

Ray never returned to the sofa after my call ended, which meant only one thing. I turned off all the lights and tip-toed up the stairs toward my bedroom. Ray lay curled up on his old side of my bed, drooling on the extra pillow. Most of the times when that happened, I slept on the couch. Too many times, I woke up to a hard temptation humping me into an impulsive decision. I swore never again.

Perhaps, extreme emotional tiredness propelled me forward. I pulled back the soft and warm comforter, stretching out underneath. I stared at Ray's sleeping face, noticing a few new fine lines between his eyebrows and deeper grooves in his forehead. He looked good for thirty-five, better than thirty-three. Back then, his drinking got out of hand, and his reckless behavior made me fall out of love with him.

In quiet moments like now, I remembered why I wanted him back and placed the love spell on him.

One night, my last fling, dubbed the 'new guy,' showed his true colors in front of a bar full of his friends. The drunken slurs vomiting from his mouth disgusted me. We had talked about our morals and values, but he spoke his true feelings. I exited the bar and walked into a taqueria with a back entrance on the occult side. I thought I drove there, but one glance over my shoulder proved I walked the five miles across town with no memory of the distance.

The door opened, and the Brujah with a scar slashing across her nose, appeared in the doorway. My conversational Spanish sucked, but nothing mattered. She knew what I wanted and needed. The red candles with black wicks shaped anatomically correct of a woman and a man waited on the table. A once living vine with thorns laid next to them.

"*Usalos esta noche*," the Brujah instructed. I understood Spanish more than I spoke. I had only tonight to use the spell. "*Dura un ano*." The spell lasted one year.

I had wondered if the vine would shrivel up or the

candles might melt without the aid of a match if I waited too long to do the spell. The elderly woman, with her skin sagging off her bones, kissed my forehead like my *abuela* did and shooed me off as if I snatched a piece of guava out of an unfinished tart.

A cab waited outside the closed restaurant. The driver took no payment for the trip back to the bar. I thanked him, and a kind smile appeared on his tan face. My awful date's car remained in the furthest parking spot, so drunken idiots would not mar the perfection. *His words, not mine.* Temptation almost lured me over there with my sharpest key. I resisted the urge.

I flew home, avoiding all the known police traps. My car rattled after I sped up to eighty. Nothing slowed me down until a drop of my blood spilled onto the foil take-out container holding the candles. A thorn on the vine pierced my skin deep enough for a steady set of blood droplets. I smeared my blood over the female candle.

I searched my house for any trace of Ray hidden inside my world. I gave up until I remembered his aftershave buried in the clutter of my bathroom closet. I dosed the male candle with the spoiled cologne. At the stroke of midnight, I lit both candles with a match, not an automatic lighter.

A flash of light streaked across the sky, followed by a rumble of thunder. The lights in the hallway flickered, and the clock on my cable box flipped back to midnight, blinking every other second. I had enough brightness from the flames extending off the quickest burning candles I had ever seen. The man and the woman bound by blood-stained ivy melted together. Her breasts and his chest became one as the wax dripped down.

The flames extinguished themselves after passing the couple's sexes. I assumed the important parts were covered. That night, I slept a deep sleep unlike any other until my house phone interrupted the bliss. Kim, Ray's sister, had too many orders for her new business and asked for my help. Ray came by that afternoon and every Wednesday since thereafter.

I inched closer to Ray. His warm breath heated my face. We laid the closest we had been in a long time. As if my gaze disturbed him, his sleepy eyes opened. The strong hand I once wanted forever caressed my hip, nudging me closer.

Our heavy eyelids drifted close. A storm in the distance came out of nowhere like an errant firework shooting off without a holiday to celebrate. My body jerked when a gasp left my mouth.

"I got you, baby," Ray said with his eyes closed.

He wrapped himself around me, tucking my head under his unshaved chin. His muscle memory warmed me as the thunder warned me.

This could not happen again.

I didn't love him anymore.

****

Since the end of the summer, Ray rushed out of my house by eight in the morning. His fall semester as a history professor began a few weeks ago, and his first class started at noon. My internal clock betrayed me, waking me up right as he drove away.

I stripped the sheets off my bed, resisting smelling the side where he slept. Once upon a time, I loved his boy smell. It might be a combination of all the fanciest spices and chemicals in the world, but I only smelled him.

That morning, he picked up after himself. He placed the beer cans into the recycling, pulled the trash bin up to the end of the driveaway, but he fucked up the kind gestures in a blender by leaving a note on my dry-erase board.

We slept together. Don't tell Kim.

I rolled my eyes. His message whispered into my ear as if he spoke his baritone voice beside me. Sleeping in the same bed hardly struck me as scandalous, considering all the other stuff we had done before. We didn't even kiss! I wished I felt something toward it, but I did not.

Ray added more material for my therapist. She knew about the love spell. Ironically, Doctor Greene had been to the restaurant where I got the candles. The fact that they had an occult shop behind the kitchen had not surprised her.

For days and months after I lit the candles, sprinkled my blood and Ray's cologne on them, I thought I imagined the whole night in my head. The cut from the thorn never left a mark on my skin, and I hid the remaining evidence far enough out of arms' reach in the attic. I possibly threw out the candles permanently fused to the foil container when I had the leak in the attic last spring.

One spec of proof remained. The ringing in my ear grew louder as I placed my coffee mug on my dinette table. I hid the scorch mark where the spell stained the center of my table. The flames hadn't reached down to the varnished surface, but I had gone too far.

My pointer finger nudged the vase hiding the burn a few inches forward. If I checked it enough times, it might possibly disappear. *No such luck.*

At nine o'clock sharp, Kim called.

"You threw a bag of nuts at him and let him eat it!" Kim's voice yelled into the phone. Her kids shouted in the background. The daily chaos already was reaping havoc.

"Ray knew the consequences of his actions. He's a big boy."

"He's a big baby. He scared me half to death, barging into the kitchen, spilling the beans about the nuts, and you guys sleeping together."

So much for keeping that a secret. "For the record, we only slept in the same bed because Zombie Ray sleeps like the dead. Nothing else happened," I explained.

Kim huffed into the phone. "From how he acted this morning, it sounded like more. I don't want to overstep, but you were my friend before you dated him. Did he mention Chloe, or do I have to be the voice of reason?"

I swore the blackened spot in the middle of my table bubbled like heated oil in a frying pan. The sizzling sound accompanied it.

"Chloe? As in the college admissions lady, Chloe?"

Kim sighed. "Yup, that's the one. I feel like I'm beating a dead horse. I know you two have been over, but I think a part of me still wishes you became my sister-in-law. I'm not telling you this to hurt you or re-stink your dirty laundry. Ray is dating Chloe again. If he's going to mess around with you, he needs to break it off with her. It's the right thing to do."

Sharp pain stabbed my frontal lobe above my left eye. "Fucking fantastic. There is nothing going on between us. In fact, I shouldn't have to tolerate him if he's seeing her."

After a brief pause, Kim asked, "Have your Wednesday nights been that awful?"

"No, they're fine. I feel like things have run their course between Ray and me. Things got a little blurry last night. If he's finally dating someone, then maybe we can both move on."

Kim grew quiet. She encouraged Ray and my relationship long before the spark started. I missed the awkward dinner parties at her house with the place settings conveniently placing Ray and me next to one another. My favorite parts were the annoying, "Oh, Lena loves pandas, how about you, Ray?" games. We caught on to the charade fast. *Ah, the fun days.*

"I suck as a matchmaker. It's all my fault," Kim remarked.

"It's okay. I swear, I'll get through this like last time. Make it up to me when we are in the city."

"I promise we can go to any bookstore and stationery store."

"That's the way back into my heart. I got to go."

"Sounds good. Let's catch up next…" A large crash followed by two high-pitched giggles cut her off. "Layla, go to your room! Time-outs for both of you! Sorry, Lena, my kids are little monsters. I'll talk to you soon."

"You bet."

I finished my cup of coffee in silence. The old radio my grandfather built a mini shelf for had months of dust covering it. Mornings like these, I meditated, alleviating stress and listening to music, keeping my tinnitus controlled. Since my grandmother died in June, I'd lost that content state. My depression took it away.

Maybe I could write about that? The fresh notebook I bought for my therapy session remained empty. The stiff spine groaned as I peeled it open. A few times, I tried writing to no avail. For half my life, I journaled my thoughts. Like too many other things, I abandoned that pastime.

Doctor Greene had a lot of patience. She must forgive me.

Chapter Two

I wrote three words before I sat down that afternoon in the squeaky leather chair across from my therapist. "I am done."

"Do you want to talk about what that might mean to you?"

"It took a whole week to write it. I think I didn't want you to be upset with me for not doing the assignment."

"Lena, that's not how therapy works, but it might be a consequence of a conditioned personality trait. If you have always done things because you believe people might abandon you or grow impatient, what are you doing for yourself?"

"I bought ten romance novels when I picked up the notebook. I did that for me."

Doctor Greene laughed, scribbling in her own notebook resting on her lap. We sat in her New Jersey home office with a beautiful view of the New York City skyline on sunny days. On our first meeting, we sipped coffee on her deck and chatted like we had known each other for years. The refreshing chemistry faded more and more each time we had a session.

I cringed when she wrote things down. A bad habit probably spurred from watching too many sitcoms with a therapist episode. She assured me her notes had both good and trigger-worthy jots.

"Am I replacing insecurity with a joke?" I asked. There I went again, attempting the upper hand.

"I doubt buying ten books is a joke for you. If nothing moves you enough to write, then so be it. It's not the end of the world. Like you said last week, you are in a different state of mind than when you used to write. Do you remember any instances that made you want to write stuff down as soon as you got home or a specific time when you found it difficult to write?"

She was good. I appreciated her ease when she pried information out of me. The good times before my grandmother died, when I almost got engaged to Ray, and the bad times unfurling from deep within my memory.

"I remember the day I stopped writing. My grandmother threw me a tea party for my sixteenth birthday. She bought dozens of little teacakes and petit fours and used real tea in fancy teacups. I loved every minute of it until I finished my tea, and she read my fortune. Her happy spirit dimmed as she swished around the muck at the bottom of the cup. She didn't speak, and when she looked at her own tea leaves, the party was over. She dropped both cups, and they smashed on the dining room floor. It took two days for her to realize she had a heart attack."

"How could you not know you're having a heart attack?"

"Her left arm never hurt, and she thought she ate a bad watercress sandwich. My grandmother never used her gift again."

Doctor Greene's bottom eyelids twitched upward. These types of facial spasms ruffled my spirits. My insurance said Doctor Greene dealt with a variety of patients. Three months in, I still had my doubts.

"There is that word again. When you refer to your grandmother, you often use the word 'gifts.' Did she do anything else besides read tea leaves?"

We collided into another level of poking and prodding. I forgot I mentioned her gifts before. My grandmother called her powers her gifts. I wanted my therapy sessions separate from the other part of my life. I needed to be more careful.

"She always did weird things," I added.

"Do other people on that side of the family venture into the mystical?"

"I never asked. I usually avoid it at all costs."

Doctor Greene cocked an eyebrow. "Bullshit, Lena. What about the love spell?"

"I had a weak moment. It's over now. Ray is dating a co-worker. I never believed I made him come back into my life. Coincidences happen. I played around, but there is no witch here."

"Maybe that's why you wrote *I am done*. Your heart has healed. You can finally let Ray go."

The soft grinding of the ceiling fan rotating on the metal piston filled the air. The fresh gardenia candle's flame tilted away from the artificial breeze. The truth stared me in the face in the form of an unconventional shrink.

My defense mechanisms pressured me into silence. I wished I could disappear into the haze hoovering over the city buildings across the Hudson River. The purple walls squeezed around me.

I flinched when Doctor Greene stood in front of me with a cup of water. "You're good at your job," I muttered.

The large shoulder pads of her power blazer lifted as she shrugged. "I like puzzles, but most of all, I love when my patients figure out their issues on their own."

"What do I do now?"

"That's up to you. Try a new dating site, make some new friends, find a new hobby, plant something?"

"Read?"

"Only if you are in a café with a hot barista who can't take their eyes off you and gives you a free biscotti with your order. If not, you can't meet a man on the way from your bathroom to the couch. Trust me, I know." She dangled her ringless left hand. "I think we hit a small breakthrough today. It can be emotional when your life suddenly makes sense. Let's tack the time left onto next week's session."

I nodded. The cold water with freshly squeezed lemon felt damn good going down my dry throat. I took several deep breaths and reached for my jacket on the arm of the chair.

"If you'd like a minute alone to reflect, I can step outside." She smiled and motioned toward the door.

"I think I'm going to be okay."

Her contagious smile infected me too. I shook her hand and left the pristine room with a smile on my face. After the session, I was a complete wreck.

Is it a good thing to dig up old memories or a bad thing?

I hadn't thought about my sixteenth birthday in years. Back then, I never thought reading tea leaves could be a display of my grandmother's powers. She did it at parties after everyone slipped into a dessert coma, much like dancing with a glass of water on her head when a merengue song came on. Her predictions made her friends smile, laugh, and wonder if she told the truth.

I thought she mastered a party trick, nothing more. I missed that she was a witch, and my mother could have been one too.

In my defense, growing up, witchcraft and vampires were all the rage in pop culture, not real life. Instead of crushing over a boy band phase, my two best friends and I went through a witch phase. It was all pretend, hoping we became cool in the eyes of our peers. I doubted the reality of being a real witch most of all.

My oldest best friend bought a book and highlighted every passage that spoke to her. Our other friend, who had joined us in sixth grade, tumbled the stones from her mother's garden, carrying them with her for strength and protection. I did the opposite. I adopted a black rescue kitten and tried twitching my mouth back and forth without moving my nose. Those days weren't perfect, but something wild brewed inside me.

I believed if a person was a witch, there was no need for wands, spells, or random placement of cards to do magic. If your gifts did not come from deep within your soul, they were simple parlor tricks. I struggled to find my own *fake* powers until I realized everything I experienced was real. As soon as I started school, I began writing poems, quotes, and phrases, freestyle as I called it, for hours until my hand begged for mercy. I never looked while my hand blurred over the paper, yet somehow the words stayed perfectly in line. The handwriting was legible, only the words were not. Symbols, letters with extra loops and dips, punctuated in erratic spaces. I believed I wrote down spells for my craft. I never spoke any of the words out loud. Any time I opened my mouth to speak, my lips closed a few seconds later without a peep out of me. My secret remained hidden until my mother found the journals. I played it off as Latin homework. I thought she had believed the lie.

On my sixteenth birthday, I tried filming myself in a writing session with my grandfather's old camcorder before the guests arrived for the party. I expected my eyes to look like cloudy, unseeing orbs and watch the table levitate off the floor. No such luck. My hand froze, and my mind blanked. I couldn't write at all.

My grandmother walked into the room and chuckled in her knowing way. She turned off the camera and sat down next to me. "Lena, your gift is for your eyes only and maybe mine if I'm lucky. Don't force it, child."

"Mother, please, don't do this. It skipped me. Let it pass over her."

We turned toward my mother standing in the doorway. Fresh tears streamed down her face. Her hands hugged herself around her waist.

"Very well then. Lena, let's get you into your party dress."

I wanted to ask more about what they talked about, but my younger cousin Dee bounced into the room in a beautiful twirl-worthy dress. The topic of conversation became out of sight, out of mind.

I abandoned my gift that day. I stopped writing free-hand and typed everything thereafter. I typed fast, like a person running out of air, but every word understandable. In college, I learned the coding language needed for a high-tech communication program. No funny business until today.

I got home from Doctor Greene's house at about two in the afternoon, and my fingers itched to write. The almost empty notebook weighing down my purse pulsed against my rib cage. "I know, I hear you. Give me a minute."

As if the intimate object listened, I shushed it out loud. Instead of the kitchen table, I walked upstairs to my vanity table. It seemed silly to keep such a trivial piece of furniture, but my grandmother owned it forever. My mother even used it for a short span of time as a child. I rarely used it for its actual purpose, except to check the warped mirror for lipstick on my teeth every now and again.

A magnetic force drew me toward the wooden table with the drawers lined with wallpaper from the fifties, stained with makeup from long ago. The old stool with the worn pink cushion welcomed me as well as the aroma of my grandmother's floral perfume. If I opened a drawer, the smell overpowered the entire bedroom. Right now, the small crack in the top drawer wrapped me in its reassuring memories, smelling sweet instead of rancid.

I dragged the notebook out of my black carry-all bag and placed it on the mirrored vanity top. A simple spiral-bound red book with glossy pages, smaller than a school notebook, with a cheap ribbon, already fraying at the end, dangling out of the spine. Natural light streamed through my bedroom window, casting a small glow on the gold embossed moon and filigree on the cover.

Much like I did for everything nowadays, I set an alarm for a half hour, and to my surprise, when the annoying bells sounded, I had twenty pages of gibberish bleeding through the back of the pages. I pried open my dry mouth, the middle of my lips sticking together for a moment. My pen fell from my shaking, aching right hand into my lap. I did it. I wrote more after all that time.

I slammed the notebook shut, cursing myself for using the notebook designated for my therapy sessions. Pacing the carpeted room helped calm me down, but the retched notebook glared from the table, almost as if it laughed and said, "Told you I'd be back."

My hands ached to put it away, tuck it into one of the vanity drawers until next Thursday's meeting with Doctor Greene. I caught my reflection in the old spotted mirror. Ink stained my hands, and smudges of the blue peeked through my bangs and dirtied my cheeks.

"Lena, what did you do?" I said out loud. Cold water and half a container of soap did not clean my hands of the ink. My fingertips and palms became an odd shade of blue, as if I had oxygen issues. The nagging thought that I never truly gave up my hope of being a real witch poked at my mind.

An incoming text cracked through my manic episode.

—*What time are you getting to the club?*— Amy texted.

—*You mean, the mall?*—

—*Yes, the mall. I might be a little late.*—

—*K, I'll buy some stuff I don't need at the bookstore while I wait.*—

—*No, go to the club. The seating is first come, first serve.*—

—*All right, later.*—

I forgot about Amy and my girls' night out. She had underlined every passage in her occult book she bought at a church charity sale back in high school. Kim took her tumbled gravel stones and made her side hustle gift basket business a reality. We stayed friends these past fifteen years, but Kim and Amy had a falling out. Neither of them ever mentioned those days when we tried becoming our own coven.

Both girls never thought I took our witch phase seriously. I kept my automatic writing a secret. My crazy grandmother seemed normal at our sleepovers, and I played the disinterest card every time they brought up how they saw something or felt the plastic planchette on the *Quija* board move. I annoyed them with my nonchalant attitude and eye rolls until the day we all scared ourselves.

Let's see if my therapist can extract that painful memory in a session. I'll pay her double if she can.

Chapter Three

Our town's comedy club resided in the mall. Every comedian spent at least five minutes of their opening monologue on the fact that they bought underwear and marshmallow cereal on their way to their night gig. It got old fast.

Amy won the tickets at her job's company barbecue picnic over the summer. Cheap prize, if you asked me. She spent double the price of the early bird comedy show on the raffle tickets.

After waiting behind the velvet rope for twenty minutes, they ushered people into the bar lounge. I almost fell asleep on my feet when I leaned against the glass wall. I had forgotten the drop in my energy and emotions after practicing my rusty gift. The tension of Ray that morning and my therapy session dragged me down, too.

—*No more plans on a weeknight*— I texted Amy.

—*Once you laugh, you will wake up. Set an alarm. On my way.*—

I slid onto an empty barstool nearest to the door of the auditorium. A bodyguard with an earpiece stood in front of another velvet rope connected to two fake gold podiums. The beefed-up security for a non-celebrity comedian performing in the suburbs made me laugh.

"Would you like a drink, miss?" The bartender tapped my arm.

"Yes, a *Tequila Sunrise*, please."

The bartender nodded and took quite a lot of care mixing out the grenadine, orange juice, and tequila. He flashed a sparkly white smile as he shook the cocktail shakers. My polite grin slid off my face. The awful mood lighting strobing through the small lounge stole my attention away in the mirror behind the bartender.

Shadows from the changing lights cascaded long, finger-like tendrils over his angular face. One second his piercing blue eyes were visible, and the next, his hidden gaze could be anywhere in the room or peeking my way. He towered over his present company by a few inches, making his face pop and his blond hair shine. Our eyes met in the mirror, but I broke the contact first.

He looked like the man who came to my grandmother's memorial with the weird people after I thought everyone had left. I still wondered what the old woman, the leader, did to annoy him enough he barked an order in another language. I thought a lot about those odd ten minutes of my life. My mother and I laughed off the coven comment as a joke.

Movement invisible to the naked eye ruffled the hair escaping my bun at the back of my neck. I checked the mirror again, but the tall man no longer stood with his group. I tugged my skirt down and rested hard against the back of the chair. It took every ounce of my willpower not to glance over my shoulder.

The bartender sprinkled a circle of sugar on the top of my cocktail. He then drew out an automatic torch from his back pocket and lit it on fire.

"Be careful with the flames. Didn't anyone teach you not to play with fire?" I knew who the deep voice belonged to as I stared above the bar at the television playing comedian clips. The soft timber of his soundwaves vibrated almost like fingers caressing my skin.

"I've always been bad at following directions." I picked up my drink, blowing out the flames.

"I can't tell if you're flirting with me or just ignorant?"

I spun around on the swivel barstool, smacking the side of my thigh against his long legs. He stood behind me with barely a spare inch. You would think from our proximity, his smell, the natural essence oozing from any man who lived a day in their skin, would be fucking with my own pheromones. He glared at me, devoid of everything except his stare and that damn frown.

Insulted or not, no one spoke to me that way. "If you're going to talk to me like that, you can leave me alone."

Up close, his dark eyes were a deep blue. He hid his beautiful, cerulean gaze while he scratched his brow. "I'm sorry, it's been a long day. I didn't expect to see you, Lena."

"Clearly, I planned out my ambush. I don't know your name, where you live, or anything about you at all. I took a wild guess that you liked Matthew Benko out of all the comedians in the world."

His chuckle toned down his harshness. The man might be pushing forty, but his smile lightened his aura tenfold. "Are you waiting for someone?" he asked.

"My best friend should be here soon."

"Come with me for a minute."

"Only if you tell me who the hell you are and what happened at my house?"

His nostrils flared. I knew nothing about him. Did

he react out of anger? Desire? Heat from one or the other blazed through his gaze.

"I feel both. Come on."

"What?"

He turned around, leaving me with my mouth hanging open. Damnit, he read my mind. He paused at the side exit door. I scrambled after him abandoning my drink and weaving through the patrons.

I spotted his tall frame weaving through the night-time shoppers rushing around the mall. In his dress slacks and velvety purple shirt, I easily kept an eye on him. The noise of swishing bags full of unnecessary garbage mixed with people pounding their feet rose high in the air amongst a sea of incoherent conversations. The man I followed rubbed his right ear. Did the deafening clatter bother him too?

A lady screaming into her phone clipped my shoulder, spinning me to the right. She muttered an apology, then resumed her shouting. I scanned in front of me. I veered too close to the forward marching people. The rushing faces, in a spectrum of dirty looks, overpowered my vision.

"Lena!" My name thundered through my head. I jerked back, right into the embrace of the strange man I followed.

"I lost you," I said. I gasped for breath. The hard column of his body held up my frantic stature.

"You will never lose me. This way," he instructed.

Without looking down, he interlinked our sweaty fingers, nudging me toward the restroom hallway ending with a set of doors with a Restricted Area sign. I tightened my fingers around his, tugging back before we reached the end. He never wavered at my resistance.

The unlocked and non-alarmed door opened and closed, shielding us from the noisy chaos. After a short narrow hallway, the ceiling shot up to the height of the outer mall. The backdoors of the stores looked like a carnival funhouse with all different colored labels and fonts.

Immediately, an unease flitted through me. I pried my hand loose but followed a few paces behind. We turned another corner toward a staircase hidden behind the other line of stores.

"Why is there a staircase in the back of the mall?" I asked.

"It's the emergency exit for garbage pickup. Have a seat." He sat down on the first step leading down to the lower floors.

"I need a name, bucko, before I do another thing with you." I tapped my heeled foot.

"Arthur, my name is Arthur."

I scoffed and sat down.

"You don't believe me?"

"I thought you looked like an asshole. Sometimes I'm wrong."

He chuckled, but it morphed into a long exhale. His hands rubbed together, then he smoothed out the bunched fabric stretched along the tops of his thighs. He cracked all his knuckles next, and the abrupt sound sliced through the quiet space.

"You're nervous. Why?" I asked.

"There isn't an easy way to say what I need to say."

I checked my phone. We had twenty minutes left until the comedy show started. Ten minutes until the lounge seating began. "We are running out of time. My friend is already going to chew me out for not being the first person in line for a front-row table."

"Right, so yeah, we met in a weird way. I warned my mother not to steal your grandmother's powers, but no one listened to me. The dramatics were ridiculous. Rose wouldn't have wanted people to mourn her life but celebrate it, just like you did. Also, my mother and her coven ignored the protection spell on your house. I felt it miles away. They ignored me." Arthur stared straight ahead while he ranted. When he tilted his head toward me, he frowned, ruining every bit of his good looks.

"The leader is your mother?" I blinked a lot. Clumps of my mascara irritated my tear ducts.

"Yes, Babushka."

And that was my cue to leave.

"This is crazy. I'm late for a stupid comedy show. I will see myself to the door."

Arthur remained seated while I bolted back toward the door leading into the mall. I speed-walked away from him while warning bells reverberated in my head like a symphony of cymbal players crashing the metal together on the wrong beats.

"Lena, wait."

"Find someone else to believe your bullshit," I called back.

I made it through the restricted door and back into the long white hallway leading out to the top floor of the mall before he caught up.

"Lena, let me explain. Please, I'm not lying." Arthur grabbed my forearm. I stopped running as soon as I passed the door. I never thought he would hurt me in any way, but I did not need another weirdo in my life. I halted in his hold, hoping no extra attention would be drawn toward us if someone walked by.

"You must have mistaken my grandmother and me for some other family. We are not witches. We have no powers."

"Tell that to the mole on the side of your eyebrow. You may be avoiding your birthright, but you can't deny you feel it in your skin, your bones, your heart." His pointer finger touched my sweater over my heart.

"Oh my God, it's a mole. A small bundle of tissue that gets irritated every time I wax. That does not mean I'm a witch. I feel nothing in my heart other than your finger intruding into my personal space."

He scoffed, dropping his hand down to his side. "You were a witch at some point. Maybe a hundred years ago or a thousand years ago. You might have been a flower child witch who died at twenty-seven like the great musicians. I don't fucking know, but your mole, your mother's mole, and your grandmother's are the telltale signs of women born into witchcraft whether they like it not."

"Moles are common as fuck. Everyone has them. There is nothing special about mine." I shrugged. Countless mediums and psychics told me the same song and dance. I heard a lot of crap about witches, and that was the biggest lie.

"I heard your mother had one on her nose. They removed it when she was ten. Rose said it stuck out right at the tip like generations before her."

"Do you understand how insane you sound?"

"Yes, I do. I don't understand why you're playing dumb with me. I'm not trying to make fun of you or embarrass you. I know what you are, and I want to talk for real about your family. Rose never told us much about you. Why did you turn your back on witchcraft?"

He thrust his hands into his pockets, and the harsh scowl on his face lightened. His long eyelashes should be illegal over his sapphire gaze. He licked his dry lips, dropping his gaze to my mouth.

"I realized I never paid for my drink, and it might have set the whole lounge on fire if the bartender didn't blow it out."

"You're stalling, and you blew it out yourself." A frustrated growl exited Arthur's mouth. I backed away from him up against the hallway wall. He stepped forward, caging me in, hiding us from the bustling mall goers. His face inched close to mine. His breath stunk of rum.

"Let's try this again. Lena, my mother meant no harm by trying to take your grandmother's extinguished powers. Rose wasn't going to use them anymore anyway. I don't understand why she didn't give them to you."

Questions flooded my mind, but I only squeaked out a plea. "Please don't do this here."

A flash of concern in Arthur's gaze alleviated the tension creasing his face. "You don't need to be alone. Whether you use your powers or not, you should have someone to guide you. If you never use them, you will lose them forever."

"I have no intention of using my gifts." I lifted my chin and folded my arms under my breasts.

"Then how come I feel like you're lying? Did you use them today? Is that why you distracted me? I can smell the ink on you. What did you do this afternoon?"

"I went to my therapy session, and that's it." I ground my blue palms into the sides of my stomach, hiding the ink stains. He knew. *How the hell did he*

31

know?

Arthur looked up at the ceiling, scratching his finely manicured scruff on his cheek. "You're not taking this seriously. This is not a new hair color or a diner where you decide to swap pancakes for French toast. This is your life, Lena. You are almost at the crossroad."

"Writing gibberish in a notebook does not make me a witch. It's not a big deal." I covered my mouth with my palm after my careless omission. I blurted out too much.

"No, it doesn't, but a love spell does."

He must be reading my thoughts. I cursed myself for not clearing my mind. Arthur tensed with frustration. He sighed so loud our personal bubble burst. The obnoxious blowing of an automatic hand dryer in the bathroom leaked out into the hallway, then a woman screamed into her phone in another language while someone screamed back at her in the video chat. The commotion from other people passing by the alcove we ducked into blasted through the space, whipping its force around us.

"When you're ready to give up being an obstinate child, come find me." He twisted his fingers in front of my face, producing a business card from thin air. I scrambled to catch it as it fluttered to the ground like a leaf submitting to the wind. The off-white card landed face down on the cracked concrete floor.

His magic trick turned disappearing act provided him enough time for his escape. The mall herd of people gobbled him up when he turned the corner back toward the comedy club.

The simple business card adorned with a crystal ball advertised a fortune-telling shop I passed all the time when I visited my parents. They had coupons in the local town flyers and emails promoting two-for-one palm readings. The person of contact's name: Anita Belarush.

My phone buzzed in my purse. I let it ring, immobile from my second interaction with Arthur. His livid glare sent a chill down my spine. I arched my neck. My old tic signaling the limit of my contained anxiety might be threatened. I needed more than the slight bone crinkling. I lifted my chin until my muscles squeezed.

"Lena, hey, Lena," Amy shouted from the open doorjamb of the hallway. "The show starts in ten minutes."

She snapped me out of my stupor. I stepped away from the wall and scurried up to her. "I'm sorry, I had to use the ladies' room."

"That's not what that guy said. A man told me you were over here 'collecting yourself.' Hot as fuck, but something seemed off."

Amy slammed the hammer down on the final nail. In another set of circumstances, Arthur's attractiveness was off the charts, but his off-putting, demanding nature disturbed me. Arthur had given me the creeps when his piercing stare mowed me down at my grandmother's wake, and now, he insulted me multiple times. He knew too much about me to be playing a game. I kicked myself mentally for heading straight to defensive mode the second he mentioned my grandmother.

We made it to the show right before it started. I suspected Arthur played a hand in guaranteeing us a table front and center. The usher brought us right to the table with a black reserved sign. I looked for him on the lower level, but Arthur's group sat on the top. His stern, scolding manner vanished while he laughed with his friends or coworkers or whoever the fuck they were to him.

I tried not glancing over my shoulder, but I got sucked in when the woman on his left kept whispering in his ear and drawing her nails over his bicep. I watched until he caught me staring and quickly separated himself from her. He raised his glass, saluting me. I averted my gaze back to the opening act, a kid from the local college reading his material off his cell phone.

Heaven, help me.

The jokes, the two-drink minimum, and the greasy finger foods could not snap me out of my haze. I felt foolish sitting here, listening to bad sex jokes, political garbage, and more fascination with having a comedy club in the mall. Amy encouraged me to laugh a little toward the end of the headliner's set.

After the lights came back on, the host of the show, the starving artist act, notified the room about autographs and CDs for sale. Amy stood up, much like everyone else, grabbing her coat off the back of the chair.

"Hey, hold back a few. I hate pushing through people," I said.

"I think I want to get the college guy's CD. He was funny."

Amy missed every cue I slung at her. She had no idea what had happened before the show. I glanced at the people moving down the stairs from the upper floor of tables, and my gaze met Arthur's. His blank face gave no reprieve. No snicker, no disappointed scowl, no smile, only his resting face peeking over until he stared straight ahead, leaving with his group. His hand rested on the back of the pretty, petite woman who sat next to him at the table.

Once he left through the door, I took a deep breath. "Go, Amy. I'm going to finish my drink, and then I'll come find you."

I expected her weirded-out expression. She mouthed okay and joined the people forming a line through the exit door. I tried my best not to freak my best friend out on the regular, but Arthur fucked up tonight.

How much did my grandmother tell him? He had no right calling me a child. I avoided the witch part of my life comfortably for years. It was stupid stirring up the cauldron with the love spell and writing down nonsense. When I get home, I must throw away the notebook and tell Doctor Greene I accidentally dropped it in the tub.

Whispered echoes of laughter and merriment rippled through the vacant space as if each patron remained in their seat. I sat alone, accompanied by my exhaustion. As if weights sat on my chest, I hardly had the strength to finish my strong drink. I had it bad before, but ever since my altercation with Arthur, my eyes barely stayed open.

How could I be emotionally drained after talking to a stranger?

"I'm not a stranger. We met at your grandmother's funeral."

If anyone else snuck up on me like that, I would have jumped out of my skin, holding onto the chandelier dangling from the ceiling. Arthur's return calmed me, and his mind-reading skills baffled me.

"Is that your gift? You can read minds?" I asked.

"Why are you so certain it's a gift?"

I thought the same thing for years. I hid from mine for so long I barely remembered it until the day I wanted Ray back. Even then, shame befell me for casting the spell. I regretted it for days.

"My grandmother called it a gift. How could my

grandmother assign a joyful name to something that caused her harm?"

"She was a good witch." Arthur sat down across from me. "Look, I'm sorry I fucked up your night. You didn't laugh once. It wasn't my intention to steal your fun."

I shrugged. "You don't know my sense of humor."

"All right then, just be careful with whatever you are doing with your life."

"Where are my grandmother's gifts? If your mother failed, what happened to them?"

He flicked his hands up, fingers splaying wide. "Probably in the urn with her ashes or halfway to the black hole in the center of the universe. No one can take them now. It's too late."

"I guess that's a good thing. Confusing, but I'll take it." I swallowed the last swig of my drink. I resisted the cough as the liquid spilled down my throat awkwardly.

"My offer to talk still stands," Arthur reminded.

"Are you on a date?"

His look destroyed all reasonable thought. The cocksure smile, his arched eyebrows, and the small nod back and forth. "Nope, not even in her wildest dreams."

Arthur rose from the chair, distracting my gaze toward his obnoxiously large silver ornate belt buckle I missed before. He buttoned his dinner jacket, hiding the monstrosity.

I expected another snappy retort or something along the lines of, "Yes, I know you checked out my junk. Let's bate each other again in another hallway." Nothing more happened. He pushed in the chair and walked out the entranceway.

"Uhm, he's hot."

The waitress, who could have stood there the entire conversation, stared after Arthur. She slid the black dinner bill envelope toward me. I snapped out of my fog and opened the booklet. The bill had been paid by Arthur Prince.

"He paid?" I mumbled.

"He wants you. Let him have you," the waitress said. She still stared at the open door.

"Okay, thanks."

The momentary hypnotism ended on the waitress. She swallowed hard. Her gaze ran wild over the empty tables as if she sleepwalked into the room.

"We must disinfect the tables before the late show. Please use the exit on the left." The monotone, scripted response returned.

I found Amy and got the hell out of there.

Chapter Four

I never walked up to my bedroom last night. I dusted my grandmother's urn and returned it to the mantel in my living room. I kicked off my shoes and collapsed on my couch which smelled like Ray. My dream conjured another man.

Arthur kissed me breathless behind the mall stores until the grimace returned to his face. The back doors of the stores opened simultaneously. One by one, women stepped out into the hidden space. Their faces shielded by their long hair. They each wore a crown of red roses.

"Look behind you!" I screamed into Arthur's face, backing up against the unyielding concrete wall. I wanted away from them. The women made my skin itch as if their presence disturbed my existence.

Arthur glanced behind him. The first woman removed her crown and jammed it onto Arthur's forehead. The next followed her precedent, then the third woman. A harmony of water droplets sounded in my ears like a leaky faucet. The piercing drumbeat of a falling liquid grew louder. After the fifth woman thrust her crown on top of the others on Arthur's head, blood dripped down Arthur's face.

"*Stop!*" I cried out. My hands waved through the thick air between Arthur and me, but my fingers never reached him. The stench of blood and roses polluted the air around me. I coughed until my eyes watered and my throat swelled. I gasped for fresh air. Arthur turned back to me. A veil of blood covered Arthur's once beautiful, scowling face. My scream lodged deep in my throat as he captured my lips with his own.

The stench of stale beer muted the dream. I opened my eyes, peering at the stained back cushion of my couch. A blanket covered me, even though I had no memory of pulling it out of the basket next to the door. My awful dream blurred to nothing as my living room comforted me.

The short-lived respite ended when the sides of my head pulsed with pain. The drinks must have been too sugary. I rubbed the soft parts on either side of my forehead and noticed my shoes back in their normal place on the drying mat. Only Ray and my mother put my shoes there.

"Ray?"

"No, it's me." My mother popped her head out from the kitchen. "Are you back with Ray?"

Oh, right, Friday was family history project day with Mom. Lately, it transformed into more of a gab session between us.

"No, Mom. I'm sorry, I got confused." I shuffled into the kitchen and glanced at the clock. It was already ten o'clock in the morning. "Shit, I overslept."

"Don't worry about it. I got here late anyway. I had this crazy dream about you. Your father said I tossed and turned, mumbling and laughing. All I remember is walking you up and down the stairs as a baby, trying to get you to sleep. I never dreamed of you when you were a baby. Now, it's all I think about."

I sat down at my table, and without asking, my mother made me a cup of coffee. "I think pacing and stairs might mean you are trying to get somewhere or escape something bothering you. Or you could be pregnant?"

"Lena, I went through menopause ten years ago. I tried soothing you, but the more I did the things that used to work, you cried louder and harder each time. Are you doing okay?"

The chance meeting with Arthur slithered into my mind. I appreciated him apologizing for ruining my night, but the entire evening and the fucked up dream left a chill down my spine.

"Remember I told you about those people who came last minute to pay their respects to grandma? Did I mention a hot guy who didn't come in but closed the door when his mother left?"

"The leader was his mother?" My mother's mouth gaped open.

"Evidently, she is. I saw him last night. I went to the comedy club in the mall with Amy. He happened to be there. He said a lot of weird stuff."

"Is he single?"

I gave her my worst expression, probably with makeup left on one eye and my hair sticking up on the sides.

"I'm teasing. Did he say anything more about the funeral? I have no clue who they are."

Mom sat down across from me with her favorite mug I kept here for her and handed me the matching pair. I sipped the steamy liquid and contemplated how much I should reveal about my interaction with Arthur. Maybe his name would ring a bell.

"He's an odd duck, for sure. His name is Arthur Prince. He called his mother Babushka. I think her first name is Anita. Do those names mean anything to you?"

Her full lips turned down in a frown, and she shook her head. "Babushka is probably not his mother's name. I think it means old woman in Russian or German. Prince seems like a common name. I bet they shortened it if they came from another country."

"He spoke in another language to his mother at the funeral, but last night he didn't really have an accent. He sounded American."

Mom pulled her phone from her back pocket. She furrowed her brow and opened her social media. "I haven't been able to access grandma's social media profile except viewing it as her friend. I wonder if I need to send a death certificate to get her password. It's nuts how hard things are when someone dies. We can check her friends' list if it isn't hidden. Maybe he's on there."

"She died at ninety-three years old. She couldn't possibly have a reason to keep her friends hidden," I surmised.

"I don't know. She knew more than me about that stuff. She loved it."

We had no luck with her profile. Forty names and I knew half of them. There was no Arthur Prince listed. I showed my mother the card for the fortune telling shop he gave me, but nothing rang a bell.

"How many people showed up for grandma, again?" Mom asked.

"About twenty people crammed into my living room, grieving like their own flesh and blood died. They stayed about ten minutes and then vanished."

"They couldn't have disappeared. Maybe they took a bus?"

"I would have heard the engine. It was fucking

weird, Mom."

She shrugged and retrieved the bag of grapes I bought the other day. "Lena, you really should take fruit out of the plastic bags, or it will go bad faster."

"Yes, Mom."

I knew when she stopped listening. She reminded me of something she told me a hundred times yet failed to do. I took the cue and dropped the subject. I retrieved the box of photos and the new album from the small table near the pantry closet.

"I think we should buy at least three more of these books. They will all be the same and organized."

"Yes, Mom."

****

After an hour, we organized all my grandfather's World War Two photos and secured them to the sticky scrapbooking pages. I kept out two photos with my grandmother in them. She stared into a teacup in the black and white photo dated September 1965.

"She always did that trick. A few times, it came true. She told me I would meet your father under a wave," my mother said.

"You guys met under a waterfall, not a wave."

"Magic is never a hundred percent right, but she had a miraculous track record. Maybe those people were the coven she checked out a few years ago, or she lied about joining a crochet group with a bunch of nuns at a senior home."

"I thought the coven thing was a joke. Both of you kidded how she joined a cult by accident."

My mother rolled her eyes and scratched her neck. Another habit of hers I learned too well.

"Lena, your grandmother never joined a cult. She

attended a few meetings of a local witch group, but she never went back after a full moon festival. There were too many younger people, so she stopped. They probably took off their clothes and danced naked in the moonlight. She was a bit of a prude."

I jumped at the opportunity. My mother forgave me for a lot of things. She will forgive me for this too.

"Why didn't you want to become a witch?"

"The same reason why you stopped writing," she said. She answered before she took another breath. Her trembling hands took our empty coffee mugs with the mother and daughter lions to the sink. My mother hunched over the sink, gripping the edges.

"What scared you, Mom?"

I hated pushing her for information. She was not a fragile woman, but she had her guards and limits. I blew past them.

"I had a miscarriage when I was very young. I ran away from home with the man I thought I loved. He thought my gift would be birthing beautiful, powerful witches. When I lost the baby, he left me. He drove me back that night with no more use of me."

I got up and hugged her from behind, laying my cheek on her back. Her hands gripped my forearms, pulling them tighter around her.

"Fuck, Mom. That's awful. I'm so sorry."

"I was so afraid that I wouldn't have a child. Ten years later, I met your father and had you. You are so special to me. I don't want anything bad to happen to you. If that man you met yesterday scares you, stay away from him."

"I will, Mom."

"Your grandmother respected my wishes. Please

don't seek out other witches. They can be cruel, unkind, and disastrous to your self-worth. If they can't use you, they will throw you away like a piece of garbage. Don't follow that path. Let it go."

My mother's body shook from her sobs. Guilt activated my own waterworks. "Okay, Momma. You're okay. I'm okay. We're going to be okay."

She turned in my embrace and hugged me tightly, only like a mother could do. "My precious daughter. I love you more than life itself. Please be careful." She glanced at the oven clock. "I have to go shopping. Do you need anything from the wholesale store? You should always keep bottled water in the house in case of a power outage."

"I might need more coffee. I have a little more than a week's worth left."

"There is almost a whole box left! That lasts you a week?"

I smiled and batted my eyes. "I work long hours. Hopefully not for long."

"You really are going to try to sell your program?"

"Fingers crossed. I'm having dinner with a potential buyer next month when he is in town."

"I'm proud of you. You got this!"

I walked her out of the house with another kiss on the cheek and told her to tell Dad I loved him. Against everything I promised, my feet flew up the stairs back to the old vanity table. The red notebook already sat opened to a clean page a few past the last time I scribbled nonsense.

The pen felt odd in my right hand, even though I was a righty. I switched it to my left hand, but that felt worse, so I put it back in my right. I stared at the blank lined page so long I swore a hole formed as if someone held the end of a lit cigarette to the page. A few blinks took away the mirage.

"I'm forcing it, aren't I?" I said to whoever listened when I sat alone.

I grabbed my personal laptop, not the one I used for my presentations, and opened a fresh document. The words flowed about my therapy sessions, my bizarre night with Arthur, and my mother's revelation.

As soon as I stopped typing, two alarms went off simultaneously.

City Day—Tomorrow with Kim, minus the kids. I remembered that one. I looked forward to it every few weeks. The second one I had no fucking clue what to do with.

Love Spell—Ray. Ends tomorrow at midnight.

A year passed by in the blink of an eye. I placed my phone back on the vanity, screen side down. Finally, it would be over. I wondered if Ray would suddenly not show up on Wednesdays. Would it work that way? Time will tell.

Chapter Five

Kim and I rode the express train into New York City early Saturday morning. Ray had Kim's kids for the day. I waited in the car while she got ready. Ray waved with the kids from the window.

I loved shopping in the city with Kim. We hunted and explored Manhattan for the next stand-out item for her gift baskets. If we could not buy it in bulk, she used the excuse of limited edition for increasing the price. Today slightly deviated from the normal routine because instead of gift baskets, she received a last-minute request for adult goodie bags for a trash-the-dress party tonight.

"I hope her wedding dress wasn't too expensive," I commented.

"She's rich. She probably bought it at a sample sale and fought to the death in an all-out brawl. She heroically stole it out of another woman's hand, who bashed her head against the floor, but she had to have this one-of-a-kind dress from a *who the fuck?* designer, or else her wedding would have been ruined." Kim stuck her finger in her mouth and fake gagged.

"Hey, those are your customers, Kim. Don't judge the big wallets." I wagged my pointer finger.

"You're right. I'm bitter because I'm so tired. I never thought this would take off as well as it did. I am grateful, but without you and Ray, I would be so fucked."

I waved off her gratitude. She paid me for helping.

Ray only got free dinners when she had time to cook with two toddlers, a pre-teen, and a husband deployed overseas. Kim made it work.

A pop-up market in the middle of Union Square beckoned us. My stomach growled, but we had an hour before our lunch reservations. I ran best on empty. I searched the small, cubed stores for something out of the ordinary. Kim's clientele expected quality and uniqueness for the price. If we packed cheap fish tank rocks instead of real gemstones, they noticed.

She splurged on twenty sterling silver chains and white gold dress form charms. They complemented the party theme, but she needed to spice things up. A weed truck advertising cheap gummy bears caught my eye. "Should we check this out? The host is paying you for the goodie bags, right?"

"The maid of honor is paying us. I'm not sure about the pot. I don't want a lawsuit because a high-as-fuck woman jumped off the roof."

"That's oddly specific, Kim?"

"Sorority days." She flicked down her sunglasses, winking, and then stared off at the busy city street. As someone who never joined one in college, I took her word for it.

"Okay, nix the gummies. Mini champagne bottles? Booze candy?"

"Yes! We're on the right track. The party is going to be fun. You're coming, right?"

"Yup, I'm down. My schedule is free." The party provided a perfect distraction from the love spell and Arthur.

"Awesome. The bridesmaids are trashing their dresses too. It might get messy."

"Aww, they didn't shorten the dresses and wear them again?"

"Hey, lady-who-wore-her-bridesmaid-dress-from-my-wedding-to-a-'Day of the Dead'-party last year. You can't talk about what people do with their ex-bridal attire. It's your dress after the pictures."

"I stand corrected."

Kim laughed it off, and we continued walking toward a candle booth and a hot chocolate stand. I tried finding something for my mom, but nothing jumped out. She didn't call me in the morning like she always did. I'd let her have the space she needs.

The entire second and third rows of shops sold more jewelry along with lotions and candles. Burnt onions wafted our way from a nearby barbecue truck. Weed, smoked meat, and shea butter were a horrible combination of smells.

At the end of the last row, Kim's gaze landed on a neon hamsa hand light hanging from the top of the vendor booth. She jumped at the two for one palm reading special. For the past two days, everywhere I turned, something magical found me. My bullshit meter dialed up full blast.

The young woman abandoned the typical song and dance show I grew accustomed to in her line of work. She wore a black turtleneck, a simple long-sleeved black dress, and leather gloves. Her ensemble concealed every inch of her body except her gaunt face. The discolored gray skin under her icy eyes hindered her beauty and aged her another twenty years.

She decorated the back wall of the booth with pictures of her so-called ancestors sitting at a round table with a similar quilt thrown over a wooden claw-footed table. I distrusted their authenticity. These days, people printed the images of seances, palm readings, and fortune-telling off the internet.

"Hi ladies, my name is Idalia. Who would like to go first?" the woman asked.

I always went second or last if we were in a large group. Kim went first every time. She believed the hocus pocus conjured up from palm reading and the ever-delicate crystal ball. I yearned for her fresh, open mind. Even though I had living proof of the supernatural, my skeptical thoughts doubted anyone who asked for money.

"Me! I would love to know how many kids I'm going to have. Is Jeremy really the one?" Kim spewed out.

I leaned against the metal pole connecting the tents and blew out a long exhale. Another thing I did when fortune tellers and psychics found me, which they always did, was keep quiet for as long as possible. Idalia worked Kim, using the questions she asked as jumping-off points for the stories she weaved. She told her about the four children she saw in the crease of Kim's right hand. Idalia's gloved hand traced the fine lines enhanced by Kim's upturned palm. She also saw diamonds, meaning wealth, in Kim's future. Kim's spunky spirit sprang to life after her reading.

I sat down in the warm seat and pressed my lips together. Idalia squinted. Her blue irises looked like snowflakes chilling her pupils, almost like the blank stare of death. The hair on the back of my neck prickled. If I believed in otherworldly things, Idalia would be one of them.

She wiggled out her arms and gazed into the crystal

ball. "I don't see anyone for you today. This doesn't happen often, but silence can be a good or a bad thing."

"My loved ones could be resting."

The lines in Idalia's forehead crinkled up. She unzipped the cuffs on her leather gloves, used the hand sanitizer, and reached across the table with her left hand. I glanced at Kim, who urged me on.

I snatched my hand back after feeling Idalia's chilled skin. I sweated in the September sun, but Idalia felt like she came from a walk-in freezer.

"Sorry, I'm anemic. I should have warned you. My hand will warm up in a minute." Idalia rubbed her palms together, blowing between them.

I felt bad for pulling away. I wondered about her bad circulation. Her breath came out in raspy pants. Dead things didn't breathe. She lived.

"It's all good," I lied. I didn't want her touching me. "Can you put your gloves back on?"

"This is embarrassing, but I'm having trouble reading you. Skin to skin helps if that's all right." Another psychic once told me I had too many lines; therefore, palm readings were inconclusive. *What will Idalia's excuse be like?*

I nodded and placed my hand palm up in hers. Her cold fingertips traced along my lines. I fought back a flinch.

"I see busyness, mixed blood, variety. Your fate line is strong, but you have another break ahead of you. What was the first break?"

"Excuse me? What do you mean, 'break?' "

"Have you changed careers? Moved across country? Been ill? It's hard to pinpoint years. It's so high up near your middle finger. You were young, but after sixteen.

Anything odd occur?"

"How did you know my age?"

"The lines on your hand change throughout your early life. Some say sixteen. Others say younger, cements your fate. Your second fate line is more straight, less choppy, but the two lines are far apart without meeting. A third one, which is a rare sight, faded away. A scrap of it remains. You're at the end of something once important to you."

The love spell on Ray ended tonight. I assumed that would be part of my love line, not fate. *Was that what she saw?*

"You are not the first child. Your mother lost a child before you. You have powers from both you and the other. You are a witch."

I yanked my hand out of her grasp, standing up. "Thank you for your time. You wanted thirty dollars, right? Two readings, fifteen bucks a pop."

Idalia's hand dangled in the air before she processed my dismissal.

"Um, yes, I'm sorry if I upset you. Wait, forget paying me. I didn't mean to blurt that out. I'm new at this. Please accept my apology."

I snatched out a twenty and a ten-dollar bill from my purse and slammed the money down on the table. "Have a nice day."

I backed away from the tent until I stumbled to a seat on the concrete ledge of a fountain. Idalia jammed her hands back in her gloves. The crunch of the zipper ripped through the air. I became hyperaware of everything. The honking horns, the cacophony of incoherent voices blurred together, dogs barking, the wind creating music through the stems of the flowers hanging onto the summer sun.

"Forget the third path." The boom of Idalia's voice roared over the overpowering sounds. I slapped my hands over my ears. I shut my eyes tight, fearful of her standing in front of me, whispering more into my ear.

"Go away! Leave me alone!"

"Lena! Lena, what's wrong?" Kim's warm hand caressed my upper back.

"Is she gone?" I muttered.

"Who?" Kim's answer flew my eyes open. My gaze scanned the booth I had fled from seconds ago. A red rope tied from one end to the next barred off the unused space. A bare black folding table sat in the middle of the tent space, and a sign rested on a small easel on top of it. The advertisement read, *Vendors Wanted.*

"What the fuck? I'm losing my damn mind. Didn't we get psychic readings from a blonde woman named Idalia? Creepy, young, dressed in all black. She wore leather gloves. She said you would have four children."

Kim tilted her head to the side, and her top teeth gnawed on her bottom lip. "Did you start your new medication yet? I just finished paying for the jewelry. I thought I lost you until I saw you over here."

"That's impossible. That empty booth had a lady in it. She looked like a walking corpse. She read your palm first, then I don't know where you went."

I hated the sympathetic smile and shoulder pat she gave me. "Lena, you walked off a few minutes ago. Maybe you sat down and nodded off without realizing it. Your eyes were closed."

"I wasn't dreaming. No one can fall asleep like that. What the fuck did she do?"

I rose from the stone ledge and searched around the

tent. All traces of Idalia and her stuff vanished. A faint whiff of coconut lingered in the air.

"I think you need to eat. Let's get a cab to the restaurant. Our lunch reservation is in fifteen minutes," Kim shouted. She checked her high-tech watch on her wrist. The reminder flashed on the screen.

Kim truly had no memory of the last ten minutes. Meanwhile, I dashed around the vacated space like a crazy person. I still felt Idalia's icy touch on my hand.

"Lena, there is nothing in the booth. Are you sure you're feeling all right?" Kim asked.

"No, let's get out of here." My racing heartbeat drummed inside my head as I followed Kim toward Fourteenth Street. I chanced another glance at the empty space. Magicians master disappearing acts, but Kim forgetting the whole interaction stumped me worse than the mysterious woman.

We stayed back from the end of the street, apart from the other people waiting at the red light. A black SUV with a T on its license plate stopped in front of us. Kim stated the restaurant's name and address. Once I had my seat belt on, I chewed off a hangnail, doubting everything in my life.

What the fuck just happened?

Chapter Six

After inhaling the fruit appetizer and several breadsticks, I realized two things about the incident in the park. The readings happened because twenty minutes had disappeared. I checked my phone when we reached the fortune-telling booth. We had a lot of time before lunch, and we used it on the palm readings. Also, I no longer had the thirty dollars I slammed on the table.

There was a slim chance I read the time wrong off my phone. With the money issue, I knew I had given Ray cash last week for picking up groceries. Maybe I never replaced the money.

The formal waitstaff began the rotation of the main course choices for the brunch. Kim commented on each breakfast item, along with a matching story. She barely allowed a few seconds of silence, jumping in with a new topic or yet another thing the kids did. She hated silence, especially when her brunch partner was distracted over a fresh supernatural experience. I stopped listening at the Eggs Benedict story.

An odd sensation roamed over my right hand in the path Idalia's fingers traced. I gazed at the parted line between my thumb and pointer finger. The natural crease stopped and continued a centimeter later. *Could a small patch of lines expose me as a witch?*

"Ray ate the quinoa in the omelet and threw up an hour later at the winery. I had told him not to eat it because it smelled funny. His stomach growled the entire car ride, then at the wine tasting, then all the way back home. We should have stopped at a drug store or something," Kim rambled.

I forced a chuckle for Kim's sake. She talked faster, the more nervous she got. The laugh from me brightened her smile. I had this day marked on my calendar forever. Our schedules had not been meshing well, and we both had cleared our schedules for today. Kim somehow thought nothing had changed from when she bought those cheap necklaces.

"Do you feel better now?" Kim prodded.

"Yeah, maybe I was dehydrated," I lied. I hated lying to Kim. I could count on one hand how many times I had done it. Smiling through a mouth of French toast covered in berry jam, she believed me. I knocked back a mimosa too.

After brunch, we visited our normal go-to shops, the street addresses by word of mouth only. I spoke when Kim asked questions and nodded occasionally. Five stores later, Kim purchased enough backstock for at least three months.

"We can go to your favorite bookstore, now? If you'd like, I can pick up a to-go order of those short-rib pierogies from next door while you shop?"

"I think I want to head home. Maybe I'll fit in a nap before the party." The yawn stretching my mouth wide was real. As if my energy meter dropped to empty, tiredness weighed me down.

Kim placed her palm on my forehead. "Well, you feel fine, but I have never known you to pass up a trip to a bookstore. Are you upset about Ray and Chloe?"

"I swear, I'm fine. I'm just tired."

"I might have a solution to the middle-of-the-night-crunch-time help. I'm thinking of converting part of my garage into a workshop. I would have a designated spot for all the baskets and merchandise, so you can help me during the day. It also might solve your Ray situation."

"That might work. The Ray thing is fine until that happens. I'll have to keep some extra beers in my fridge for a little longer. It's not a big deal. He kills the spiders and takes out of the trash if I leave dinner for him," I dismissed.

"If things get serious between Ray and Chloe, it's going to be awkward as fuck if you two spend Wednesday nights together."

"I plead the fifth." I hustled down the steps into Grand Central's main concourse ahead of Kim.

"Hey, now. You could have been my sister-in-law! I don't want to get involved, but I think I said this before. If something is going on between the two of you, he needs to end things with Chloe or stop messing around with you."

I took a few minutes for my answer. Just like the first day of the spell, my life shifted in an instant. The love spell ended tonight, and Kim found a solution to eliminating Ray's weekly trips to my house. I shook my head back and forth while checking for a train track number. The love spell must truly be over if Ray got back together with Chloe. How fitting I found out about everything today?

When we found seats on the train, Kim nudged my forearm. "Well, Lena, what is it? Are you going to get back together with Ray or not?"

"No, we aren't. That ship sailed away peacefully."

"Okay. My husband will be back in the States for

56

the holidays. I'll start working on the garage remodel in November."

Layla, Kim's oldest daughter, texted her mother with a fury. I processed anything on my phone screen, granting me some space. I scrolled my social media.

A part of me missed Ray and the late Wednesday nights already. My marathoning thoughts rotated like a constant weathervane blowing around in the wind. The love spell ran its course and failed.

Laughter bubbled in my gut. The jovial air burst out of my mouth a few moments later. My body couldn't hold it back much longer.

"What's so funny?" Kim glanced up from her phone as more text messages came in.

"You wouldn't believe me if I told you." Pain pulsed along my abdominal muscles. My cackling continued until I lurched forward.

"Is it the garage? Jeremy? What is it? Ray?"

"Ray! You're going to laugh your ass off. Do you know I cast a love spell on him? Literally, the next day after I did it, you asked me to help with your business, and now, the last day of the spell, you told me I won't have to work with Ray anymore. If this isn't fucking hilarious, I don't know what is."

Kim patted me on the back. "Uh, that's a crazy coincidence. The universe works in weird ways. I hope my sane friend, Lena, is going to show up tonight at the Trash-the-Dress Party. She was supposed to be my sober ride home."

"Don't worry. The crazy will be kept to a minimum."

Kim pursed her lips together and nodded. She peered down at her phone, huffed out a breath, and called her daughter. I shouted "Hi" to Layla and rested my head back on the orange-padded seat. I stayed quiet long enough. I almost fell asleep for real that time.

Nothing weird or supernatural had happened for years, then months after the love spell. *Why did I disturb the cauldron?* My time with Ray officially ended tonight. One less component of my stressful life.

My aching body sank further into the unyielding plastic seat. I hated long walking days. It drained my energy in addition to the bizarre lady disappearing from the park. Kim tried explaining about a band her daughter liked, but I fell asleep while she talked. It wouldn't be the first time.

****

Kim didn't mind me sleeping most of the train ride. Her twins fell asleep in the car all the time. Off the train, we rushed over to my car. A meter maid had tucked a red and white ticket under my windshield.

"What the fuck is this?"

Evidently, my registration expired in July. I owed fifty bucks. I jammed the parking violation into my purse's abyss. Little things like that irritated the fuck out of me, especially when half my day got already screwed up and my lingering headache throbbed.

My phone automatically registered home on my screen. I switched it off. Another destination overpowered my thoughts. I dropped Kim off at her house and headed downtown.

A large "Available" sign hung in the front window of the taqueria. Newspapers taped to the inside of the glass concealed the empty restaurant. No static, no tingles, nothing greeted me as I peeked through a small, uncovered part. The counter and tables remained, but dirty menus and leaves littered the floor. It looked like a tornado tore through the space.

I walked around the back through the bank's parking lot next door. Four warped, wooden boards nailed to the door frame covered the burnt back entrance. The unmistakable stench of old smoke clung to the black, charred door.

Kitchen fires happened all the time, but there had been no visible fire damage in the dining room. The yellow walls, the multi-colored garland hanging from the ceiling, and the glass display cases remained unaffected.

I dragged my hand over the worst part of the fire damage. For a split second, heat warmed my fingertips, then stopped. I snatched my hand back from the wood. I didn't want another strange occurrence without explanation, today.

I found nothing online about a fire, only that the restaurant was temporarily closed. Hopefully, no one burned the old Spanish lady as a witch for a love spell gone wrong. Events like that never made the news. The sun disappeared behind the row of trees behind me, casting a grim shadow over the exit. I took the hint and left.

Just my luck, the coffee shop a few stores down closed late. I ordered a caramel latte and sipped the hot liquid back in my car. Even though the coffee perked me up, my body held onto the tension from the day. I rubbed the muscle knot over my shoulder blade with no relief.

"Ray will be fine," I said. I searched the internet for what happened after a love spell ended. The first response eased my discomfort. If the love was not reciprocated at the end of the spell, the recipient would wake up as if they had been in a long dream. *Fingers crossed.*

The odd situation in the park still left a sour taste in my mouth. I did not imagine it. Idalia pissed me off, but the vanishing act made my blood boil. I might need Arthur Prince's help after all if crazy shit kept happening.

Chapter Seven

I arrived at the party's house address a comfortable twenty minutes late. A large cardboard cutout of a bride and groom stood on the front lawn of a small, blue cape cod house, but the groom's head was mysteriously missing. I gritted my teeth at the macabre image. The pink van parked in the driveway had streamers attached to beer cans hanging from the back bumper. On the trunk, someone wrote, "Off to Hell." The trash the dress, my marriage was done theme screamed loud and clear.

Music cranked up past the speaker's tolerance boomed from the house. *How long do they have until the cops shut this hen party down?* No one heard the doorbell ring. I knocked hard, but the festivities raged on.

I texted Kim. Her face popped out in between the parted curtains. I waved, but she left.

"Long time, no see." Kim opened the door wearing her old fairy costume from the Renaissance Faire. She curled her hair, slathered her face with glitter, and fluffed up the skirt into a horizontal tutu. I barely managed a shower, emails, and running a comb through my wet mop of hair.

"You didn't tell me this was a costume party." I crossed my arms and tapped my boot.

"If I mentioned it, you wouldn't have come."

"I can dress up. I would have worn my devil horns." I poked the edge of her stiff, tulle skirt. "Did you use a whole can of laundry starch for this height?"

"No, the tutu is from Layla's dance costume last year. Come on, everyone is raving about the champagne gummy bears."

As Kim turned around in her kooky ensemble, her large purple fairy wings smacked my nose. "Hey, be careful with these things. Did you do a wing training course?"

Kim's gaze barely focused on my face as she swayed to the left. I steadied her shoulders. "Ha-ha, yes, Lena. It was online, and I passed." I arched my eyebrow, straightening out her lopsided elastic wings. "Sorry, I'm a little drunk. The sob stories are hitting too close to home."

"Then, let's switch you to soda. Lead the way, Kimmy," I said. She pranced into the sitting room until she wobbled on her feet. She held out both of her hands at a one-hundred-and-eighty-degree angle, catching her balance in her stockinged feet. *Soda wasn't going to help her now.*

From the cars outside, I expected a few people, but at least thirty ladies, also wearing assorted costumes, circled around a woman chugging a bottle of wine in the middle of the kitchen while standing in an empty kiddie pool. The red fermented liquid dribbled down the sides of the bride's mouth, landing on the sweetheart bodice of a white mermaid-style wedding gown. Aside from the new wine stains, the dress looked good as new until each woman grabbed a spray bottle of paint and peppered the new divorcee with red and black splotches.

"Oh my God!" The words escaped my mouth. I had heard about brides taking unusual photos in their wedding dresses, but I never heard about it happening like the madness occurring in front of me. Women took photos at the beach in their gowns. The pictures came out lovely. Amusement parks and gardens, yes, those too. Spray paint? No cleaner in the world would be able to get the paint off the intricate beading on the hips, and the lace train bustled high on her ass.

"Go Fiona! Woohoo!" A lady in a black corset, holding a helium-filled penis balloon, shouted. She probably got her Bachelorette and Trash-the-Dress party signals crossed. Chanting and clapping came next. The bride kicked off her black ballet flats, and two ladies caught them. The loud music and the cackling women completed the scene, heightening the chaotic energy expanding throughout the room.

I backed away from the hysteria. Kim nudged me toward the hallway on the other side of the kitchen. I squeezed through the fairies, the vampires, one pirate lady, and the rest of the bridal party in their lime green bell-shaped gowns.

The moment I crossed from the linoleum flooring to the carpet, my heartbeat settled enough to think again. I walked further into another sitting room, where four women sat on folding chairs. These ladies wore renaissance wench costumes, not mystical fairy.

"What's next? Did someone hire a naked man to come out from behind the curtains?" I asked. I placed my hand above my brow, inspecting the room around me. The wood paneling screamed the nineteen eighties and the mustard-colored carpet. "Or is the ex-husband chained to a chair in his boxer briefs?"

All the ladies' heads jerked toward me together as if I disturbed their sitting in silence.

"It's not that kind of party," the woman sitting next

to an empty chair said. "We are supporting Fiona. Who are you?" She scoffed and crossed her legs.

"I helped make the goodie bags. I'm sorry for offending you with my presence." I held my hands up in the air, surrendering.

"You *should* be sorry. Fiona is having such a hard time. Please be more mindful of her feelings."

Shit, tough crowd. I regretted not purchasing some marijuana gummies for the favors, but I should have picked some up for me.

"Dark humor is not the best here. Got it," I remarked.

Inaudible chatter filtered in behind me. "Thank you, miss. I'll do it every night."

"You will feel better within a week. Thank you, Michelle. Who is next on the list for a palm reading? Deirdre Weiss? Are you here?"

I recognized her voice before I turned. The fortune teller from the city stood in the hidden doorway leading into another room. She smiled pleasantly, looking more disheveled than earlier. Same all-black outfit, her hair frizzy around her forehead, and the chilling stare. At first, her gaze overlooked me on the side of the den. When her next pawn hadn't announced her presence, she spotted me on her second glance.

Idalia's grin morphed into a deep frown. Crackling bones like a mummy awakening filtered into my eardrums.

Kim fluttered in from the kitchen, holding a wooden tray with half-full plastic champagne glasses. She placed a fallen strawberry back on the edge of one of the glasses.

"Who wants champagne?" Kim shouted. She held down the tray in front of the sitting ladies. "The toast to freedom is in five minutes."

Idalia and I stared each other down. I wished I hadn't blinked. She was not leaving the party until I got answers.

"Hey, Lena, the fortune teller from the city is here! Isn't that weird? It just hit me where I saw her before. Maybe she can finish your reading?" Kim smiled, innocent as ever.

"*What?* You remember now?" I yelled.

Kim tilted her head to the side. "Of course, I remember. How could I forget?"

"Shit," Idalia muttered.

I lunged at Idalia. If I knew how to shoot fire from my fingertips, that woman would be toast. The magnitude of the violent rage shocked me, but I had no reflection time. Idalia's long blonde ponytail whipped around her face as she fled into the kitchen. I ran seconds behind her, tasting her fearful, tart gasp.

We dashed into absolute chaos. The ladies' throwing paint resembled wailing banshees throwing talismans into a fire. The bride sat in the kiddie pool, hugging her knees, rocking back and forth. Her wedding dress train floated behind her, half submerged in the brownish purple liquid. Her now black veil hid her audible sobs.

The pure anarchy distracted both Idalia and me. One minute we saw the bride, and like a sea of sirens, the women sang in moans, circling the distraught woman.

I seized the preoccupied Idalia's forearm and squeezed. "Got you," I screamed. A sloppy, drunk fairy crashed into our tussle, spiraling Idalia and me to the floor. My heavier body pinned Idalia's lithe frame to the linoleum. She thrashed and arched her hips upward with no prevail. Her palms and knees slipped on the splattered wet paint. After two more attempts, she laid still below me.

"We need to talk," I whispered in her ear. She slammed her eyes shut, mumbling incoherently. "I don't want to hurt you. I want to know what the fuck happened this afternoon!"

Her eyes opened, and a strangled cry wrenched out of her throat. If I wasn't pinning her down, watching her breath push away stray hair fallen over her face, I would predict she was the undead. A foul odor of rotten coconut wafted off her body I doubted a night's worth of showers would fix.

"Please, let me up. I can't breathe," she croaked. I didn't believe her. If only I had spare handcuffs in my back pocket. I sat on her ass, my thighs straddling her tiny waist. She breathed fine.

"I'll get off you if you talk to me."

Her sharp inhale, followed by a nod, caught the attention of the dancing fairies.

"Fight, fight, fight!" a chant started.

Hell no, I was not going to be a part of this animalistic ritual. Against my better judgment, I rolled off Idalia's hips. She coughed, rolling onto her side. I wasn't impressed by the theatrics.

"I'm waiting." I poked her back. *Yes, my impatience was a bitch.*

"Fine, I'll tell you all I know."

"Lena, what the fuck?" Kim stood over us, her gaze ping-ponging between Idalia and me. Idalia played the pity card with her pouty mouth and sympathetic stare. I crossed my arms over my stomach hard enough to sting.

"She put a spell on you. You didn't remember

anything about the reading after it happened." Kim furrowed her brow. I pointed back at Idalia. "For your information, your spell didn't work on me."

The lady who had bumped into us before, cackled, throwing her head back. "Oh, witchy, kitchy, don't be bitchy."

Kim chuckled, scratching her glittered cheek. "I forgot? That's not like me." She reached out her hand. I took it, rising back to my feet.

I offered my hand to Idalia, an olive branch of courtesy. She waved it off, crawling to the nearby desk, and pulled herself up. Her ripped stocking at the knee revealed a large bruise she must have had before tonight. Bruises didn't appear that fast. She looked fine otherwise except her gloves were missing.

If I guessed her age, I pegged her for mid-thirties. She looked younger in the daylight. Her liver-spotted hands told a different story. She had the hands of at least a fifty-year-old. Scars, brown spots, bulging veins, and bony fingers.

"Did you bring your gloves?" I asked.

An odd look passed between us. Recognition, maybe or perhaps understanding. "I left them in the room."

A woman dressed in normal clothes, jeans, boots, and a sweater, walked between Kim and me, handing Idalia her gloves. Idalia's hunched shoulders relaxed as she tugged the unforgiving leather onto her fingers. "Thank you, Janet."

"The ladies are waiting," Janet urged.

"They will have to wait. I have unfinished business."

Chapter Eight

We stayed with the rest of the party for the champagne toast. The bride resembled a euphoric kid after winning a mud fight, chugging back her drink. The only things left white were her teeth and her sclera.

Idalia and I left the kitchen, reeking of paint, skunked perfume, and mini hotdogs. *How could they eat after inhaling all those fumes?* I wanted to leave by the time the ice cream bar rolled out.

Idalia led me back to the other sitting room with a downstairs bedroom attached. She closed the door behind us. The empty room lacked the tedious care taken with the rest of the house. Only a table and two chairs sat in the center. Nothing else, not even a window, adorned the space.

"There are no windows in this room?" I questioned.

"It used to be the live-in maid's room," Idalia explained. "It gives me the creeps."

I cocked my head almost from ear to shoulder. "You are spooked? Lady, you made my friend forget about you for six hours, and you accused me of being a witch from a line in my palm. You're not supposed to be frightened."

She bent her body over the small table and held her forehead in her hands. "I get it. You're mad. I'm sorry about earlier. I don't make it a habit to blurt out sensitive stuff. You had no protection. I went too far."

"Please don't take this the wrong way, but every

68

time you speak, I'm going to have more questions."

"I know, I'm fucking this all up. There are a lot of things to talk about here. Hold your questions for the end. Have a seat." As if she sensed my hesitation, she laid her hands on the table, palms up. "I mean you no harm. I wish to aid in your journey, however that may be. Come here, Lena, and place your palms over mine."

I ignored the warning, an invisible scratching like nails on dry skin coursing over my body. The gain outweighed the potential fear. I wanted all the knowledge she had and more.

I sat down on the glazed wooden chair and stared at Idalia's gloved hands. As if she remembered earlier today, she removed her gloves again. Her bare hands resembled the weathered bark of an old tree. The lines, grooves, spots, and protruding veins popped out of her wrist. I hardly wanted her touching me, but a connection had to be made.

"Lena, I promise I'm not here to hurt you. We don't have much time. I wouldn't put it pass Fiona's friends to storm the door down."

I rolled my eyes. I hated being rushed. "All right, I'm ready."

I slid my palms over hers and pushed down slightly. Our hands were almost the same size, except my fingers stretched longer by a fraction of an inch.

"Hold steady. Keep the connection. Don't move your hands," Idalia instructed. While her hands were braced by her elbows, a stiffening started in my right arm. I held the awkward position for at least two minutes before she spoke again. "Lena, please answer yes or no to my questions. Answer as truthfully as possible."

I exhaled a deep breath and nodded. Idalia's chin

drooped to her chest. Her neck rolled back and forth. If her head rotated a full three hundred and sixty degrees, my scream would be heard ten towns over. She hummed, but her lips spoke intangible words at the same time like a ventriloquist.

"Am I supposed to understand what you're saying?" I asked.

I gasped as her head popped up. Her blue eyes gleamed purple off the candlelight. She met my skepticism head-on, and her lips formed a menacing sneer.

"Were you born a witch?" she asked.

"I don't know."

"Yes, you do. It's in both your maternal and fraternal lines. The correct reply is yes."

"Yes, I was born a witch."

"Do you practice your craft?"

"No."

"You will lose your powers after the twentieth full moon."

"That's not a question."

"Where do you think your unused potential will go?"

"The end of the world. I have no fucking clue. What happened to the yes or no questions?"

"Your grandmother had protection, but she left you vulnerable, exposed, unarmed."

"I don't want that life."

Her eyes narrowed into black slits, and her head cracked to the side of her neck. "You think you have a choice?"

"Yes."

Idalia paused her bullet questions. Her left palm

twitched beneath mine, drawing my gaze toward our joined hands. I half-expected the pulsing energy, the repulsion of opposites, to force our palms apart, but no. We held our embrace, whether I liked it or not.

The muscles in my arms burned from floating in the air above her. They could be wretched off my body for all I cared. I had to keep the connection.

"When does the full moon countdown start?"

"It has already begun. You're fading. They're growing. Drain, poor witch, drain."

The wooden table rumbled like an earthquake affected only the round top. The candle inched toward our hands.

"Stop this. Right now," I shouted.

"No. Are you willing to break the eternal line?"

"Yes."

"You hollow-hearted swine, how dare you deny your power!"

"It's my power to deny! Fuck you!"

"Hahaha, if only you followed the proper rules. Run away, child."

"No, finish this, now!"

"Under the garden, below the squirming worms, entombed beneath the souls. That's where the craft will go when abandoned. The moon will shed tears for your death, the rest of time a sniffling bore. Watch out, for the flames kidnap the light."

The liquid wax splattered over my knuckles, missing Idalia's hand completely. The momentary pain snapped me back to the surface.

"Let the earth, moon, and sun cry for me. I don't want to be a witch."

"You don't have a choice. You're already his. He's

here."

"Who?"

The doorbell rang, echoing throughout the house. I swore the walls shook from the clattering bell sound.

I tore my hands away from Idalia. Her body slumped forward over the table, her cheek colliding with the surface. Spasms raked through her prostrate body. I cradled my burnt hand, watching the rest of the show.

Women's voices grew louder like buzzing bees swarming throughout the house. If my true love was here, I would be taking the back exit.

"Lena, are you ready to begin?" My focus switched back to Idalia rubbing her eyes and yawning wide. "Place your palms on top of mine. It's easier to show you how I did the spell instead of telling you."

"My hand is hurt from the spilled wax. Just tell me, please."

"What wax? What are you talking about?

"*Dalia!*" A man's voice boomed through the house loud enough my hair whipped around my face in a windowless room.

"I have to go," Idalia said. She blew out the lit candle on the other side of the table and snatched up the circular board we hoovered our hands over.

"Like hell you do. Who's here? Tell me!"

"My brother," she said. "Don't worry. He has no clue you're here."

Someone pounded on the door to the room we sat in, jerking our attention to the left. "Madame Prince, your brother is here." The woman shouting through the wooden door turned the doorknob to no avail. The brass hardware turned every which way, remaining closed.

"There's no lock on the door? Are you keeping it

shut?" I asked.

She cocked a shoulder up. "We better go before he blows this house down."

I got up from the chair on wobbly legs. I pitched forward, slamming my palm onto the table for balance.

"I feel weird," I muttered.

"Try being me. I feel weird all the time."

"*Dalia!*" her brother screamed.

Our door flew open, and fairies of all shapes and sizes rushed into the room. "A man is here for you," someone said.

"Where is he?" Idalia asked.

"He won't come inside."

Idalia huffed out an exasperated breath. She lifted her gray woven messenger bag over her shoulder. "I'll deal with him."

She hustled through the fairies with me trailing not far behind. They tried closing the parted space she blew through, but I cocked my elbows out. Whatever the fuck happened back there left me with more questions.

"Dalia! Invite me in!" Her brother's voice stopped me cold in my tracks. I slammed my back against the wall at the edge of the kitchen.

"It doesn't work that way! Give up that crap. You're not a vampire!" Idalia shouted.

"Dalia, invite me in."

When he spoke slower, enunciating each syllable, I was certain. I never feared him when he lured me away from the comedy club two nights ago, but tonight I gritted my teeth, and my hands trembled. He was pissed.

"Fiona, can my brother join the party?" Idalia asked.

The dirty bride left a trail of filthy paint in her wake. Ex-bridesmaids fell to the floor, cleaning it up as she passed.

"I'd fuck him. Can I fuck him?" Fiona said. Her slurred voice scratchy and used.

"Eww, no. Invite him in," Idalia said.

"Ugh, fine. Hello, baby, come inside. Will you strip for us?"

"No, thank you." Arthur's feet pounded on the hardwood floors inching closer to the kitchen. My breath came faster, and my heart pounded in my ears. I flattened out my back against the wall as much as my body allowed. My breasts protruded, and my stomach stuck out in my peplum top. If he looked for me, he would find me.

Idalia ran back into the destroyed kitchen. Arthur passed me right by. "What the hell happened here?" Arthur scanned the mayhem and marched up to the fairy guards gathering around Idalia. His black trench coat flared behind him from the fan on the floor, making the disgusting odors in the room worse.

"I got my first alimony check, motherfucker!" Fiona shouted.

Arthur ignored her. He stared over the ladies' heads at his sister. "What the fuck does all this mean?"

"I'm not having this conversation in front of my friends."

"Friends? You think these glitter bombs are your friends?" Arthur grunted and ripped off his coat. He extracted a fist full of cash out of his pocket and threw the bills in the air. "You want more money? Take my cut! These clients are paying customers only. We're leaving!"

"She's not a customer." Idalia's gaze followed her extended pointer finger right at me.

I slid against the wall, moving away as fast as I could before Arthur made sense of where his sister pointed. I looked back, dooming my escape in the process. Arthur's lips parted. An audible gasp left his throat.

"No men allowed. No men allowed." The pirate with the loudest voice chanted, and the other women joined her. They crowded Arthur, circling his tall frame. He threw his head back, running his hands over his face.

I took the chance and threw open the screen door to the backyard.

"Lena, I'll take care of you next!" Arthur said.

I'll be waiting, asshole.

Chapter Nine

I closed the loud screen door and ran into the backyard. There were no outdoor lights, or back patio, just a short, pebbled walkway. From the light of the kitchen, an old yellow swing set lurked at the tree line. Flowers, surrounded by a rock garden, tilted sideways in the breezy air hugging the backside of the house. Crickets swished their legs back and forth, filling the air with their music every few seconds.

I stepped onto the walkway and gagged from the fresh stench of vomit on the non-flower side of the small stone landing. As my gaze adjusted to the starless night, I noticed a pergola draped in vines standing parallel to the swing set. I hauled a lawn chair off a stack by the vomit and made my way into the shadows.

From my position in the middle of the shielded space, I had a clear view of the screen door. The noise from the party made its way through the walls and the propped-open bathroom window. A deep, tiresome yawn rumbled through me. I sank deep into the chair, resting the back of my head against the top.

I barely processed the latest mind-numbing ten minutes of my life. Idalia was Arthur's sister, Idalia Prince. I thought back to the day of my grandmother's funeral. Had Idalia been there? She did not recognize me in the city. *How could this be happening?*

"Are you hiding in plain sight? I can see you,"

Arthur's deep voice stated. I jolted upright, and my tired eyes snapped open.

Arthur flicked the light on his phone toward my face as he shuffled through the grass. He already had a lawn chair under his arm.

"I had enough of fairyland."

"It makes them feel free. They are escaping their lives for the night." His voice softened from the aggressive tone he had inside.

"I guess I'm too serious of a person to let go that easy," I remarked.

"I bet." Even though it was the third time we had seen each other, he extended his hand. I shook his cold flesh. "I want to apologize for my outburst before. My sister shouldn't be here. It's too close to the new moon."

"Is she a werewolf?"

"Ha-ha, no. They don't exist."

"Are you sure about that?"

Arthur cocked his chin up while a smile slid across his lips. I barely made out his features in the dark. We sat face to face in two different worlds. My legs crossed at the knee cut off all blood flow, and his jean-clad legs spread out wide, aiding his perfect slouch. I stared him down while he pondered my werewolf comment.

"I think werewolves belong in old black and white movies our parents talked about when we were kids."

"Thank you for clearing that up. If you have a moment, there are a lot of things I need explained."

"This is not the place for this type of conversation."

"Then I should have scooted around to the front and left this shit storm." Without the moon or the stars casting any light, I swung my legs apart without flashing him. I rose from the chair and headed back toward the house.

"Lena, wait." His touch on my arm shocked me, and it wasn't from static shock. "I didn't follow you out here to flirt about werewolves. I want to help you." Heat as if he held hand warmers for half the night seared into my skin. A faint flicker of red light, like fading filaments in a Christmas lightbulb, illuminated the space where we touched.

"How are you doing that?" I asked.

"I was about to ask you the same question." He released me, and the cold air chilled the spot.

"I need to go." I made a big mistake by walking past him instead of around the wooden edge of the opening arch.

"Lena, please." Arthur reached for me again but hesitated. I almost reached the screen door until his voice stopped me dead in my tracks. "Your love spell worked. It's cursed, but it worked. Release him now while you still can."

I squeezed my eyes shut and thrust my palms over my eyelids. "The spell is almost over. I don't need to do anything!"

"This is why you need me. The spell is still active. Find your beau. Release him before midnight."

"Buddy, I have had enough shit from you and your cracked-out sister. Do you take care of her? She needs help more than I do."

He spat off to the side. "Deal with your boyfriend first."

"He'll be fine. He's already dating someone else. I won't have to see him again unless I want to. Everything else was a bunch of convenient coincidences."

Arthur ran his fingers through his hair, groaning at

the sky.

"Why do I always run into you when I'm in a shit mood? The spell will end tonight, but only if you put a stop to it. His life depends on it."

"How did you even know I would be here? I'm so fucking confused!"

"We'll fight about it later. Go, now! The man could die, Lena! Save an innocent guy before it's too late!"

Arthur walked into the perimeter of light from the kitchen. Panic lurked behind his gaze. Before he breathed an inch of the same air as me, I bolted. I threw back the screen door, ignored the party, grabbed my purse, and headed for the front door. I dialed Ray as soon as I got in my car.

"Are you at my house?"

Ray stammered, "Well, I ran out of beer, and I had left a case when I came over this week, so I only stopped in to grab a few."

"Ray, it's eleven o'clock on a Saturday night. You're at my house, say it."

"Yeah, I'm here. You have that streaming channel I like, and they just released a movie for free that is in theaters."

I ended the call through my car. I had enough of his beating around the bush. I did it to him. I was the reason why he felt destined to be on my couch forever.

I broke every speed limit racing home. The dial twitched once my car leveled out at eighty miles per hour in a thirty-five zone. I slammed on the brake in front of the upcoming red light. The car stopped, but my breath kept panting faster.

I made it home in minutes, turning off my car without putting the car in park. The car restarted, and I jerked the gear into park. Ray stood in the beams of my headlights, drinking a beer without a label.

When I stayed in the car, he walked to the driver's side. The car locked itself the second he tried opening the door. "Lena, what's going on?"

I loved him. Deep down in the pits of my soul, shitty timing and bad luck snuffed out our potential life together. We should have been happy, riding the high of a possible family life, but the cards dealt had other plans.

He tugged at the locked door again. "Hey, unlock the door?" The car window became a microscope, magnifying the confusion on Ray's face. "Lena!"

If I stayed in the car, we remained trapped in our horrible dance. The parasitic spell fed off the kernel of real love. As much as I hated Arthur and his weird sister, I felt like I was meant to meet her and see him tonight. I needed the warning. Ray deserved more than being a plaything of a dream long gone and needed to be released correctly from the spell.

I waved my hands at the window, shooing him back. The car door opened, and Ray pulled me out.

"What happened? Did someone hurt you? I'll kill them." His cold hands cupped my cheeks, and his gaze searched mine for answers.

"That's what I'm afraid of. Ray, I have a confession to make."

The side of Ray's mouth curled up. Deep down, I suspected he wanted our relationship back even though he had Chloe. I put off the end for far too long.

"The other night changed things for you too?" he said. His bedroom eyes, half-lidded from the ungodly hour bewitched me, but I fisted my hands, squeezed my eyes shut, and exhaled a deep breath.

"Ray, I release you from my spell. You are free."

The damn motion sensor garage light turned off the moment I broke my claim on Ray. As my gaze adjusted to the darkness, his head pitched forward, our foreheads resting together. I had smelled cheap beer on his breath, but now the strong whiff of the aftershave I bathed his candle with a year ago assaulted my nostrils like he reapplied.

"Lena, I love you," Ray stuttered. The crisp, windy air enveloped his body, chilling the skin touching me. His hands turned frigid, and our foreheads stuck together like a wet tongue to a pole.

"I release you, because I love you," I commanded.

I stepped away from his embrace, activating the light above the garage. Ray shielded his eyes from the glaring lights, bright enough to kill a vampire. His vacant stare filling with tears destroyed me. My body shook with the emptiness washing over me. Our love crumpled between us.

Ray wiped tears off his puffy face against the sleeve of his thermal shirt. He almost turned away, but the logical part of my brain tuned out for the next few minutes. I saw what happened, even if I didn't believe it.

He lifted his right pointer finger up to the sky, almost begging for a lightning strike. Like the other night, when we slept next to each other, a rumble of thunder rolled through the sky. I followed his finger up to the darkness, then back down onto his face. Ray thrust his finger down his throat, gagging and choking until his wrist passed his lips. I tried touching him, preventing the ultimate suffocation in such a compromising position. He scurried away across my lawn, hunched over like a wounded animal.

"*Ray!*" I followed his swift movements. I screamed his name again until I spotted him near the bushes separating my yard and the neighbor. He stretched up to his full height. The streetlamp illuminated part of his face. His visible eye bulged red. He tried blinking, but an invisible hand pried his eye open. "Ray?"

Tiny bones cracking forced my hands over my ears. Ray's muffled scream brought me down to my knees. "Stop this! Please! He doesn't deserve this!" I pounded my hands against the grass like it would help the situation.

"I told you the spell wasn't over."

Like the wake and the party tonight, I hadn't heard him come until he announced his arrival. I scrambled up from the ground, running toward Arthur.

"Please do something! Help him!" I shook his unforgiving biceps. His hands stayed in the pockets of his jeans.

"I would if I could. I've never seen a spell turn so ugly. He's going to break apart."

My nostrils flared, and my fists pushed off his rigid chest. "I don't know what else to do! I'm not a witch!"

"You're more powerful than you could ever imagine, but this isn't your doing. The Brujah cursed your spell. We must hope it ends."

A loud scream interrupted our exchange. Ray, my poor Ray, thrashed and gnawed his hand. I ignored Arthur's riddles and lunged toward Ray. I grabbed ahold of his slippery arm. Saliva and something darker, probably blood, dripped down his arm. I yanked my sweater over my hand, gripping his arm, and heaved back with all my might. His tortured scream grew louder.

"It's almost midnight. The spell might end then."

"And what? He will turn into a pumpkin?"

"When did you cast the spell?"

"A year ago."

"No, what time of the night?"

"Midnight."

Arthur glanced at his watch. "Three minutes to go."

"How long does it take someone to asphyxiate?"

"I don't know. Hold his left arm down. Let's try to get him to stay down."

Ray's skin burned from the cold. Either he would freeze to death or suffocate. Another strained cry for help broke me. I held in my tears the last few minutes, but all respite left when he turned his head, pleading with his gaze.

"Hold on a little longer, man," Arthur said.

More blood dripped down Ray's arm, which thrust further down his throat. "Ray, stop moving."

"He won't stop until he reaches it."

"His stomach?" My hold on Ray faltered. The last sharp jerk of his hips and kicking overpowered me. I angled my weight over the side of his body, trying as hard as I could to keep him immobile.

"His heart. He's trying to give you his heart."

An unbearable, searing pain ripped through my back. Ray's free hand clawed at me. Arthur pulled him back, and his possessed body thudded to the ground.

The more we tried controlling Ray's movement, the intensity of his flailing grew harder. While another rumble of thunder slipped through the sky, Ray's body stilled and grew slack.

"One minute left," Arthur said.

I laid down into the crook of Ray's arm, mimicking how I slept on him countless nights of our relationship.

My head rested on his chest. His wild and frenzied heartbeat thumped against his ribs. The pulsing rhythm slowed, growing softer until I barely heard it all.

"Is he dying?" I asked.

"You can't live without your heart."

Unlike the fairytales, my tears drenching his shirt were not magical tears, bringing forth light to anything they touched. They held nothing but my grief, ignorance, and shame.

"Time. Ray, get up," Arthur ordered.

A hand smoothed across my hair. I deserved no comfort for murdering Ray. Arthur kneeled next to Ray's motionless body. Ray's hand stilled on my head. I sobbed, until Arthur wrenched Ray's hand out of his throat.

"Who the fuck are you?" Ray's chest raised with each new breath. He cradled his damaged hand. Arthur and I helped him to his feet. He wobbled as if his pending death still had a grip on him.

"I'm a friend. Let's get you back into the house," Arthur said.

"A friend of whom?" Ray questioned. He sneezed and coughed, clearing some of his raspy voice.

"Can we get inside?" I offered.

Ray woke up a little more. In the shining light of the solar-powered spotlights near my front door, I saw the state of his arm. Bite marks filled with clotting blood ran up and down his forearm and wrist. He wiggled his fingers.

"I have to go home. I'll get my stuff another day."

"Ray," I called. I stepped closer to him, but Arthur held up his hand, shaking his head. I ignored him. "How many beers did you drink tonight?"

"Not enough. Goodbye, Lena."

Ray hopped into his pickup truck and never looked back. Arthur started leaving, but I stopped him. "You're leaving too?"

"I warned you to be careful with your gifts. I almost didn't follow you home, but for that man's sake, I'm glad I did."

"I meant no harm."

"Well, now you know."

I tried not taking his cold stare to heart, but I felt like a child who played with matches after her parents distinctly told her not to do it. Arthur walked toward the sidewalk and passed the bushes, where Ray almost died. A shiver, not quite from the cold air, forced me inside.

The television show Ray had been watching played in the living room. He never hit pause when he met me outside. The characters laughed until it grew awkward for them, and they resumed their superhero nonsense. His telltale snacks of cashew pieces and cheddar popcorn mixed with caramel popcorn sat in a big bowl.

On autopilot, I shut off the television and dumped the junk food in the garbage. The doorbell rang, rattling my own heart in its cage. Arthur yawned but waved on the other side of the fisheye glass of the peephole.

"What now, Arthur?" I shouted through the door.

"Can I come in?"

I opened the door, and like the first time Arthur stood behind the threshold, his knuckles braced against the old doorframe. "It's over. Thank you for your help."

"I came back to check on you. Are you okay? That wasn't exactly a normal break-up."

Nervous laughter, or perhaps manic gasps of breath sounding like amusement bubbled out of my body. "I'm fine. Thank you for checking."

"You're not inviting me, are you?"

"Not today." I slammed the door in his face. A harsh gesture, but I had enough for one day.

Chapter Ten

I woke up feeling like I had eaten sandpaper for a midnight snack. Nothing alleviated the ache inside me. My knees cracked as I sank down into my tub, filled with jasmine-scented bubbles. The calming oil sedated the rambling chaos of my thoughts.

Ray almost died because of me. I owed Arthur big time. He saved Ray's life. Shit like that was exactly why I avoided witchcraft in the first place. People got hurt, good souls worthy of living their entire lives without some foolish girl wrecking it all.

I sunk down into the soapy water until the back of my neck rested on the edge of the tub. Usually, I laid a towel down, dulling the harsh porcelain digging into my spine. Today, I welcomed the pinch of discomfort. I deserved the pain from my actions yesterday.

My therapist would have a field day if I told her the truth.

Masochist thoughts were steps backward, not forward. I knew what I did wrong. I could not allow it to happen again. If I talked to Arthur, he could help me.

Arthur created a whole other set of problems. Three times, he had ruffled my feathers, disturbing my peace. His piercing gaze felt like a red laser beam zeroing in on his target. Who the fuck was he anyway? Some asshole whose mother was in a coven that steals dead witches' powers? The very thought of that festered the awful taste in my mouth.

For all I knew, the fucker could have a tail.

He had rosy lips, his sandy-haired mustache hanging over them. If I kissed him, would it be scratchy or soft?

I closed my eyes, rolling my head back and forth, shaking off the thought. A kiss seemed like the opposite of something he would do. But what if he kissed softly, trailing down my body until his lips brushed against my innermost parts, arching into his touch?

My hand already slipped down into the water, circling and rubbing myself beneath the remaining bubbles. His mustache must be soft, like his full lips caressing my body.

In the darkness behind my eyelids, Arthur and I fucked like our lives depended on it. Our bodies undulated together, building an unstoppable inferno. The powers I desperately ignored and squashed down flew out every natural hole and slits in my skin into his parted mouth. Flames flickered from our fingertips until mine burned out and his raised higher than the tiled ceiling. I clung to his body, riding his cock past a natural limit of thrusts. We never stopped fucking. Lust slammed us back toward the ground. Arthur's smoking fists clutched heaps of grass, leveraging himself over my shivering frame. The orgasm strangled us both, crushing the air out of our lungs. We died in the field that once was a bed that started out as a tub.

"Lena, knock, knock!"

Nasty water flooded my mouth. My eyes opened and my mother stood in the doorframe with her hand covering her eyes. I jerked upright, spitting out the bathwater I drank while I slept.

"Hey, Mom," I sputtered.

"Lena, please remind yourself to set an alarm while you're in the tub. I thought you were dead."

"I died in my dream."

"I hate when that happens." My mom scrunched up her face as if she sucked on a lemon. She put the toilet seat down and sat.

There were enough bubbles for my modesty, but the last time my mother and I had a heart-to-heart while I soaked in the tub, I wore braces and pig tails.

"So, Mom, what brings you around these parts?"

"Ha-ha, your master bathroom? Well, I don't have great news."

"Who died?"

"Not this time. They are closing your grandmother's nursing home. All the nurses and staff are going to have to find new jobs, and the seniors will be relocated," Mom said.

"That's a shame. I'm sorry to hear." Mom inhaled a large breath and held it as she cracked her knuckles. "What's the matter? It's not your fault. They probably lost a lot of people from the pandemic. Weren't they going to close a few years ago?"

"Yeah, it's finally happening. I'm headed there today. Um, the twins, Dolores and Elona are asking about you. They would like to see you before they are transplanted somewhere else."

The lukewarm water I waded in became cold in an instant. "I vowed never to go back there. Mom, I swear something bumped into me."

"I know. A ghost hit your shoulder on your way out with your father. Your shoulder felt bruised for a week. Lena, we were all stressed that day. Besides the twins, the staff would like to see you too. They took such good

89

care of my mother. I think the least we can do, is stop in before the last day."

"Can we talk about this after I'm done with my bath?" My wrinkled fingertips had enough. God knew how long I slept while I had the worst and hottest sex dream of my life.

"Okay, I'm going to make some tea. Do you still have the vanilla chai?"

"Yup, I buy it just for you."

"Thank you, don't stay in too long. You will look like a prune."

I wobbled out of the tub as soon as my mom left the room. Sharp hunger pain in my stomach reminded me I still lived, regardless of the twisting thoughts muddled in my mind. I wished yesterday never happened, and now I dreaded today.

Before I went downstairs, I contemplated reaching out to Ray. His usual —*I'm home*— text missing from last night. He always did things like that in case I worried. After gathering my ponytail too tight against my skull, I chickened out and checked my social media for Ray's page. Low and behold, he blocked me. A few posts back, he liked an image. I found it, and my suspicions rang correct.

Did he remember what happened last night?

"Lena, tea is ready!" my mom yelled.

I'll think about Ray later and deal with Arthur, too.

****

My mother wore me down, and we went to the nursing home. The twins were sweet Albanian ladies whose grandchildren only visited them on holidays. Half the time we saw them, they murmured nothingness in their native tongue. I asked them one day to write down what they said. Instead, they wrote in perfect English, a poem unlike anything I ever read before. They must have lived by a meadow, for the descriptions of the crisp mountain air lifting them up countless times appeared too vivid for lies.

They sat in their spots in the television room, writing again. One of the aides, who specialized in occupational therapy, peered over Elona's shoulder, smirking at the words written in perfect cursive. "What spell are you casting?" she said.

In unison, both Elona and Dolores placed a finger to their lips, whispering, "Shhh, they're letters." Their heads wrenched my way. I ignored the universe for the umpteenth time. As if I imagined the abrupt jerking of their necks, when I looked back at them, they continued writing to no one.

I faked a phone call and searched the eating area for the artificial floral arrangement I made the facility last year. The once vibrant assortment gathered a lot of dust. I grabbed a cloth and sprayed the polyester blend with a little water.

"Your grandmother always smiled at your gift. Even with her advanced dementia, I swore she knew you made it," another nurse aide said. She pushed her cart of fresh linens, protein drinks, and coloring books passed me.

"I was her favorite," I commented.

"Oh yes, we all saw that with her. You were the baby." The nurse had a slight Caribbean accent and walked with a limp. I forgot her name, but I always said hello.

I thought she turned the corner, so I allowed the tears to fall from my eyes like a river. I held it in for too long.

"Sweet child, have a seat. Crying is okay. We all

need to cry."

The nice lady guided me over to the seat my grandmother sat in for mealtime. I swore a part of her lingered in the spot, wrapping her arms around me from behind. The echo of her life remained here. A soft pressure like fingers dragged up my left arm.

The man who ran the cafeteria curled his fingers in front of his mouth, blowing into the enclosed space like a kazoo. I jerked out of the seat, startling another elderly woman I often saw when my grandmother lived here. She spotted me and smiled a toothless grin.

"Rose, the governor is coming tonight. You must get dressed. Roderio, fix my hair when you can."

"Don't worry, I'll be ready," I said.

The woman twirled an imaginary necklace around her bony finger and fluffed her hair. Buzzing like an intercom on the fritz engulfed the room. The volume increased, and the pitch sharpened. The cafeteria man and the old woman's words faded into the noise. My breath wheezed out of my mouth. I held on tight to the rickety table's edge.

"*Mom!*" I hoped my vocal cords worked even though no sound made it out of the dome I resided in. She must be on the other side where the first incident happened by the bedrooms. No one reacted to my yelp.

It was time to go.

I ran back the way I came in. The muscles in my calves burned from the sudden sprint. I had the heavy door leading out of the dementia wing in my sight, but then I realized the key, too high for any patient to reach, did not hang down from the top of the door frame.

My mother's hand gripped my shoulder. The warmth, our blessed connection, unfurled the tension rumbling through me. If she stood by me, it stopped. Whatever 'it' was at the time.

"Lena, are you okay?" I turned toward my mother and wrapped my arms around her shoulders. She used to be taller than me, but her narrowing spine brought her down two inches to my height. I dug my chin into the hollow of her neck, begging for escape without words. "We're almost done."

We separated. Our gazes, her green eyes and my hazel eyes, understood each other.

Sound came back, first with an alarm and shuffling of nurses' sneakers. Dolores, the nimbler of the twins, stood in the doorway of the television room. They were not allowed to walk around freely unless with a nurse. Mom and I gasped at her standing straight ahead.

"Dolores, get back to your seat!" a nurse shouted. She grabbed Dolores's elbow, nudging her back.

"No, she must learn! Read the prayers. Stop them. Don't let them take what's rightfully yours." Dolores crooked a shaky finger at my face. "Take it! Take it all! Fight back!"

"Shush now, Dolores. Dinner is starting,"

"My book! Give me my book!" Dolores swatted at the nurse hard enough that I instinctively reached out to help.

"Dolores, please calm down. What book?" I asked.

The nurse retrieved a notebook from behind the wheelchair. "This is what she wants. Dolores, I won't give it to you until you sit down."

"Give her the book. Give it to her! She must be protected!" Dolores chanted again and again.

"I'm sorry, Ms. Martin. She has not been well," the nurse said.

From behind my mother, like a child shying away behind her mother's skirt, I nodded.

"I'll take the book." My mother, my best line of defense, retrieved the composition notebook from the nurse's hand. The creased once-stiff cover looked like it had been run over multiple times. Mom clutched it away from her body.

"Well, look at the time. We should get going. I'll email Doctor Javerz when I get home." Mom faced me and gave me the signal we worked hard perfecting a few years ago. "Lena, say thank you, and let's go."

"Thank you."

The nurse unlocked the main door, the alarm shrilling in my ear for the last time. Mom hustled to the nearest garbage can in the long hallway back to the main entrance.

"Can I see the notebook?" I shouted.

Her fingers gripped the notebook, which looked filthier in the light of the hallway. Ink smudges and food smears stained the cover and pages.

"Lena, this is garbage. There is no magic here."

"I never thought there would be. Please don't throw it out. I want to look at it."

"They don't do what you do. This is nonsense."

We hadn't spoken about the elephant in our lives since grandma stayed in the hospital twenty years ago after my sweet sixteen party.

"Mom, she wanted me to see it."

"And I said no. Let it go, Lena."

Mom's pained expression made me back down.

"All right. Throw it out." I gave in.

She stomped over to the garbage can and threw it inside. I passed the notebook atop the regular trash and felt nothing.

****

As always, my mother switched to nagging questions as soon as we got to the car and then back at my house. I thought she would drop me off and be on her merry way, but no.

"Any luck with the new drug subscription?" She pushed her glasses high on her forehead, inspecting the written prescription tacked to the fridge.

"Mom, I haven't had the time to do enough research on it. I have an early presentation tonight, so I might do it later."

"When did time stop you from doing anything?"

"I've been busy."

"Don't put it off for too long. Your health is a priority. Have you done anything more online for the family history project?"

"Not much. I fell down your grandmother's third husband's family rabbit hole, but I'm struggling with your grandfather's side."

"I don't understand. They might have come here illegally, but how can there be nothing? There must be a marriage record. My grandparents met here in the United States."

I hated letting my mother down. My father's family research found itself. I had enough information from him and my cousin. My mother's father's side was another story. Two pictures of her paternal grandmother were all we had left, along with an address for the old grocery store, which was now a bar, and census reports from the early twentieth century.

"They update records all the time. Maybe there will be something in the next batch of new stuff."

"You're right. At least you have made some leeway on the German side of your family."

My family history project was years in the making. I hit a wall, then something new popped up on the website I used, and bam, the addiction returned full swing.

"I can't believe your great-grandmother looks so much like you."

The picture was worth a thousand words. If I hadn't made the connections I did, I'd never have known my great-grandparents were in the photo. Oddly enough, they were the only two people not staring at the camera on New Year's Eve in nineteen eighteen. My great grandmother, already in love, laid her head back against the Kaufmann's knee, aka my grandfather.

"I know where she's buried," Mom added.

"You know where everyone's buried."

"And where is the problem?"

"People are more than their graves."

"But, sometimes, stones and bones are all we have left."

"You're right. I judged wrong."

Mom ruffled through a finished album as I pulled my credit card out of my back pocket.

"Lena, how many times do I have to tell you? That's such a bad habit."

"Yes, Mom."

"How's your knitting coming along?"

My mother's favorite diversion tactic in full bloom. She had to be running out of inquiries.

"I abandoned it months ago. I had no idea Ray was allergic to wool."

"Now that you guys aren't together anymore, give

knitting another go?"

"Maybe."

"All right, let me get out of your hair. You should sleep a little more. I can't tell if you have dark circles under your eyes or smudged make-up."

I shrugged. "A bit of both. I will. Bye, Mom."

After she grabbed her keys from the kitchen table, she stalled again. "I'm sorry about what happened at the nursing home. I should have given you the notebook."

"It's okay, Mom. I know you had good intentions."

She opened her mouth but decided against that final thought. Her car door slammed shut, and her engine roared to life. She started talking to my father, the volume at the max, through the car speakers. Her tires scoffed over the deep slanted curve in the road.

I picked up one of the pillows from my couch and screamed as loud as possible into the worn fabric. My throat ached after the third yell. I needed help.

Chapter Eleven

My first Wednesday night without Ray sucked. I
made dinner alone and ate in silence.

I half expected him to overpower the broken spell,
but I understood if he stayed away. A photo on his social
media profile of a beautiful, red-haired woman saluting
their tuna rolls together at a restaurant's grand opening a
few minutes ago proved he wasn't coming over.

I wished I heard silence in my misery. The hum of
the refrigerator, the buzz of the electricity powering up
the world, and the swift turning of the fan disrupted my
thoughts. I stepped outside, retrieving my mail, but the
outside noise hurt worse. Cars zoomed by, a powered-up
lawn mower roared, and a car horn beeped from the stop
light down the street.

The migraine relief pills stopped working an hour
ago. I trudged back into the house, searching for aspirin.
I came across the small piece of cardstock I tucked away,
but frankly, no hiding spot was good enough. The card
kept magically appearing, piercing my thoughts,
reminding me who worked there.

Arthur's shop was about five miles away. He hadn't
tried contacting me since the night with Ray. He didn't
have my phone number, but worst, he knew where I
lived. I half expected him to show up unannounced over
the past few days. However, it had been radio silence
since I slammed the door in his face.

I ignored the allure one more time. I tried eating, but I was so messed up I lost my sense of taste. The pasta and vodka sauce tasted like nothing. I pushed the plate away and grabbed my car keys.

I drove past Arthur's psychic shop at least once a week, never with any intention of pursuing the place. The sale sign giving half-price readings Monday through Wednesday rubbed me the wrong way.

I paid for parking at the curb and stood outside the darkened main entrance. The closed sign swung back and forth against the glass window hanging inside the door. I peeked inside the main room. They must be obsessed with the color burgundy. The floors, the walls, the furniture, and the thick curtains were all a dark red shade, like pooled blood in a deep cut.

I'm officially freaked out.

My phone alarm sounded at seven-thirty p.m. I had a training call at eleven tonight. Arthur had three hours left. I knocked without any tingles.

Arthur opened the door a few seconds later. He looked out of breath in a white T-shirt and dark wash jeans.

"Hey," I said. After an eternity of judgment, he said my name. "Am I too late?"

Arthur waved me in and locked the door behind me. The first zap of cold feet straightened my spine.

"You're right on time. I locked the door because too many people don't read what's right in front of them. I don't want to be interrupted." He pointed toward the closed sign, swinging back and forth again. I understood why it dangled now. Arthur had shut the door seconds ago, but why did it move before I came in?

"You were expecting me?"

99

Arthur smoothed his hands together as if he reapplied hand lotion. "Yes, but why do you think you're here?"

"All right, I'm going to bite the bullet. I have no idea why I'm here. I was home, minding my own business, until I came across your card, again."

"You know why you came. You couldn't wait to see me again. I excite you more than I unnerve you." Arthur winked and crossed his arms over his stomach.

"And I'm leaving now." I almost swiveled around in my flats.

"Can't take a joke. Got it. Lena, you're here because you played witch, did a powerful love spell, and almost killed your ex-boyfriend. The residual decay lingers on your skin. You're marked. It will fade, but it's red hot now."

I should have left when I peeked through the window. Any potential excitement for tonight disintegrated. His words slapped me in the face. I hated that he knew what happened. He stripped me of my confidence, unleashing tears filled with shame.

I bit the side of my hand, stifling the muffled gasp stuck in my throat.

Strong, soft hands on my forearms guided me over to an old wooden chair. He dragged the strap of my purse down my shoulder and massaged the tight knot of muscles above my right shoulder blade. I wanted distance from him, yet his movements calmed my embarrassment. I missed his caress the second he pulled away.

"We all try a love spell. It's nothing to worry about. It's over," he said.

"How the fuck did you know about it? I barely told

anyone about the spell. I forgot about it until a few days ago." I looked at his stern, unreadable face. His gaze looked miles away, and he rubbed the stubble on his chin.

He sat down on the other side of the small round table. A crystal ball clouded with natural swirls in the orb sat on a pedestal of fake talons in the middle of the crimson tablecloth. If I wasn't drawn toward the arch of his back, the stretching out his long legs under the table, and the sound of his knuckles cracking, I would have scoffed at the fortune-telling setup.

We mimicked our positions the other night in the dark garden. Now, we were out in the open. The natural light of the sunset shined through the bay window of his shop, and the glow off several colored glass lamps twinkled rainbows over our hands. I felt as though I saw him clearer when the shadows hid his face.

"There is never going to be a right time to tell you, so I'm sorry if this turns your world upside down. Do you want a drink?"

He can't be serious. I nodded, tucking an errant strain of hair behind my ear. "Lemonade, if you have it."

He smiled, the first one since I came in. "I made a fresh batch earlier. I'll be right back." Arthur rose from the old chair and disappeared past the stereotypical beaded curtain. The beads falling back into position resonated louder and louder. I covered my ears and squeezed my eyes shut.

"Lena, what's affecting you?" His muffled voice made it through my barrier. He came back with a pitcher and two small glasses.

I opened my eyes, and my fingertips rubbed the fleshy part on the side of my forehead. "The beads. The clicking hurts my ears."

"How long have sounds disturbed you?"

"My whole life. Look, Arthur, it's getting late. I work nights. Can we get to the gist of it, whatever the hell that is?" I said

"All right, let me know how the drink is, and I'll tell you everything."

The sweating glass of lemonade looked mouth-watering. He even wedged a small slice of lemon onto the rim. I took a sip, and the perfect mixture of lemons, water, and sugar burst into my mouth.

"Delicious."

Arthur sat there watching me as if he waited for the poison he slipped into the drink to strike me down dead. My heartbeat pulsed fast against my ribcage, but it had nothing to do with the lemonade.

"I'll tell Babushka you like it. It's her recipe," Arthur remarked.

"You're stalling, Arthur."

"Do you moan every time you taste something sweet?" He folded his hands over his stomach, snickering.

I took another gulp of the drink, catching a piece of ice between my teeth and crunching it loud. "Objection, relevance?"

"You're a lawyer too? I thought you designed computer programs."

"I'm out of here." I grabbed my purse and headed for the door.

"Oh fuck, wait. Lena, damnit," Arthur pleaded.

I whipped around so fast we almost collided. Finally, the crackling air sparked between us. "Make me stay."

"My mother knew the Brujah who sold you the love spell. Her name was Corrine. On her deathbed, she told me everything. There is a witch who doesn't want to be her birthright, dabbling in things she doesn't understand. She cursed the spell to teach you a lesson. It was fucked up, in my opinion. She should have warned you." He sucked in his lips.

I took a step forward, and he retreated two moves back.

"Tell me more." A foreign strength curled its tail inside me, searching for a weak spot in the air surrounding Arthur.

"You are a double-hereditary witch. Both your mother and father have it in their lineage. I don't know which side is stronger, but I think it's the Spanish side."

"My father's side."

"Yes, Lena. Corrine suspected fear kept you from exploring your options, or something traumatic made you abandon your gifts. If a witch doesn't use their craft, they will lose it." He waved his palm through the air between us. "The abilities of your ancestors are fading. If they leave you, they will be gone, permanently."

"What if I want it to leave me?"

Arthur placed his hand on the back of his neck, chuckling. "Then you're not my true love."

My mouth opened for the snappy comeback, but only a small squeak emerged. Arthur walked back to his chair, pulling a candle from the sales floor. A foot-long match with a black tip appeared from behind his ear. He performed magic tricks while I got my head cut off by his last admission.

Oh yes, we were getting along splendidly.

The flame sparkled as the lit match fired up the

fresh, new wick. The unmistakable whiff of sage masked by eucalyptus and citron watered my eyes and swam up my nose.

"Can you blow that out? I'm allergic to sage." I sneezed twice in a row.

"Do you actually have an allergy, or do you wish me harm?"

I ignored him, "Do you know how much time I have left to decide about my gifts?"

He shook his head and shrugged his shoulders. "You have some time left because you were able to stop the love spell, but how much is unquantifiable."

"Is there a test?"

"A test to determine if your powers are going to leave you or not? Not quite. There is a test to determine if you are a true witch." Arthur blew out the candle and moved it behind him.

I tapped my foot, waiting for his answer. He poured himself half a glass of lemonade and drank it in one gulp. "And?" I insisted.

Arthur's gaze shifted back to me. "Find death, not your own, but someone else's. Do not become a murdering hand, for that is immediate damnation. If you find your quest is futile, your time is done." Arthur spoke in a monotone voice as if he quoted a book passage he remembered by heart. He squeezed his eyes closed, rubbing his forehead.

"So I find death, and then I can fly on my broomstick."

"Come on, I'm being serious."

"Fine, your sister mentioned something about twenty full moons. Will I find death in the next year and a half?"

He shook his head. "You are way past twenty full moons. Stay away from my sister. Her goal differs from mine."

"Oh yeah, about the other night, she never told me how she made my best friend forget about meeting her. I suppose her spell wore off too quick. Is she a witch?"

Arthur dropped his hand from his face. He pursed his lips together, groaning. "She did what?"

"Oops, am I going to get her in trouble?"

"Forget that ever happened. She shouldn't have been at the party."

I smirked, "Too late, Arthur. I remember everything."

He tongued the inside of his cheek. "She fucks around with hypnosis. Your friend might be one of those lucky few who can fall under her spell."

"Are you making up this bullshit as you go or is that a line you use a lot?"

"There are more important things to attend to here. Forget about Dalia. I'm going to give you some stuff to help you find death if it is your true path." He rose from his chair and selected items from a glass buffet table. "Take these. They will help."

"Rose hips and Chai tea?"

"Yes, drink it daily."

"How the fuck is tea going to help me find death? I'll drink a cup of tea and die?"

"It might help calm you. My mother brewed it after death found me." Arthur said the last part and sucked in a big inhale. His large hands covered his face completely.

"You're a witch, too?"

After a pause, he continued, "Fortune teller, palm

reader, gamer, magic trick specialist, and yes, Lena, I am a witch."

"I feel like an idiot for not asking you."

"If it makes you feel any better, I hide it well."

"What about your sister?"

His phone buzzed on the table. He glanced over at the name on the call and rejected it. "We are getting off topic. You want to figure out if you should keep your powers or not? Death will determine if you truly are a witch or at the end of your line. It's the only way." Arthur tapped his right hand on the table next to his phone.

"Am I keeping you from something?"

"He can wait. I can't give you a lot of details because it will impede your discovery."

The phone rang again. Before I saw the name on the black screen, he palmed it, dragging the phone off the table into his lap.

"Can I call you for help?" I asked.

"I'll do what I can." Arthur listened to a sound only he heard, tilting his head sideways. "We'll talk soon." He answered the call and walked past the beads, leaving me alone.

I scoffed at his dismissal and walked out of the room, looking more like the inside of a body with red tendons oozing blood and muscles disguised as tapestries and paint. A police officer lifted my windshield wiper and tucked the small red and white ticket under.

"Ma'am, your registration sticker is expired. Free parking also starts at 8 o'clock."

I flipped the man the bird, grabbed the ticket off the glass, and slammed my car door shut. I turned the radio up all forty notches. The popular singer screamed where

I could not. I was utterly fucked with more questions than answers from the last fifteen minutes.

Chapter Twelve

How exactly does a person find death? I visited
cemeteries all the time and never felt anything off kilter.
I despised funeral homes from the year of death five
years ago. Every time I answered the landline phone,
someone died. At first, it came in threes. One person
close would die, then a celebrity of some sort, and then
another person associated with someone in my life. Then
death forgot its own precedence.

On second thought, my hatred of funerals went
further back. My *abuela* died around my eighth birthday.
She was my great-grandmother on my father's side, but
Abu to me. The first death kicked off the learned skill of
etiquette for when someone died. They laid her out for
two full nights, four hours of hugs, shaking hands, and
withholding my tears until the end. I practiced the Lord's
prayer over and over, repeating it under my breath
throughout the time, even though my mother insisted on
printing it out for me for the funeral mass.

As we left the funeral home after the second night
of the wake with the stench of formaldehyde clinging to
our black clothes, I turned back and wished I hadn't. Abu
sat up in her coffin, clutching her chest, then kissed her
dead palms, blowing it my way. I remembered smiling
back, not at all frightened. My mom, ignorant to the
occurrence, urged me out of the room, zipping up my
coat.

"Abu will be okay. She's sleeping soundly." Even at a young age, I knew the comfort tactics my mother went through at great lengths for me.

I told my parents and my grandparents what happened after the funeral. My father's mother wailed and cried for days. We made a special trip to the supermarket for more tissues. Mom insisted I forget about it. I had a child's rampant mind, after all, back then. Now, as I stood in my therapist's office watching a ferry float across the Hudson River to New York City, skeptics hindered my thoughts.

"If I crashed a funeral, would you judge me?" I asked Doctor Greene.

My therapist's bottom eyelids twitched. "I don't think it's a crime, but if you use me as your one phone call in the middle of the night, I will be pissed off."

I wasted half of my weekly therapist session on thinking about how to find death. My therapist thought I pondered places to meet men. The dead person could be a man. Arthur never specified a man or a woman.

"I doubt I'd be arrested. I can say that I knew them in passing," I surmised.

"What does that mean? You knew them as you passed by their coffin?" She placed her notepad down on her desk and removed her reading glasses. "Lena, putting psychology aside, breaking up with someone sucks. You can either learn from the experience, remember good memories you might want to do with a future partner, or better yet, learn traits and patterns to stay away from in your next dating experience. I think there are much better places to meet men than funerals. You're not seeing the real person, either. They are in a state of grief. You weren't yourself after your grandmother died. I wasn't myself after my cat died. Let's brainstorm more productive places to meet a potential boyfriend."

"I picked up Ray in a bar, so they are out."

"Come on, don't be stubborn. How about a brewery? Go to a trivia night. Try hot yoga."

I tilted my head. "Hot yoga?"

"He'll have tight pants on so you can check out the goods, and you will find out what he looks like as a hot, sweaty mess. Don't forget to smell him too."

She had something there, but I had no time for a relationship now. *What about a gym?* A gym addict might naturally go into cardiac arrest. I could use Kim's membership for a while, check out anyone who looked like they were exercising extra hard.

"What the fuck am I thinking? I think I lost my mind." I shouted, burying my face in my hands. Another wave of fatigue dragged a yawn from me.

"Do you take any supplements?"

One yawn followed the other, and now my therapist yawned. "The usual crap."

"I think you should go for your yearly physical soon, get some bloodwork done, check your vitamin levels. A couple of weeks ago, I started taking vitamin D, and I honestly feel better."

"You're the second person that told me to start taking vitamins. I'm a naturally pale person, and it's almost fall. I'm in my element."

"All right, let me know if you change up anything." She sat back down at her desk, rustling through the papers and notes in my file. "How's your family history project going?"

I knew she had many patients, but the fact that she looked up a topic disheartened me. There were other places I wanted to be other than here if she needed to scrounge up information.

"It's fine. Can we make this only a half hour session today?"

"Insurance doesn't care how long you stay, only that you showed up. The co-pay is the same at a half-hour or an hour. Am I keeping you from something?"

"I have a lot on my mind."

She leaned forward, arching her perfectly plucked eyebrows. When I said nothing, she asked, "Well, what? I guess you could crash a funeral. It might be a good 'how did you two meet?' story one day."

"I moved on from that idea. When is the Day of the Dead? It's after Halloween, right?"

"You're losing me here. Are you worried about dying? Did anyone else you know recently die?"

I was lost days before I got here. Arthur and his wacky sister, Ray, and now a quest for death were fucking up my life. I appreciated Arthur saving Ray, but now I'm obsessed. I checked Ray's profiles all day long. I guess it wasn't my power forcing Ray's hand down his throat, but the unease remained. I skipped breakfast today because I was at such odds with what happened.

"I finished my grandmother's estate paperwork. Last week, I closed out all her credit cards, sent her death certificate to the department of motor vehicles and the phone company. I cried for an hour. I miss her so much," I said. My therapist bought the partial lie. I did close out her bank account, but all the other stuff sounded good clumped together.

"That is hard. I'm going to write you a prescription for a mood stabilizer that doesn't have to be taken every day. It lasts about four hours. If you get upset and emotional, take half of a pill as needed."

It worked. She wrote the illegible prescription on the blue pad and keyed in the information on her tablet. "Thank you. I'll let you know how I feel once I start taking them."

Her caring smile slid across her face. "Get some rest. I'll see you next week."

"Can we move our sessions to every two weeks?"

"If you think you are feeling better, sure. I can alter my schedule to every other week. Unfortunately, if I cancel your upcoming appointments, they will potentially be filled up with another patient."

"That's fine. I will see you in two weeks."

She reached over to her desk, and for the first time, I noticed the tape recorder in the plastic magazine folder. The red power button dimmed out.

"Hey, we are off the clock, and I'm not recording what you say. What's up, Lena? You seem more than just depressed about your break-up with Ray."

"I swear I'm fine. On and off the record, I'm okay."

"All right. Be well, see you in two weeks."

****

I was not okay.

The rest of my Thursday turned into a wild goose chase about death. I stayed off the computer because the last thing I needed were cops knocking on my door, questioning everything I looked up. Instead, several torn out notebook pages cluttered my bed with ideas.

I paced the small span of my bedroom, peeking back at the insanity:

Visit a cemetery.

Morgue at a hospital

My grandmother's retirement home

Funeral home
Hospital, in general

They all had potential issues. Since the pandemic, hospitals were fortresses. If I broke a bone, I would have a reason to be lingering around the hospital. What if I posed as a grieving relative and visited a funeral home? I just happened to get lost on the way to the bathroom, which is always downstairs, to the left, through a maze. In my quest to pee, I stumbled upon the morgue or a viewing room and touched a deceased person.

My great-grandmother's dead flesh haunted me for days. I had touched her bare wrist as I pulled the lace cufflinks further up her arm. I scrubbed my hand raw afterward.

The hot water scalded my hands as I ran the faucet in my bathroom. The memory of the day never dulled.

My reflection looked pale in the afternoon sun. The little weight I lost sucked in my cheeks. The hollow now there had the same hue as the dark circles under my eyes. The white streak on the left side of my bangs spread over a few more dark strands.

"You're out of your mind." My mirror image smiled and laughed. *What the fuck was I doing?*

I crumbled the death options, one by one, and threw the papers away. My four o'clock alarm sounded. Amy and I had plans for dinner tonight. She decided on the restaurant last time. I picked tonight. I needed the break in the madness.

Chapter Thirteen

I hated the tavern in the middle of town. I only went once and regretted it. The naysayers claimed the table in front of the fireplace was haunted. My terrible date and I had sat at a table furthest from the hot spot. Invisible hands pulsed against my throat. I struggled to breathe. I went to the ladies' room, confident I experienced an allergic reaction to an unlisted ingredient in the food. I breathed easier in the back of the place, away from the dining room. As soon as I re-entered the room, I walked right out of the side door.

My feet left the restaurant of their own accord. I rationalized the experience as a warning. I hadn't felt fear for my safety, but the awareness of a dead presence fucked up my mind for months.

Maybe it'll try and touch me again. *Does a ghost touch count?* One minute I'm cursing myself for attempting to find death, and then I'm purposely playing with fire.

Amy and I met at the tavern at half past six o'clock. Amy had never been there, but she knew the stories too.

"Can we sit at the haunted table?" Amy asked.

"I knew you were going to ask. Yes, I requested it." I brought up our reservation on my phone and showed her the special instructions box.

Amy clapped, bouncing up and down. "I thought it was the one by the fireplace on the left side?"

"No, the right side is correct. That's the trick. We aren't entering the restaurant through the original door. From our direction, it's the right."

"But even the place says it's on the left."

"Exactly, because then they can determine who is having an actual experience or not."

Amy nodded, hiking her purse higher up her shoulder. The owner returned to his podium and grabbed two menus from the inner shelf. "This way, ladies."

Unlike last time, I felt fine. The windows were opened, allowing fall air to circulate throughout the room. Our table sat directly in front of the unlit fireplace with scorched wood for character. An elderly couple, eating in their blissful silence, sat on our left. Two men in business suits were to our right.

Amy nudged her knees further under the table and spread her hands out on the white linen tablecloth. "I've always wanted to come here. There is so much energy swirling around the room."

"Uh-huh, do you want to split the stuffed mushroom appetizer with me?" Yes, I tried changing the subject, and yes, Amy sneered my way.

"How can you look at the menu already? Don't you feel it? It's here. I know they're here."

"All right, Carol Ann. Reel it back. If you're dead set on having a paranormal experience, it's not going to happen. Pretend like you're at a normal dinner with your best friend, and who knows?"

"Who knows what? George Washington might sit down and tip his captain's hat my way. I want to feel a ghost. If I stay perfectly still, that might help."

"Hi ladies, Welcome to the Washington Tavern. Can I interest you in something to drink?" the waiter asked.

"White wine spritzer, for me. She will have two fingers of honey whiskey," I ordered.

"Miss, are you all, right?" the waiter asked. He checked out Amy.

Amy's eyes were closed, and her hands remained glued to the table. "Yes, I'll take the whiskey."

"While you are feeling shit out, I'm going to the ladies' room," I said. It had been a while since Madame Amy felt anything besides her cat scaring her by jumping onto things.

I chucked my cloth napkin onto my plate and got up from the creaking wooden chair. The side entrance door opened, sucking the warm air out like a vacuum. I stayed on course and did not ditch Amy.

The frigid bathroom held no respite. A crying woman dabbed under her eyes in the mirror.

"Are you okay?" I asked.

She nodded, blowing her nose on the mascara-stained paper towel. Stick to the path. Toilet, then wash your hands, then back to Amy. As soon as I got in the stall, a man's voice whispered into the ladies' room.

"I'm sorry, Shelly. Please forgive me."

"Sorry means shit to you, Robert. Get out!"

"Not until you accept my apology."

I rolled my eyes. The last thing I needed was to be held prisoner by a soap opera at the sinks. I said to hell with it and interrupted the couple. They gave me dirty looks like I was the weird one interrupting them.

The bathroom doorknob turned, but something blocked the door. I made sure it was unlocked and tried again. Not a budge.

"Is there a problem?" the man asked.

"Just my luck. The door won't open," I said.

He stomped over, opening the door without a problem. I ignored his side eye and headed out into the hallway. The waiter rushed toward me. "Ma'am, your friend is causing a scene. Can you quiet her down, or I will have to ask her to leave?"

"What the hell are you talking about?"

The young man sighed like this happened all the time in the hot spot and shuffled back to the main dining room. I turned the corner and gasped. Amy had her head thrown back as far as it naturally bent, her mouth opened, and her right hand shook on the table.

"Oh my God, you idiot. She's having a seizure. Call an ambulance, now!"

"Fuck me." The boy scrambled away.

Amy, shit, she hadn't had one in months. I pulled my chair over next to her and clasped my hand over her trembling one. I checked the back of her neck, and luckily her head rested on the high-back chair. She was as safe as she could be.

"The EMTs will be here in ten minutes," the waiter informed.

"Thank you."

Amy hummed low in her throat as her head lolled to the side. She closed her mouth, clearing her throat.

"Amy, it's Lena. You had a seizure. Can you hear me, hun?"

Her unfocused eyes opened, staring at my chest. When these happened, her recovery took several minutes. She once told me to remain calm and be patient with her. Eventually, her speech came back after a mini coughing fit.

"I'm sorry, Lena. My neck hurts."

"It's okay. Drink some water." She did with shaky

hands. I covered her warm hands with my own, helping her. "They called for an ambulance."

"Thank you. My chest hurts."

"They'll check you out. You're going to be fine."

Cold air whooshed through the entire restaurant. The paramedics arrived. I rubbed Amy's back over her chunky sweater until two men in green walked her toward the quieter part of the restaurant in the back. Like magic, the other diners continued eating and resumed their idle chatter. I pulled Amy's purse strap off the back of the chair and snagged her coat from the empty seat. I sat for a moment, catching my own breath. It's hard fighting the sense of helplessness. I did what I could for her.

A burning fire crackled next to me. Since I returned from the ladies' room, nothing had been right. Ever since my grandmother passed away, complete and utter madness followed me around every corner.

The orange and yellow flames mesmerized me as they warmed the right side of my body. An ornate iron gate encased the fire inside its hearth. I laughed at my silly thought. There was no way a fire burning as bright and fierce would allow a simple blockade to stint its fury.

I sat far enough away, but my cheeks flushed while a bead of sweat rolled down my hairline. Wave after wave of scorching heat flew toward me. I turned my head away from the inferno. No one else appeared bothered by the fire. It was only me.

Someone gripped my shoulder, keeping me from rising out of the chair. The pressure almost stumbled me to the floor, away from the blaze.

"Excuse me. *Stop!*" I flicked the air over my shoulder. My fingers drifted through the air, feeling nothing. The weight holding me down released.

I popped up to my feet, the chair hitting the back wall, rattling the hanging memorial plates. No one stood behind me or near me except the dwindling fire.

"Miss Pearson is asking for you. Miss?" the waiter said.

"I'll be there in a minute."

It's hard collecting your belongings when your hands are shaking as bad as mine. I knew I hated this fucking restaurant. *Did I touch death, or did death touch me?*

The last of the fire burnt out in my peripheral. When I went to the bathroom, the fire had not been lit. I chanced a glance over my shoulder. The patrons ate, laughing, talking, spitting disgusting food into their napkins, reaching for the bread. They sat completely ignorant to the experience ensnarling me. To them, nothing happened. Fuck them all.

"Lena, can you take me home?" Amy yawned, rubbing the back of her neck where it rested on the top of the chair.

"Of course. Can you leave your car here?"

"The owner said it's okay. I'm sorry, Lena."

"Never apologize for being sick. Are you sure you don't want to go to the hospital?"

"Yes, I want to go home."

"Come home with me."

"I have to go home and take my medication."

"All right. If you change your mind, I can come over."

"Lena, you're flushed. Are you okay?"

"It's hot in here, that's all."

I rushed us along, faster than I should have after her

incident. When we sat in my car, and I flipped on the radio, I felt better. The further away we got from the restaurant, the more I berated myself for thinking I experienced the ghostly hand on my shoulder.

"I need to go back to the moon festivals. I need more essential oils, candles, and crystals. Does Kim have any extra back stock she would let you rummage through?" Amy asked.

"I'm sure if you asked her, she would let you take a peek."

"No, I don't want to see her. If you remember, please mention it."

Right, I had forgotten over the thousand times I tried. Amy and Kim had not spoken in ten years. What will it take to get them back together?

"The new moon is coming up. Are they having a festival, then?" I asked.

"I think it's every new and full moon. I'll check."

"Cool, let me know."

I dropped her off, and she promised to call me before she went to bed. I sat in her driveway, debating my next move. I copped out on driving over there, so I called Arthur's shop.

"Death touched me. Does it count?"

"What? How? When?"

"Washington Tavern. Touch on the shoulder. Twenty minutes ago."

"Ghosts don't count. Try again."

"Ghosts are the epitome of death."

"Too old. Try again."

"So, ghosts are real?"

"Yes, but werewolves are not."

"Arthur, are you crazy?"

"Yes, ma'am."

I sighed, rubbing my shoulder. My alarm sounded on my phone. I had a demo in a half hour and a call with a potential buyer in the morning. Real life called and I got back to it as soon as I could.

Chapter Fourteen

My first official stop on my journey was the last thing that popped into my mind. I went to the largest cemetery in the historical part of town, surrounded by the oldest streets in America. Almost every building had a blue and yellow plated marker highlighting a historical event happened there. All I wanted to know was who died there.

I parked on the gravel driveway by the covered rock salt dunes on the outskirts of the cemetery. Most of the official parking spots were now occupied by food truck patrons. A large, garish purple van bought a permit for the open field next to the graves. It rubbed me the wrong way to eat pulled pork sliders next to my grandmother and great-grandmother's final resting place.

A long freight train rattled through the neighborhood. The conductor blasted the horn every few minutes distracting me. I had no idea what I expected from coming here. *Maybe I should order some food and head home.*

I passed the newer section, with flower arrangements covering freshly filled-in dirt, near the damn food truck. The more I thought about it, the higher my anger rose. There was never quiet over here except for the middle of the night when everyone should be sleeping. Even without the music blaring from the food truck speakers, the constant traffic on the main road interrupted the deepest prayer.

I marched forward, walking up the path toward the older graves. In case anyone asked, a simple college assignment brought me to these muddy hills in search of answers to the town's history. In my bookbag, I packed tracing paper, black crayons, and my expensive camera for the photography phase I sucked at a few years ago. It seemed like a good alibi for my cause.

My cold fingertips grazed the top of a marble stone from the late nineteenth century. Violet Faust died at forty years old in eighteen ninety-two. Her husband, buried next to her, died the same year at forty-five years old. I wished they had more details back then. *Did they die together?* It could have been an accident that caused their lives to end.

I took out the camera and snapped a picture of the moss-covered grave. At least the moss grew on the sides, away from the raised block writing. I checked around for anyone looking for a lunatic attempting to touch death. No one came back to the older sections anymore. I had the dead all to myself.

I sat down on the wooden bench dedicated to someone in the town and leaned my back straight against the chilled surface. I hadn't remembered nodding off, but when I opened my eyes, the tracing paper had black smudges where I wrote a few verses of nothingness.

How many times in one week was I going to scare myself?

The trek back to the car made me feel like an idiot. I crumbled up the paper and threw it into the first trash can I passed. My mother would be screaming if she knew where I was right now.

I walked a little faster and tripped on a raised root

between the graves. The ground smacked into my cheek, knocking sense into me. Then the people walked by. High heels, dress shoes, and sneakers passing by a few rows down. The front of my body hurt from falling, but I scrambled onto my knees, wiping my dirty palms on my thighs.

A funeral in the old section of the cemetery? I squinted at the crowd forming around a coffin on the gurney over the deep hole. I shook my head in case they were a mirage from years before. When I heard a cell phone, and someone yelling, "Yeah, we're at the cemetery. Park by the food truck. The lot is full," I knew I wasn't imagining anything.

Copious amounts of flowers lay on top of the closed casket. I blessed myself out of long-forgotten habits. I shouldn't be here disrespecting the dead, hoping to touch the right headstone or lay across a sensitive stretch of dirt with enough power for what?

"Are you okay, miss?"

An elderly man with white hair, bright red cheeks, and a small smile stood two gravestones down. His head tilted to the side, inspecting my disarray.

"Yes, sir. I tripped on a root." I got up and rubbed my palms together. "I'm sorry for your loss."

"Thank you for your kind words." He slightly bowed his head in my direction and continued toward the seated group of people. I smiled back, but he'd already turned toward his family.

A red-headed woman hustled over to the group, clutching her muddy high heels to her chest. "Grandpa, wait for me," she said. Her gaze peered over to me. Dark freckles covered the woman's face from her cheeks over the bridge of her button nose. Her thin lips pursed together.

"I was just leaving." I scurried out from the line of cracked, faded graves.

The woman's eyes widened, then squinted into black slits. "Did you know my brother?"

"No, I'm sorry. I was doing a project for school and fell. I'll be going now."

"Your car is blocked in. Come, stay for the funeral. Pay your respects."

"I wouldn't want to intrude."

"His name was Michael. His voice chirped like a songbird. His haunted melodies sank their teeth in deep. He would've wanted you to stay, Lena."

My head snapped her way. *Who the fuck?* "How do you know my name?"

"We went to Saint Helen's together until fifth grade. Remember me? Christine."

As if her face morphed back to ten years old, I saw the resemblance to her younger self. "Oh, wow. Yes, I'm sorry, again. Where is my mind, lately?"

"My mind is gone. I can't stop crying."

"Christine, come." A woman dressed in black waved her over.

"Please stay. I could use an old friend," Christine said.

"Whatever I can do to help."

I folded my hands in front of me and stood with the other friends. The number one reason why you shouldn't randomly hang out in cemeteries. You got sucked into a damn funeral.

After the priest said his prayers and the mother shared another story about his life, I thought we were done. Everyone stood in the soggy grass with downcast eyes and their hands thrust in their pockets for those lucky enough to have them. But then, Christine touched the coffin, followed by her father and her grief-stricken mother. As they pulled back, blessing themselves, more family members touched the shiny wooden box under the flower arrangements.

Death lay right in front of me on the raised platform. If I touched the coffin, game over. I would be done. My feet stayed cemented to the ground. Gravity made my arms weigh a ton. By the time the wave of people reaching out got to the friend section, an unheard pass flitted over us. I stood immobile like the tree watching over funerals day in and day out behind me.

I missed my chance. Two men from the family side removed the cascading flowers from the top of the coffin. One more prayer later, and the mechanical whirring of the pulley lowered the coffin down into the opened grave.

I barely moved from my rigid stance until Christine hugged me, searching for comfort in an unlikely place. I wrapped my arms around her upper back, pulling her in for a deeper hug.

"Thank you for staying. It would have meant a lot to Michael."

"Of course. I knew I had to be here today."

"If you would like to come back to the house, we will have refreshments."

"I have to meet my mother. Reach out to me on social media. Let's catch up soon."

We hugged again, and I grabbed my backpack from the floor, walking away toward the food truck. The anger I expected for letting that opportunity pass never struck me. Tears instead overpowered me. I walked to my grandmother's grave and sobbed over the newly grown grass.

"What am I doing, grandma? What the fuck am I doing?"

I leaned back on her gravestone and patted the earth where my *abuela* lay next to her. The garden angel I bought a few weeks ago sat in the small space between the two stones. I swore the stones moved closer together every time I visited. A hair of a centimeter each day, unnoticed. One day the angel will be in front of both joined stones.

The music from the food truck resumed. They must have turned it down for the funeral. I stayed until storm clouds rumbled in and a few warning raindrops pelted down. I ordered a pulled pork sandwich from the food truck and went home.

Chapter Fifteen

The cemetery visit bothered me the rest of the week. An impenetrable unease settled in my thoughts, my bones, my world. I cracked my neck a dozen times, desperate for the knot to be gone. Nothing worked.

My erratic sleep schedule turned a corner as well. I dreamed of Arthur two nights in a row. The first one, I stood in a gray room, bargaining with him for more information about death. His stoic, mute stature enraged me until I walked over and tapped on his cold, marble cheek. Tiny cracks fractured his face until a pile of dust and rubble laid at my feet. The second dream, we talked about nonsense until we kissed ourselves breathless. I woke from each dream drenched in sweat, catching my breath.

It took every ounce of energy I had to visit Kim in her garage test run setup. I had to do something normal, or else I would be calling Doctor Greene for the numbers of the nearest psychiatric wards.

For now, Kim simply had two folding tables situated in the garage. It worked. We jumped right in and prepped a couple kits in half the time it usually took us. Like any best friend, she knew something upset me.

"Ray isn't going to be home," Kim said.

"Thank you, Kim."

"He's not seeing Chloe anymore. I think he's seeing someone new."

"Thanks for the update. Can we not talk about Ray?"

She grimaced and muttered an apology. "Layla is seeing someone."

"Great, my thirteen-year-old god-daughter has a boyfriend, and I don't."

"Ha-ha, don't compare yourself to Layla. A guy gave her a piece of gum a week ago and now they are Romeo and Juliet. Their cruel parents are keeping them apart because of homework."

"Oh, dear. Then her life will be over in another week when he gives another girl two sticks of gum."

"Exactly. Shit, that stings." Kim got a paper cut from her info cards she stuck into small envelopes. She sucked her bloody finger into her mouth.

"Eww, wash your hands, vampire."

"Be right back."

When she walked back into the house, I released the loudest yawn. Since I visited the cemetery, a restful night's sleep eluded me daily. I tried writing when I got home, after eating the most delicious sandwich I hoped not to like, but nothing came. Something held me back from writing and touching that coffin.

Was it too easy or the cause of death not, right?

"Sorry about that. No zombies will be made from these baskets." Kim wiggled her bandaged finger.

"Yeah, that wouldn't be good for your reviews."

"Speaking of weird shit, what happened with that guy at the party?"

"What party?"

"Damn, you are closed tight. The trash-the-dress party. The strange fortune teller's brother. He was hot."

"Oh, Arthur. He's hotter from afar. He can read minds and works at the palm reader shop in Northfield."

"If my husband knew my thoughts all the time, I doubt we would still be married."

"He can tell when you are faking it?"

Kim threw a ribbon roll my way, slow enough that I dodged it. "Hey, no fucking with the merchandise."

"It's my merchandise." We both laughed. "Oh, Lena, I missed you. I should have set this up a year ago. Ray got to have you all to himself. Ugh, I'm sorry. Every topic I don't want to pester you on keeps rolling out of my mouth."

"I missed you too. It's all right. You're allowed three more taboo questions."

Kim rolled her eyes. "I will think long and hard about them before the night ends."

"*Mom!* The twins aren't eating!" Layla called from the kitchen.

"Put on the TV!"

"Tried that already!"

"Excuse me." Kim rolled her eyes and left me alone again. I turned on the space heater, Ray installed for us. The area even smelled like him. I leaned my head against the wall under the rush of hot air. The warmth welcomed me, and Ray's scent calmed me.

A text message came through from Amy.

—*Moon Festival, tomorrow night? New Moon*—

I checked my calendar and my alarms. I was free.

—*What time? Where?* —

—*Pound Point Camp, six o'clock*—

—*I'll drive*—

I set up the reminder for tomorrow night at four-thirty in the afternoon.

"Was that Arthur?" Kim asked.

"No, two questions left. I'm going to one of those

moon festivals with Amy tomorrow night. Do you want to come with us?"

"I can't leave the kids on such short notice. Scope out the situation, report back, mole."

"Can I be a spy instead of a mole?"

"Ha-ha, sure."

"Still not talking to Amy?"

"It's my turn to grill you, not the other way around. Back to Arthur, are you going to ask him out?"

Once again, Kim avoided talking about Amy at all costs. The subject of Arthur, on the other hand, remained a mystery. "Is chivalry dead enough that I have to ask a guy out?"

"I don't know. I've been married forever. I even met my husband in person."

We both exaggerated our gasps. "Maybe Arthur could be something. Who knows? One more question."

"What are you going to do about your new white hair?" Kim flicked at my bangs turning whiter each day.

"I'll get around to dying it eventually. I kind of like that it's a streak."

"It seems a lot more than it did at the party. We're getting old, Lena! I don't want to turn into an old hag."

"I feel fine. Excuse me while I throw out my hip, picking up that dropped ribbon." I groaned, picking up a stray bow.

"At least we will grow old together."

****

I left Kim's after eight o'clock. I missed our nights together. A part of me wished Amy and Kim talked again, just one more time to bury the stupid hatchet. It would be a perfect night with the two of them.

Before I realized my diverted path, my knuckles

knocked on Arthur's shop door. I whipped around toward the street, but my car was parked directly behind me. I drove here without realizing it.

The closed sign laid still against the glass door. No lights shined in the red interior. I grabbed my phone and dialed the number on the window. The nightly message kicked in.

"We are currently closed. Please leave your name, number, a brief message, and we will get back to you soon."

"Hi, Lena Martin here. I'm outside your shop at eight twenty, Tuesday, September…"

"Lena, hey. I'll be at the door in a second," Arthur said. His breathless tone sped up my heartbeat. He hung up before I uttered another word.

Arthur threw open the door with a video game controller in his other hand, and he wore a headset with a small speaker in front of his mouth. "Lena, I wasn't expecting you."

"I don't know why I'm here either. Can I come in?"

"Yes, of course." He stepped back into the darkness. He didn't turn on the main room lights but led me beyond the noisy beads, where light shined. "I'll play in the next heap, or maybe the one after that. Company," Arthur said into the black mesh microphone.

We turned the corner, and a guy with a hat on sat in one of the two gaming chairs in front of a big-screen TV. He moved the joystick fast but wailed as the word *DEFEATED* appeared on the screen.

"Hey, this is my buddy, Carter. Dude, this is Lena." The guy waved and looked me up and down. His tight smile told me I interrupted the last whatever of their game.

"You play video games in your spare time?" I asked.

"And you read, what's the difference?"

"How did you know that? That's like first date stuff."

Arthur pointed at the soft part of my temple. He caressed a finger, smelling like pizza, down my cheek. "You look like a reader, and I can read your mind."

"Do you guys want me to leave for a bit?" Carter said.

"I'll go. I didn't mean to interrupt your guy night," I replied.

"You just got here."

"I'll talk to you later, Arthur."

"Hey, wait, don't go yet." Shooting and computer-generated army voices asked troops to get ready behind me. Arthur stomped after me through the dark front room. "Lena, please."

I turned back. I only saw the part of his handsome face that caught the shine from the streetlight lamp across the street. "I'm having trouble with the test. I missed a chance a few days ago. Will that be my only option?"

He stepped closer and removed his headgear. "Did you miss it, or did you choose not to?"

"I could have touched the coffin, but I didn't."

"It wasn't your time. Like I said, stop forcing it."

"But what if that was it? I felt like someone handcuffed my arms behind my back. I couldn't move. I stopped breathing."

"Something probably did stop you. You look tired. Go home, rest. We'll talk about this another day."

"You want to go play video games."

"Ah, I play all the time. I don't get to see you all the

133

time. Please let me know you're okay. You're shaking."

"I'm cold. I'll head out."

I pivoted back toward the sales floor. A tug on my right shoulder propelled a gasp from my throat. I whipped around with my fists raised.

"Woa, Lena. It's just me. What was that?" Arthur shielded his face with his hands, palms up.

"I'm sorry. I'm not sleeping well."

Arthur's gaze roamed over my face. He removed his headset and flicked off the blinking red light. "Has anything tried hurting you?"

I shook my head, but I bit my fist, thwarting my tears.

"I don't believe you," Arthur said.

"Nothing has harmed me, but I have been bumped into and something touched my shoulder."

"Do you ever catch a glimpse of it? Even if it's a split second in your peripheral."

"No, never."

Arthur lifted his arm toward me, then dropped it back down to his side. "It could be a family member protecting you."

I shrugged. "You make it sound positive."

"I don't think you're ready for the other possibility."

"Hey, Artie, they're killing me here. Are you joining the next mission?" Carter asked.

Arthur glanced over his shoulder. He tugged his bottom lip in between his teeth.

"Go, we'll talk another day. I have a call soon."

"Here is my cell phone number. If anything scares you, call me." He handed me another business card for his mother's shop with his cell number scribbled on the back.

"All right, Arthur. See you soon."

His eyes burned a hole in my back until I looked at him again with my hand on the doorknob. If I didn't walk out now, I would never leave. The slight aroma of a burning candle mingled with rosemary followed me home.

Chapter Sixteen

I kept my promise to Amy and bought us tickets for the Moon Festival. We parked and trekked toward the campgrounds.

"I'm shocked you were down to go. You're never eager to do this weird shit with me anymore," Amy inquired.

I had to tell someone. After the dinner, Arthur, Idalia, and my mom's weirdness, I had to tell someone.

"Well, I might be a witch."

"I know that, but what changed?"

"Amy, I don't mean the pretend stuff back in high school. My ancestors were witches. My grandmother was a witch."

Amy smiled and flicked her hand up. "And? Are you going to tell me something I didn't know?"

"So, everyone knows I'm a witch, except me?"

She held up her pointer finger and her thumb an inch apart. "A little bit? Hey, I'm not faulting you for abandoning it. I remember your sweet sixteen. That shit was real."

"I miss my grandmother."

"Me too." Amy laid a sobering hand on my shoulder. "Let's get a spirit board and see if she will say hello to us."

"Oh no, we are not disturbing any of my family members. Let them rest in peace."

"Fine, we'll see if my Aunt Tina wants to talk. She never shut up when she was alive. Maybe she will gab about the afterlife."

"I don't think it works that way."

Amy danced away, ignoring me. While we walked the crazy distance to the lake club entrance, I downloaded the tickets from my email. At the main entrance, a woman dressed like a fairy, wearing gothic black wings, greeted us, waving a smudge stick over our heads. I held back a sneeze. There must be sage in the bundle.

"Enter with peace, love, and open-mindedness," the woman sang.

"Thank you, I love your costume," Amy boosted.

"Only eight more months until the Renaissance Faire! Huzzah!"

Amy giggled and pinched me in the arm. "Come on, Lena. Drop the serious act for one night."

"Sorry, I think everyone but me has a fairy costume in their closet. You have one, don't you?"

"Oh, look, there is a map of the place!"

Amy had one in green. I squeezed the plastic purple and black bracelet over my fingers onto my wrist. Amy did the same, already giddy from the proximity. I coughed as we breached the first row of vendors.

"Allergies?"

"Always. I can barely walk by the candle store in the mall without having an asthma attack. At least this is outside."

"Do you have a mask with you?"

"It won't help. If I randomly walk away from you, don't be offended. I don't want to freak out anyone by sneezing and coughing all over their stuff."

Amy nodded, and we joined the herding crowd. The Moon Festival had become a viral hit overnight. One video knocked the place out of the water. A gathering of a hundred people became a thousand people with multiple areas for vendors, chants, and sideshow acts.

The line for the drink cauldrons snaked around half the main part of the first section. Young witches and wannabes donned black-brimmed witches' hats, flocking to the booths with the real witch stuff. We walked for twenty minutes, and Amy already bought a spirit board, a satchel of crystals, and got two books from the book fairy. I tripped on a rock, had a sneezing fit from a candle booth, and a boy dressed like a mushroom told me my aura was red. All the psychics were booked until eleven o'clock at night.

"I think there are three more sections of vendors," Amy announced.

"Oh my God, why?" The energy, the vibe, the scene bothered me. I didn't want to be out here when the sun went down. The trees themselves stared, branches lurching back and forth in the steady wind. The bustling people in their costumes and black gothic attire drowned out the sounds of the forest. A headache nudged my temple. *Just what I needed.*

"Hey, Lena, do you know when we plan to head home? I got a text from the psychic. She has an opening at ten-thirty tonight."

"Amy, it's only seven o'clock. I don't know if I can stay here for three and a half more hours."

"Do you have a presentation later?"

"No, but that's late. It's an hour's drive home from here."

"I'll call a car service. Go home when you want. I

don't want to keep you up."

"It's fine. I will stay."

"Your eyes look red. Did you bring any allergy medication?"

"Nope, I can't drive on it. It puts me out."

"Fuck, Lena. I would have driven. I feel like a shithead."

"Don't worry about it. Go shop. I'm going to go down by the lake."

Amy wrapped her arms around my neck. "I'm sorry."

"We're okay. Remember, spices are cheapest in the supermarket."

"Ha-ha, very funny. I'll see you in a little bit."

Apart from the shoppers, the pressure in my chest eased up, and my body calmed down. I took off my flats and stuffed them in my bookbag when I reached the end of the wooden trail toward the shoreline. The sand lacked the finesse of an ocean beach. Coarse pebbles tormented the bottom of my feet until the calm water lapped at my toes. I managed a deep breath, then another.

If I turned left, a beautiful sunset filtered through the puffy clouds, but if I turned right, darkness waited, ready to take over. I walked straight back to a picnic table stuck in the line of dusk.

The people sitting at the bench looked at their phones and quickly got up. A circle of people, some with floral crowns, some with horns, others in normal clothes, swayed together on the retreating light side of the beach. I had a prime spot for the show.

As I watched the people chant and hold hands, a woman dressed like a gypsy, including a cheap scarf belt with fake coins, obstructed my view. She shook out her hands and legs, rolling her neck at the same time. If I wasn't at an event specializing in the occult and spirituality, her erratic behavior would be unusual.

She wandered down to the edge of the sand. The tiny, rippling waves kissed her feet. Her bandana flew off her head in a gust of wind that hadn't reached me, even though I sat close, staring at the woman. Soft mumbles came from her mouth.

Another woman, also wearing a similar fortune-teller motif outfit, shuffled through the sand. She stood next to her, and both women craned their heads toward me. I gasped, standing up abruptly.

"I'm sorry, ladies. I did not mean to interrupt." I tugged my purse more securely on my shoulder.

"You didn't, dear. Please, stay a while. Can I join you?"

"Sure, you and your friend can both sit with me."

The woman sat down. Incense wafted off her skin. "What friend?" I looked where I thought I saw two women, but the other gypsy disappeared back into the crowd.

"Forget about it. Are you having a rough night?"

"There are too many people here. I can't focus on one person. My frequency is all over the place. I can't tell whose thoughts are who's. Are you married to a boxing champion?"

"No, I've never been married." I held up my ringless left hand.

"See! Someone here is married to a boxing champion or a karate sensei. I hate when this happens. I need to clear my palette." She ruffled out her hands, flailing them around like a disgruntled flamingo. "Have you ever been to Prague?"

I shook my head. "My best friend in college sent me a postcard from the Netherlands. Does that count?"

"No, that's too far removed. Did you dislocate your wrist falling off a stage?"

After a few rounds of questions, none of them about me, the lady wiped a tear from her cheek. She took a deep whiff of her wrist, blowing out her exhale. I squinted, and she held her wrist up to my nose. The strong scent of lavender oil hit me straight in the face. "It's supposed to be calming," she said.

The night sky, almost at the other edge of the horizon, reflected beautiful light against the still lake. The serenity relaxed my limbs, along with the lavender. I hadn't realized she stopped asking questions until she started again.

"Did you sleepwalk out of your dorm room in lingerie?" she asked.

My insomnia paired with situational narcolepsy wrecked my college experience. I woke up one day mid-conversation with my mother on the phone, no shoes, and only a lace slip on.

"I did once back in college."

"Bingo, okay, I'm getting warmer."

"You lost a flower a little while ago. She meant a lot to you. Your mother has her gifts. You weren't ready, but the time will come. Is that right?"

"My grandmother's name was Rose. She passed away in May. She always said I had powerful gifts."

"She loves you very much. She's picking wildflowers in the fields like you used to do with her and making pizza just the way you like it."

The dam broke on my pent-up tears. It was her time. I was lucky to have the borrowed time with her the past few years when she moved back here after my grandfather died. I shouldn't cry because she had a beautiful life. None of that mattered now. I needed the crying to feel again.

"There, child, it's okay. I didn't mean to upset you." The gypsy woman rubbed my back and offered me a tissue from a small plastic pack she held in her lap.

"That reading is mine. That's my grandmother, all right. Is she peaceful?"

"Very much so. I only get flashes, like snippets a second or two long. It's my gift. She had a smile on her face and a rolling pin in her hand."

"I fought my cousins for that damn thing." My tears finally morphed into laughter.

"Forget about an alarm system when you have one of them. I think I can go back to my booth now. Thank you, sweetie, for allowing me to see your beautiful life." She rose from the chair, touching my shoulder once more.

"Wait, let me give you something for the reading. I don't have much cash, but do you take cards?"

"You are too kind. Most people don't offer to pay me when I give a free reading. Please keep your money and support another witch trying to make an honest buck."

"Thank you. I owe you one."

The gypsy narrowed her eyes, rubbing her perfumed wrists together. "Has anyone ever told you what your gifts are?"

"No, I'm just the designated driver."

She nodded with a wide smile. "Your time will come. Thank you again, Lena."

I never asked her name but watched as she

disappeared into the crowd of darkened figures. Amy found me, and we walked through the last two sections together. After her reading, we left. On the way out, I searched for the woman dressed as a gypsy, but never found her again.

"You're acting weird again, Lena." Amy poked my arm when we got back onto the highway.

I yawned and opened the window a crack. "I'm tired."

"Did the gypsy give you a bad reading? I'm not too thrilled with mine."

"Actually, it was a wonderful reading."

"Then, what is it? You didn't buy anything. If you think you're a witch, you need supplies, spells, something."

"Nothing jumped out at me. I'll talk to Arthur about what I need."

"Who the fuck is Arthur?"

"Promise me, you won't tell anyone what I'm about to tell you."

"Who am I going to tell? My cleaning lady? You're my only friend. I work from home and barely talk to my coworkers."

"Remember the guy from the comedy club? His name is Arthur Prince. He's been guiding me a little bit. He owns the psychic shop in Northfield."

"The guy who paid the bill and almost made us late to the show?"

"Yeah, he tried to steal my grandmother's powers at her funeral. He apologized, but that's his thing. If I decide to give up my powers, he wants them. I'm torn about keeping mine, so I'm trying to find death. If I find it, it's supposed to help me decide what to do."

We passed three exits before she muttered a word, "I'm lost at the death part."

"Finding death is the test. I don't fully understand it all yet, either."

"The hot guys are always nuts."

"Seems that way, doesn't it?"

"Is Arthur a witch?"

"Yes, I just found out."

"Is his sister a witch?"

"I assume so. They're twins. He knows a lot of stuff about me, but I know jack shit about him."

"Is there anything I can do to help you?"

I sighed. "Amy, I think I have to do this alone."

"Is Kim helping you?"

"No, she is busy with the kids and her business."

"Lena, we both know this stuff is real. I might not be a witch, but I can still help you."

"I don't want you to get involved. I'm figuring this out as I go along. I have no clue where it's going to go."

"All right, when you are a big, bad witch, don't forget the normal folk who tried helping."

Amy meant the comment as a joke, but it shook me down to the core. I never thought of bad and good witches. My grandmother was not a bad witch. Idalia seemed too frail to be a bad witch. You wouldn't need a house to fall on her, just the right gust of wind. Arthur had his looks, but nothing he did screamed evil, yet...

"I'll let you know what happens."

Chapter Seventeen

The next morning, Amy called me with a few options I'd never thought about in my quest to find death.

"I don't want you to get involved, Amy. What if it gets dangerous?"

"Come on, I could be your familiar or your sidekick. Every witch needs a sidekick."

"A masked vigilante needs an assistant, not a witch."

"Humor me, please. I stayed up half the night looking this up."

I sighed, my tight shoulders slumping over my computer.

"I don't understand how this one could work," I said.

"The church held a funeral yesterday. Maybe the spirit is still there," Amy offered.

"Amy, I appreciate your help, but I don't want to spend an hour driving all the way to New Jersey. The traffic will be hell, and if the front door isn't locked, I don't want to be arrested for insanity."

"The church sits on top of an inactive volcano."

She got me every time. "What saint's name is it?"

I was not breaking any commandments by walking around a church. It was not a sin to walk up to the altar, bless myself, and see what happened if I kneeled on the floor at the top of the aisle. The arcade arches would not fall from the ceiling, capturing me in my transgressed state. My skin would not be scorched by the angels casting me out.

After a few turnabouts, I followed the signs leading toward the church. It was a famous church, but I had never visited. My great-grandmother married her third husband where I planned on standing and feeling. It might provide an edge of luck.

The massive church in Newark, New Jersey, loomed above me. I checked the website, and the confessionals were open today.

The heavy front door leading into the church vestibule slammed shut behind me, grazing my back. *Did it swat my ass for blasphemy or nudge me forward?* I shrugged off a chill breezing past me from the stairs leading upward to my left.

I hesitated in the small, green-carpeted space, crowded by a table holding missalettes and a basin of holy water attached to the wall. The sanctuary door creaked open, and a kind-looking priest with a half-smile popped his head out.

"Hello, come on in," he said with a slight accent.

"Hi, I'm sorry I disturbed you, Father. I'll be on my way," I stammered. The confidence I built up abandoned me. My body already pivoted halfway toward the main entrance.

"Ah, no worries. I haven't had a confession in an hour. I almost fell asleep in the booth. Thank you for waking me up." He tilted his head forward, revealing a bad bald spot in the middle.

I placed him around fifty or late forties with a thick Irish accent. His kindness urged me on. "You're welcome. Is it too late for a confession?"

"It's never too late. Are you traveling, or are you a local?"

"Traveled. My great-grandmother got married in this church."

"After today, you can say you confessed in the same church." His smile widened, and mine stiffened.

I hadn't confessed my sins since I was ten. Back then, anxiety killed the liberating experience. I feared the priest in my old parish would not forgive my sins and send me home without penance. Twenty-six years later, stepping up into the wooden booth, reeking of the last person's sweat, made me fold my hands in my lap, squeezing my fingers until the pressure hurt.

"Whenever you are ready, miss," the priest said.

The metronome ticking back and forth heightened the dread filling me up. I hated how I kneeled on the cushioned bench while the priest sat in a chair, facing the heavy curtain. I had not planned on lying, but if I told him the truth, I wanted him looking my way, staring at my unfaithful face.

"Dear Father, who art in heaven, it has been twenty-six years since my last confession," I began. I knew the verbiage was off, but the priest had not corrected me. He slapped his knee and whistled.

"That's a long time. I am happy to bring you back. How have you sinned?"

"I spoke badly about my peers behind their backs, I pulled a woman's hair a few weeks ago, I snuck out of the house to meet a boy after my parents were asleep, I staged my first car accident to hide what really happened, I lied to my mother and grandmother, I had sex before marriage, and I used the Lord's name in vain."

Fuck, I sang like a canary.

I rested my head on my folded hands on the top part of the padded bench. *Did I add enough?*

"In all those years, that's it? Not bad. Venial sins hinder daily happiness. Why did you lie to your relatives?"

"Money issues, and choices I made."

The priest accepted my bad summary of the truth. Guilt rolled around my stomach, stirring the restless acid.

"Do you have a rosary?" the priest asked.

"Yes, my good Jewish friend brought me one from the Vatican. It's blessed by the pope."

He chuckled again. "That is a good friend. Do you have it with you?"

"No, I don't have it with me."

"Please stay a while. We have plastic rosaries available to share. Complete the rungs on your rosary, and all will be forgiven."

"Amen." I blessed myself and ran out of the booth as if it caught on fire. I added claustrophobia to my mental tally of ailments.

An abundance of flowers cluttered the steps in front of the altar. The sweet aroma reminded me of my grandmother's garden in full bloom. I tended it as best as I knew how, but time will tell if they come back after the winter. A soft touch slid across the top of my right hand, almost like a small insect crawling on my skin. Neither visible to my naked eye. I processed the caress as comfort.

I grabbed a plastic rosary from the small box in front of the altar and sat in the first pew, where the widow must have sat yesterday. I felt nothing, so I tried the other side. Again, only the pitter-patter of my heart moved through me.

"Forgive the flowers. There were two funerals yesterday. The sexton hoped they would still look good for Sunday mass," the priest said. He blew out the candles on the altar. Thin wisps of black smoke floated up from each tealight holder.

My voice caught in my throat as the vapors continued climbing past any normal threshold for a small, extinguished candle flame. They hung in the air, misbehaving and distracting me.

"You can stay if you like. Saturday mass isn't until five o'clock," the priest reaffirmed.

"Thank you, Father." I bowed my head, feeding the rosary beads through my fingers. After completing the first ten Hail Marys, the stench of a freshly-scorched match tickled my nose. I glanced back at the altar, and the candles were lit again.

My gasp echoed through the pews, reverberating like a drumstick hitting a cymbal. I glanced around the sanctuary, searching for anyone who lit the match. It felt empty. The large door I came through remained closed. The priest's footsteps had shuffled down the stairs about four Hail Marys ago.

Glass falling against the concrete floor jolted me up from my seat. The sound came from my right, where an alcove of candles in red glass holders branched off. Another commotion alarmed me from my left. Crackling flames lit up the identical space on the other side of the altar.

I avoided the presence of the lingering smoke before. Now, my scream caught in my throat. A woman exited the brightened nook. A black veil covered her face and neck, but it did not hinder her sight. She lifted her hand and pointed my way.

I ran down the carpeted nave, forgoing my mission. A push against my shoulder right before the doorway, near the baptismal font, wasn't strong enough to deter my flee. Nothing stood behind me, but again like the attracted side of a magnet, the right side of my body lurched back.

"Let me go!" I peeled open the heavy wooden door toward the vestibule. The missalettes flew off the table, scattering into my path. I jumped over them and skidded into the entrance door.

A warm body wrapped its arms around me, halting me. Amy yelped as I hugged her back.

"Lena, what happened?" She tried separating us, but I held onto her for dear life. My heart thumped against my ribcage.

"We have to get out of here, now!"

Chapter Eighteen

Arthur answered after one ring.

"Lena," Arthur said my name on an exhale as if he had been holding his breath past his lung's limit.

"Were you running?"

"No, I'm home. Is everything all right?"

I didn't blurt out the truth. He warned me about forcing the path. *If he says, 'I told you so,' I will hang up immediately.*

"Um, yeah, but I need some…" I trailed off. I sucked at beating around the bush.

"Can you meet me at the coffee shop on Shoemaker Avenue? They do art in the foam."

"I can be there in an hour."

"See you then."

I waited for the relief that never came. A hot shower did nothing about my mindset. I plucked my eyebrows too thin, pinching my taught skin until little red dots of blood appeared. Eventually, the puffiness around my eyes stopped me.

My hands shook where I held onto my bathroom vanity. Thoughts raced through my head of Arthur's impending judgment. I growled into the mirror, wanting nothing more than to lift one of my porcelain pill boxes and smash it into the glass. I still looked like me. The thickening white streak in my mousey, brown hair brought life to the dullness. A few new strands turned each day. I watched the area, but the transition happened after I looked away.

I lied when I said I needed an hour. The twenty minutes of obsessive-compulsive primping landed me in my car and then the café a little after four p.m., fifteen minutes short of the requested hour. Arthur already sat at a table tucked away in the corner furthest from the cash register and baked goods' display cases. He picked at a half-eaten flaky croissant until our gazes met.

He removed his cloth napkin from his lap, meeting me halfway in the small space. "Lena."

Why does he say my name on a breath? His voice reminded me of how we spoke behind the walls of the mall's stores. He moaned my name when he talked, twisting my gut harder each time.

"Hey, Arthur. Can I buy you a cup of coffee?"

He waved me off, pointing back at the table he vacated. A waitress placed two coffees with milk hearts in the middle. She smiled and grabbed her yellow pad from her apron.

"Would you like something to eat, Miss?"

"I'll take a croissant, too, please."

The waitress brought out my food in moments. I had no idea how I should start talking. Arthur slurped his coffee like soup. He stared my way, but I couldn't quite pick my head up yet.

"I've been worried about you," Arthur said. I finished my croissant and half of my coffee before he spoke again. "Are you ready to talk about it?"

"If I blurt out a whole bunch of stuff, do you think you can keep up?"

He licked the lingering coffee foam off his top lip and cocked his head to the side. "Lena, I shared a bedroom with my twin sister growing up. We had a good relationship because I kept up with the drama."

"What started the continental divide?"

"Our father died when we were sixteen. He had been sick for about a year. One afternoon, I asked Dalia to go pick some wildflowers for Dad. We lived in Pennsylvania at the time, and there was a large meadow behind our house. She did it all the time, so it wasn't a weird request. Neither of us thought anything was off that day. Then, Dad had a horrible coughing fit while I replaced his oxygen tank. I tried putting new tubes in his nose, but he grabbed my arm. I still feel his grip on me. His eyes rolled back in his head, and he was gone. Death found me that day.

"Idalia stood in the doorway, drenched from the rain. She dropped the flowers and flung herself over Dad's chest, but he was already gone."

"Did you become a witch that day?"

"It took me a while to figure out what happened. My mother knew something was off. She never told me anything, so I researched it on my own. I became obsessed with anything related to witchcraft. After a few months and internet chatrooms, I found a coven, and they guided me on the path chosen for me."

"How did that mess up your friendship with your sister?"

"Dalia became insanely jealous and spiteful over our father's death. I had no idea he was going to die that day. She wanted to be a witch, too, even though the path chose me. She forced it until death had no choice."

"She forced death into making her a witch. How the fuck did she do that?" *She might be a zombie, after all.*

"I'm not exactly sure. That's how my mother

phrased it. I'm worried about Dalia."

"Is that why she's so frail?"

"Something like that. She's neglectful of her own life. Her jealousy overrules everything."

"Did you guys suspect you were witches before your father's death?"

"It's a funny thing. I never believed we weren't normal kids. My mother and father read palms in our hobby shop. I saw it as a skill you learned. No powers needed. I loved playing with fire, even before my dad died. I never thought I was doing anything odd."

"I knew my grandmother was a witch. I guess I rationalized the weird shit by thinking I was pretending to be her, not actually doing anything of my own. She almost died on my sixteenth birthday."

"Sixteen is a rough age."

"So is thirty-six."

I liked hearing him laugh again. He finished his food, eyeing up the half-empty display case with more treats.

"What's your favorite?" I asked.

"Chocolate Mousse."

"Good choice."

I waved the waitress over and ordered a chocolate mousse mini cake. Arthur's gaze lit up, alleviating the sadness. She brought over the delectable treat with two spoons.

"Who's corrupting whom?" he asked.

"Too soon to tell."

The rest of our interaction felt like a date. He paid for the treats and the coffee after we shared stories of our favorite sweets from childhood. If that was a date, I had a great time until the pesky death conversation roared back.

"I feel like I'm dominating the conversation. Why did you call me?" Arthur asked.

"Do you know how hard it is for me to go back to my life, hoping I will stumble upon death? My days are now torn between checking into a mental institution or rationalizing a logical way to be at a car crash at the perfect moment."

"I know it sounds crazy, but I understand exactly what you mean. You're not the only one suffering. After moving here, I have never felt right in my own clothes, my home, my job, my friends. Something happened, and it fucked up everything."

"What happened?"

"Your grandmother died, and then I saw you. She talked about you all the time but never told us your age. Her loving nature made me think her granddaughter was a little girl in pigtails. She threw me off your scent."

"Every now and again, I wear my hair in pigtails at the end of the day. My grandmother stayed with me before her assisted living got set up. She did tell the truth."

"Fine, it still doesn't help me."

"Then, forget everything you know about me. Delete my number, don't travel past my house, and find yourself a new comedy club." Ugh, one minute, I'm swooning over chocolate with Arthur. The next second, I pushed him out of my life.

"It's not that simple," Arthur lamented. He inched forward, lifting his chin up.

"Actually, it is. I went to a moon festival last week, and there are tons of people willing to guide me on the right path." I shrugged. I said the words, even though bile curdled in the back of my throat. *Would he pass my bluff test?*

"You are not losing me that easy."

"What is in it for you?"

Arthur finished the rest of his coffee, then twirled a silver band around his right ring finger. Small indents in the metal made it possible.

"This can go two ways. You might be a prophecy come true if you become a witch."

"Did an evil sorceress curse us at our births?"

"No, this isn't *a fairytale.* I'm supposed to be the new blood keeping my mother's eclectic coven going after she's gone. My future wife, also a powerful witch, will aid me in my journey."

"That doesn't sound too far-fetched. I assume you think it could be me?"

He shrugged. "That's up to your own pathway." Arthur straightened his back against the wooden wall seat.

"Love has nothing to do with it?" I asked.

"Oh, I'm certain I could love you. I like you, that's for sure." As if Arthur regretted what he said, the slight upturn of his full lips fell back to rest. His gaze went blank while he stared at my neck.

"What's the second way?" Arthur folded his hands tight on the tabletop, looking anywhere but at me. "Arthur?"

"If you decide to give up your powers, I want to be there for the moment of truth. Powers can be taken, and I am a curate." His hardened gaze piqued my curiosity further.

"Tell me more."

"Think of it as simple physics. Energy goes in and

energy flows out. It must have somewhere to go. Some people might say I steal magical powers. I say, I simply catch extinguished powers when the witch has cast them aside."

"Can you actually see them?"

"Yes, they take a small corporal shape. It's like watching ants marching home into their hills. Small, bouncing orbs, following one by one."

Arthur's imagery surprised me. Instead of ants, I thought of fireflies. As much as I felt odd about practicing my craft, an overwhelming sense of protectiveness fell over me. I clutched my cardigan tighter over my chest.

"What do you do with the powers?"

"There is a prophecy of a time when witches everywhere will be called upon." Arthur looked up, scratching under his freshly trimmed mustache. "The story differs slightly from coven to coven. The leaders will be chosen when the time comes, and the forgotten powers will help."

"Help what? Fight a war?"

"No, it's more like that expression, let sleeping dogs lie. Eventually, the dogs will wake up, and we all must be ready."

Arthur's stern expression knocked me back in my chair. He reached for my hand, but I kept them fisted in my lap.

"I feel like you're going to bolt from the room at any minute," Arthur surmised.

"I don't understand how I feel right now. Should I be freaked out? This is fucking insane shit we are talking about here. One minute I want to run away, and the next, I want to know more."

"This isn't day one. You watched your ex-boyfriend try to give you his heart. After something like that, everything else is child's play."

"I guess so."

"There are a few more things to discuss. Do you want to come over to my place? I feel more comfortable continuing this conversation there."

"Sounds like a plan."

Chapter Nineteen

Arthur lived fifteen minutes away from the coffee shop in an apartment on top of a mountain. In the living room, there were five different lamps cascading different hues of light.

"Come in. Would you like some coffee?" He rolled his eyes and scratched his brow with his middle finger.

"We just came from a coffee shop, but sure, why not?"

"Sorry, I've never been the teacher before."

"Relax, I'm not going anywhere."

We traded nods, and Arthur led me toward his dining room table. Receipts, bills, unopened mail, and other miscellaneous crap cluttered the far end. "Idalia sucks as a bookkeeper. We need to hire someone more suited." He draped a thin sheet over the papers.

"Does she live here, too?" I asked. His apartment was clean for a bachelor pad. Is he single?

"No, she lives with my mother. They live in the building across the street."

"Are you single?"

"You have to ask me? Yes, I'm single. I've been wanting to ask you out since I met you. Do I suck at being obvious too?" I wiggled my hand like a rocky boat. Arthur laughed, releasing more tension. "Let's go into my office."

The apartment wasn't overly big. A typical two-bedroom apartment with an open kitchen on the far wall. His hand trailed behind him as if he wanted me to take it. I thrust my hands in my hoodie pockets, resisting temptation.

He unlocked the wooden door to our right. Arthur's definition of office differed from mine. I stood in a cluttered space with different types of things. The most normal thing was a bookcase, but it lacked the usual mishmash of books people owned. Trinkets, antiques, decks of cards, and a lot of ornate boxes of all shapes and sizes laid upon the shelves. A piano took up the left wall, and display cases with everything from porcelain dolls to fancy crystal balls were front and center.

"Now, I know what to buy you for Christmas," I remarked.

"Ha-ha, please don't buy me a crystal ball. I'm so afraid of an earthquake or a large truck driving by, and the whole damn thing collapses."

"We don't have earthquakes in New Jersey."

"You never know!"

His collection of oddities intrigued me. "What is your favorite piece?"

He barely hesitated. He turned the small key on the display case and took out a worn, scratched-up crystal ball. "I got this one in Budapest. It's too old to use, but I love messing around with it."

"Is there an expiration date on crystal balls?"

"For me, yes. The older the ball, the cloudier the reading. Tiny traces of the memories and fortunes of the guests stick to the ball. They're impossible to remove. I've tried. Also, I don't speak the language well enough."

"Do you have a cheat sheet for all this stuff? I'm not going to remember it all," I confessed.

"Please tell me if I'm overloading you. It's been so long since I've had anyone new to talk to about it."

I tugged out the piano bench and sat down. Surprisingly enough, my tinnitus rested. Usually, when I entered a new place, everything became a distraction. Noises amplified tenfold, even if it's just the hum of the electricity from the upstairs bathroom light someone left on all the time. In Arthur's apartment, nothing disrupted my thoughts.

"Do you have a noise-canceling machine anywhere?"

He shook his head, "No, but I made a steamed pot of herbs and spices before you called. It cleansed the apartment nicely."

"Yes, it did. No offense, but I have a demonstration tonight. Now that I know where you live, I can come back another day."

"I want to try something simple before you go. Can you stand up for a second?"

I stood up, and Arthur shooed me away from him. He kneeled on the floor by his upright, spinet piano, unlocking the small padlock attached to the lid of the old piano bench. *Who the fuck locks up a piano bench?*

The rusty hinges creaked as he lifted the worn wooden seat. All the paraphernalia cluttering his living room changed into cheap knick-knacks bought from a party store as I gazed upon the real stuff hidden away from the public eye.

Arthur blew across the items, disturbing the fresh layer of dust. I expected caked-on dust like the boxes out of arms' reach in my attic. The fine layer he wiped off could be a week or two's worth. *How much witchcraft did he use regularly?*

Arthur sat down on the back of his calves, using the utmost care with the fragile items. Each item, from journals to books, along with candles and stones, looked older than him.

Once all the other items were removed, he lifted out a large book, dense like a textbook. As Arthur's fingertips disturbed the dust, the spine cracked, and the spilled tea-colored pages flipped open.

"You looked shocked," Arthur observed.

"Most people keep sheet music and photos of lost loves in their piano benches," I commented.

Arthur furrowed his brow and tilted his head back.

"My grandmother used to keep photos of her old boyfriend, Walter, in the piano bench and an old photobooth strip of her with my biological grandfather."

"Now, that's weird. In my experience, people forget about this hidden space. Let's go into the kitchen."

I chuckled. Things he thought were weird were normal for me, and vice versa. A great start for a complex evening.

Ray's scared face swallowing his wrist flashed in my mind. His uncontrollable howls filled the silence.

"Lena, we all make mistakes. Let me teach you how to do this my way. I promise no one will get hurt."

His warm lips on my cheek sparked me back. My gaze fixated on his closeness. "Did you just kiss me?"

"I gave you a reassuring peck on the cheek. I wouldn't call that a kiss." Arthur held my chin. "I should warn you."

I could stare at him forever. His gaze was like a kaleidoscope, never settling for the same color twice. Today, bright greens swam through the blue. "I'm already in the devil's lair. What more can you warn me about?"

"My powers get stronger after I have an orgasm."

"You're fucking joking." At his stern face, I swallowed my outburst.

"I may come off as an asshole with a dire need of an attitude adjustment, but I don't fuck around with sex."

I drew back from him, dissecting his confession.

"How did you notice that?"

"I used to date a witch. She wasn't very powerful, but she excelled in the kitchen. The moon controlled her life like a wave imprisoned by low and high tide. One day, she forgot how vicious the ocean can be."

I followed hot on his heels, enthralled by more of his past as we moved into the kitchen. We sat opposite each other. A dying rose wilted in a vase between us.

"Did she die?"

"She came close to it. Stevie always wanted more. We did what we could for more energy, more umph. I noticed after we were intimate, I accomplished things faster, concentrated better, focused on the magic. For her, she felt more alive near the water. From her cooking skills, I thought Stevie would be more connected to the natural shifts in the earth, but the waves cried out to her. She purposely didn't follow the rules, swam at night, and if it wasn't for a guy smoking pot on the beach, she would have died."

A shiver like wet seaweed clinging to the back of your leg on the beach gripped me. I arched my neck, rubbing at my right shoulder blade. "Can I have a glass of water or wine? Do you have any vodka?"

"I won't let that happen to you. I'm trying to be super careful." He got up and snagged two pumpkin beers from the fridge. "I shouldn't have told you about her. It was so long ago. She's married with twins."

"Is she an all-powerful witch, now?"

"No, she stopped practicing that night on the beach. We broke up a week later. I ran into her a while back, and she said she still cooked obviously, but she lost the urge for more."

"Did you love her?"

"Yes, I did. Stevie was the first woman I trusted enough to show her my very underdeveloped powers at the time. I always had been able to manipulate fire, but she made it dance in ways no one else had."

Jealousy slapped me in the face. I barely knew if I liked Arthur, but my cheek still tingled where he kissed me. The cold beer did not alleviate the burning envy coursing through my mind.

"You must push yourself to the limit, and only then will your powers emerge, but we both took it too far."

The delicate rose with its petals fanned out neared its death. Who knows how long he had the rose on the table, if he cut the stem himself at the perfect angle, or if he put sugar in the water? Is that magic? A trick of the green thumb trade. Arthur kept talking. I hyper-focused on the wilting flower, inserting beauty into the dark room.

My good ole friend wrapped in static buzzed in my right ear. A sharp rush of pain jerked my right hand toward the flower, abruptly stopping a centimeter before the satiny outer petal. The air became an instrument, and I played my fingers around the dying flower. One layer at a time perked up and blossomed anew all over again. Even the green leaves, shriveled as if they weren't in water, returned to their prime state.

Arthur stopped talking. His eyes widened in front of

me. "How did you do that?"

"Inherited magic? Bumps on my D.N.A? Spit collected in a vial from my ancestors?"

"Eww, really? Is that how your family maintained it?"

"Of course not, geez. I'm kidding. My gifts have always been sporadic occurrences, easily explained by the simplest, lamest answer. I had no idea the flower would regrow at my touch. I was getting mad and then *zap*. It happened."

Arthur scratched his shadow of a beard on the edge of his jawline. "Did my Stevie story piss you off?"

I looked up and around the kitchen, avoiding eye contact. Unlike my kitchen, there were no personal things added except for the rose. It resembled a model house, purposely devoid of anything emotional.

"I knew she wasn't my soul mate. A guy has needs. Selfish really, but necessary," Arthur added.

"Can we stop talking about her? I was jealous, okay? I've never had anyone besides my grandmother to talk to about this. My two best friends stopped talking altogether when shit got real. I blacked it out as much as I could until I almost killed Ray. Show me what I need to know to find death, or else I really don't have a reason to be here." I failed to keep the frustration out of my voice.

Arthur slumped back in his chair as if I'd dumped him. He pointed toward the door. "You are here of your own free will, Pasqualena Concetta Martinez or Lena Connie Martin. The exit is the same way you came in."

"Who the fuck do you think you are? I came here for help. You have been planting ideas and ridiculous fantasies in my head since we met. I'm out of here."

"You'll be back."

"Fuck you, Arthur."

The sad part about rushing out of there was I had no idea if the flower remained pretty or returned to its former state.

I sped home and ran up to my room, slamming the door behind me. My lungs burned from sprinting the short distance. I sat down at my vanity table, but the natural light blinded me in the mirrored surface. I ripped the darkening shades down on all four of the windows.

Like magic, every wick from the candles crackled with the newly born flames.

"*Arthur, stop!*"

The flames flickered as if he listened, debating whether to leave me in the darkness. I wrenched up the blinds on the window facing the road. Only my neighbor's son's beat-up car was parked on the curb.

I fled to my bathroom and thrust the two candles I had on the counter under the running faucet. The water roared like a waterfall off a dam.

I slid to the floor, propped up by the far wall. A metallic, sweet taste filled my mouth. I touched my lips, and watery blood slid off my finger onto the floor.

"Crap, what now?"

I felt around on the countertop for my magnifying mirror. Once I found it, I stretched my bottom lip down. The sore I had been tonguing and chewing on for days gushed with fresh blood. I must have aggravated it without realizing, again.

My fingers delved through my stringy, oily hair. I ran away from that part of my life for almost twenty years. The more I saw its use, the little I wanted to deal with it. If Arthur wanted my powers, he could have them.

An alarm sounded from the bedroom. I got up off the floor, shut off the faucet, and opened the door back to my bedroom. Darkness filled the space. Arthur's calling card trick finished.

I shut off the alarm. *"Call Kim. Weekly Basket run."*

A normal Wednesday in my old life. I pulled up the shade the highest it could go, furthest from the vanity, and did the others halfway. I placed the lid on every candle.

The small bin I kept my notebooks in whispered under the vanity table. I blinked away the hysteria, but the mechanical whirring lured me over. These episodes never lasted long. I went with the flow until it stopped.

I sat down on the flattened tuffet, ignoring my pulse drumming inside my body. My shoulders hunched over the table as my trembling hand grabbed a notebook. I squeezed my eyes shut until I only saw black behind my eyelids.

Ten minutes later, I stared down at my writing. Unlike any time before, I understood the words.

"Help Ray, Help Ray, Help Ray, Ray, Ray, Ray."

Ten pages of the same scribbling. I flipped them back over and over until I went back too far. Scribbling in a cursive I did not write covered the beginning pages. I slammed the notebook shut and read the name on the two little lines. Dolores Sopi.

A scream wrenched out of my throat. I washed my hands again and again over the wet candles, hoping for a cure-all, end-all solution. When my skin turned pink from the hot water, I stopped.

"That's impossible," I said to my reflection. Thankfully she stared back in disbelief too.

I crept back into the bedroom, flipping on the lights,

opening all the shades. There was no such thing as traveling notebooks. When I gathered up the courage, I peeked at the notebook. My name, written in black magic marker, hovered on the lines.

I gripped the sides of my arms hard enough to crack a rib. That couldn't have been one of Arthur's tricks.

"I'm out of my fucking mind."

I thumbed through the cursed notebook, and my hope that the whole episode happened inside my head vanished.

"Ray, Ray, Help Ray, Help Ray, Ray, Ray, Ray."

The words remained. I chucked the notebook onto the floor, running from the room.

Chapter Twenty

College hallways stank of sweat. Damp jean bottoms, body odor, socks worn too many days, and the faint whiff of marijuana. The shit-colored concrete walls with faded blue accents made the busy space cramped and stuffy. In the few minutes of shuffling along with the herd of students scrambling to their next class, I almost headed back out the door.

Ray's last class of the day should be done. In all our years together, I never saw him lecture his students. It would have been easy enough sneaking in and admiring how hot he looked, explaining American History. The damn guy barely remembered to pay his bills each month, but he knew the names and dates of every battle in the American Revolution.

The heavy auditorium door slammed shut behind me. Ray's squinted gaze widened as he saw me walking down the stairs. He stared back down at the pile of papers in front of him.

Yeah, he's still pissed.

"Non-matriculated students must always wear a badge. Did you check in at the main visitor center?"

His harsh voice halted my steps. I hadn't expected a warm and fuzzy welcome even after I convinced myself that we parted on good terms both times. His cold demeanor changed everything.

"Can we talk for a second?"

Ray resumed his work, writing a note in the margin of a student's paper, and said nothing in return. I approached his desk with slow, calculated steps.

"On school grounds, people aren't supposed to be within six feet of the teachers. We're too important to lose."

His double meaning sliced another cut into my fragile confidence. My legs still felt like jelly after I stormed out of my house. The dizziness passed, but the agitation remained.

I walked right up to the line of tape and the plexiglass shield protecting him from the students.

"Does it really need to be like this? You're dating someone new. I did you a favor by ending things." My voice cracked as I held in tears.

Ray placed the red marker down on the desk. The thin tube rolled toward the front edge, stopped by the small, raised metal lip. *Did I do that?*

"Unless this concerns my sister or her business, there is nothing left to talk about. We are done, Lena. I have study hours in fifteen minutes. I need these last two essays graded before then. You know the way out."

"I need to know that you're okay."

He waved his hand over his face and the top half of his body. "Very much alive."

"Okay, then I need your help with some local history."

"Go to the library. The reference librarian will help you."

"Ray, please, I did nothing wrong."

"I told you where to go. Lena, please leave."

"Ray, come on." I placed my hands on the plexiglass.

"Lena, I'm out of your life for good. Let's keep it that way. If you will excuse me, I'm late."

Ray rose out of his chair, stuffing the papers and renegade marker into his satchel. Without looking back, he stormed out of the room using the door beside the dry-erase board. The desk chair kept spinning long after he left the room.

The stadium door lurched open, abruptly stopping the possessed chair. A boy scrolled on his phone until he saw me standing on the professor's podium.

"Are you a substitute?" the boy yelled down the rows.

"No, your professor will be back soon."

The kid nodded, adjusted his junk in his gray sweatpants, and sat down in the back row. So much for having a crying moment alone.

Against my better judgment, I exited the room using the door Ray went through a few minutes ago. The empty hallway with multiple doors loomed before me. I found the history department four doors down.

The room funneled into a large open space with multiple desks. Ray sat in the corner, near the open window.

"Miss, do you have an appointment with a professor?" the woman at the first desk asked.

"Yes, I almost married him."

The woman sputtered a few sounds. We turned toward Ray, the only other teacher in the communal office. His head popped up slowly. He rubbed above the bridge of his eyebrows with his left hand and ushered me over with the right.

"Can you stop going around telling people that?"

"Only if you give me a few minutes?"

His large, expressive brown eyes glanced at the clock. "Three minutes, Lena, or I am calling campus security."

I knew I hurt his feelings, but I hadn't expected the withdrawn, aggressive version of him now.

"How are you feeling?"

"I'm fine. My wrist has been bothering me since the day I left your house. The teeth marks have healed. Do you know how that happened?" He stared at a student's paper. His eyes moved back and forth too fast for actual reading.

"You were doing some stunt you saw on the video app."

"Lena, you're a bad liar. What happened that night? Who the hell was that guy with you?"

"He's a friend." My voice pitched up.

"You don't seem so sure."

"Ray, when I got back home, you stumbled out to my car, told me you hurt your hand trying to fit your fist in your mouth, and wanted to go home. You apologized for overstaying your welcome, and we agreed it's best not to see each other anymore. My friend, Arthur, followed me home to make sure I got there okay because my tire pressure light turned on. He saw you and made sure you weren't a burglar. That's it. I came here to check on you because I feel like a shitty friend."

He touched my hand like he had done hundred times before.

"I'm okay, Lena. I've moved on. It's good to hear you have someone looking out for you. I will always be here for you if you need me."

The somersaults in my gut wanted more closure. Ray flashed me his calming side smile I knew well.

"Thanks, Ray."

"Call Kim when you can. She's taking on a lot with the garage remodel. Layla is driving her nuts. Maybe a visit with Auntie Lena would help."

"Okay, I will."

"Can I please get back to these two essays?"

"Yes, sorry. Bye, Ray."

"Oh, did you need any local history, or was that an excuse to follow me?"

I pursed my lips together, smacking them open. He shook his head and dove down back to his work.

My alarm went off, and I walked out of the office. I had dinner tonight with my potential buyer. The big day had arrived, and I almost forgot. I needed an outfit, my nails done, and my hair washed.

Ray was okay. I kept saying that over and over. We were done.

****

Of course, I was late for the most important dinner of my life. Almost the entirety of Grand Central Station was sequestered off because yet another movie was filming in the main concourse. I barely took note of the actors standing less than five feet in front of me, trying to figure out what train to buy a ticket for in the scene. If somehow I remembered the movie scene, I would boycott everything about it.

I hailed a cab on the first try, resisting the temptation of the bakery across the street. It used to be Ray and I's tradition every time we took the train into the city. Warm croissants with hazelnut peanut butter spread along with the prettiest artwork displayed in the dirty chai foam. My dented black coffee cup with the mermaid on it sucked in comparison.

The address of the restaurant flew out of my mouth to the taxi driver. "Are you famous? I heard they are filming a movie?"

"No, I'm late for a very important date."

The taxi veered away from the curb. Both televisions nestled in the back of the front seats were smashed. *How fucked up can someone be to punch a TV in a cab?* I shook my head and changed my outfit in the cab. The smudged plexiglass hid my modesty. Another little black dress hugged my frame perfectly. The skirt barely reached my knees, but I needed every bit of help.

We flew through midtown, beeping all the way. Five minutes later, we made it to the restaurant in one piece. The concierge opened the cab door, ready with an umbrella. I wished I had spare cash for a tip. The dinner alone would set me back a few hundred dollars. Hopefully, that would be pocket change after I sealed the deal.

I had only seen a small four-by-six pop-up box of the infamous Richard Flanagan, the potential buyer of my program. Nothing did the man justice. His exquisite tuxedo could make James Bond's confidence falter. The gorgeous man held out a bouquet of a dozen roses.

"Lena, it's a pleasure to meet you." We shook hands, and he kissed me on the cheek. Heat flared to the spot.

"Likewise, Mr. Flanagan."

"Please call me Richard. You don't want to scream *Mr. Flanagan* later, do you?"

"What?" I spit out the drink I had not remembered pouring or drinking. The specs of red fizzed with carbonation bubbles until tiny holes appeared in the white tablecloth. "What's happening?"

"We are about to discuss our merger after I drink this acid. It does burn good on the way down." The man sitting across from me gulped down the red liquid. When he finished the last drop, he threw the stemware behind him. No sound greeted the shattered glass on the tiled floor. I glanced behind Richard, where the swinging kitchen door once stood. White doorless walls replaced the chartreuse painted room.

I grabbed the edges of the table, holding on for dear life. The other tables with patrons, I swore I saw when I walked in, thrust upward as if their ejection buttons were activated. My scream fell on deaf ears.

"You didn't touch your food? We picked out that heart, especially for you." A pulsing heart made of gelatin wiggled on the plate. "If you don't like it, try mine." Richard fisted his chest, slipping a few fingers down until a loud crack reverberated through the air. "I have to break some ribs first."

I shut my eyes and screamed again and again. Something touched my shoulder, and I jerked up without looking. I fell for seconds, hours, days.

The weightlessness in the darkness took the bad things away until my bedroom floor met the side of my face. My legs tangled in my comforter as I kicked it off. The streetlight outside my bedroom window flashed on and off like it had been doing for weeks now.

I shrugged off a whole-body shiver, yawning deep. I hated fucked up dreams like that one. They were too normal until they all went to hell. I grabbed for my phone and widened my gaze at the time. Nine o'clock, September 15, a waxing gibbous phased moon. Rain until midnight. Ten missed calls from Richard Flanagan.

"I hope everything is okay, Lena. I tried your cell

phone. I left the restaurant. Let's talk again soon."

"Please pick up, come on," I whispered into my cell phone.

"Richard, speaking."

"*Richard!* It's Lena Martin. I don't know what to say. I'm sorry for standing you up."

"Thank God, Ms. Martin, I'm relieved to hear from you. Are you all right?"

"Yes, I think so. I started new sleep medication a few days ago, and I'm so embarrassed. I fell asleep at one and just woke up. I swear this is not like me. Did I blow it?"

"Slow down. Forget business right now. We were worried sick about you. Sleep medication is no joke. My mother almost burnt the house down one Thanksgiving. She put the frozen turkey in the oven, turned it on, but didn't remove the plastic. We had to stay at a hotel for a week to get the smell out of the house." His laugh unwound the tension in my shoulders.

Maybe I didn't fuck this up.

"Wow, that's awful. At what point did she wake up?"

"Two blocks down at her old aunt's place. Her aunt had been dead for years. She scared the shit out of the people living there now."

"Yikes, that's bad. I only messed up my imminent future."

"It was a mistake. I get it. I would tell your doctor. You can't mess around with this stuff. It might be too high of a dosage or not the right meds for you."

"Thank you for the advice, Richard."

"Don't mention it. You missed a lovely meal. They served a tasty heart attack on a red plate. Unfortunately, over dinner, my partner and I discussed our long-term goals and growth path, and we are going to pass on purchasing your program. It suits our needs now, but we must shift our focus elsewhere."

Pain erupted in my thigh underneath my pounding fist. *I fucking blew it.*

"Ms. Martin?" Richard cleared his throat. "Did you fall asleep again?"

"No, sir. I'm here." Defeat took over my voice.

"Lena, you have a great program. Please don't be discouraged by us pulling the offer. We need new products more than communication aids between the people we might have to let go. The pandemic roughed us up bad. This is no reflection on you. Keep going. You're a fresh, young mind. Keep building up your clientele. I'll be in touch."

"Thank you for your kind words. I will take it as a compliment."

"You should. Goodnight."

My tears, clouded with my eyeliner, stained my pillowcase. Grumbling, I tore it off the flattened pillow.

The fabric stretched under my mouth, barely muffling my scream. At least he packed compliments around the ice.

I called my mom, holding my sobs back until the end. It's no one's fault. It was bad timing. The thought of selling the company never occurred to me until Richard's phone call out of the blue.

Chapter Twenty-One

"Did you sell your program yet?" Kim asked.

"I fucked it up," I confessed.

Kim backed into her assigned parking spot at the country club. Due to the unseasonably warm September, the pool would be open for one last weekend. Even the leaves on the trees were late turning colors.

"You said, *fuck*," Kim's eldest daughter, Layla, said. At thirteen years old, she was wise beyond her years.

I hushed her before Kim realized she copied me.

"How? What? Did you ask for too much money?"

"Kim, you wouldn't believe me if I told you. I accidentally missed the big dinner, and they pulled the offer right after. They shifted their focus."

"But Uncle Ray said it was a done deal. You will become a big shot, forget all the little people, and move to Hollywood," Layla butted in. She leaned her elbows on the backs of the front seat. Her two-year-old siblings snored away in the car seats on either side of her.

"We don't mention Uncle Ray in front of Lena, hunny," Kim scolded.

"It's fine. I don't mind. Ray knows I worked hard on my program. It makes me feel good that he believes in me."

"I believe in you too, Lena!" Layla shouted. On cue, her brother and sister both cried as they woke up.

"The terrible two's only lasts a few months," Kim

said.

"Then, the nightmare three's start!" Layla threw more fuel on the fire.

After some help from a valet, two bottles, three pacifiers, and Layla watching videos on my phone, we got everyone to the pool area. Kim left me with the kids to sign us all in.

"So, you're not moving to Hollywood?" Layla asked without looking up from my phone. She chuckled at the same cat video she watched over ten times.

"When people sell computer programs, they don't move to Hollywood. That's more for movie stars."

"I want to be like *Sabrina, the Teenage Witch*. If I become a witch like you, can I move to Hollywood?"

Part of my duties as Ray's girlfriend was babysitting Layla before the twins came along. Her phases never lasted, but the questions often rattled me. Her old soul yearned for adulthood. I never mentioned witchcraft around her. *Who ratted me out?*

I sprayed suntan lotion on the twins, hoping I seemed calm. "I watched the original show, not the new one. Who told you I was a witch?"

"The person I'm not supposed to talk about to you." Layla leaned in and cupped her left hand over the side of her face. "Uncle Ray," she whispered. In her normal voice, she continued, "He's mad at you for casting a spell on him. His new girlfriend with a funny name said she would protect him from you."

"Chloe?"

"No, the new one. I don't like her."

"You didn't like me in the beginning."

"You wore too much perfume. A kid needs boundaries."

I laughed. Layla handed me back my phone and pointed at two girls waving from the concession stand. I recognized them from the photos taped up in her room. I nodded, and she shuffled her way over to them.

"Just me and you babies."

Jaxon and Tully smiled from their double stroller. "Baby apple," Jaxon said. At least they still liked me. I unzipped the cooler bag handing them each an apple slice. I wasn't releasing them until Kim came back.

"Did Layla find her friends?" Kim found us, holding the strings of four white balloons with the club insignia on them.

"Yup, they're over there ogling the lifeguard, and these cutie patooties have been all smiles. Who's the fourth balloon for?"

Kim separated the large one and handed it over. "I suspected Layla couldn't keep quiet about Ray, so maybe this will lighten the blow."

"Ah, I see. Did you meet the new girlfriend?"

"Yeah, but I'm biased. I will always like you best. Who's ready to go swimming?"

Jaxon squealed while Tully whimpered and cried. I unhooked my little buddy from his straps, and Kim took her daughter. I wanted to ask her if Ray mentioned anything about the love spell, but if my friendship had any potential of survival with Kim, our conversations about her brother must be kept minimal for both our sakes.

The heated pool water helped my aching muscles. I was out of shape, nearing the laziest time of my life. The sun also shined on my exposed skin, spreading heat all over in the best way. Jaxon kicked his little feet in the water gear, swimming into my arms each time I stepped back. Behind me, giggling grew louder as Layla and her friends wadded over.

I jumped around, twirling Jaxon a little above the water. Layla wasn't startled, but her friends jumped back. "Jaxon, full attack mode!" I released the toddler, and he betrayed me by swimming to his sister and asking for a hug.

"You can't teach a poodle to be an attack dog," Layla warned.

One of the girls, the older red head, leaned toward me, "Can you place a spell on him? Jaxon will do what you want then?"

Oh, no, not this again. "Toddlers are immune to witchcraft. They already see spirits and weave their own magic. Jaxon doesn't need me to help him. Look, he turned Layla into mush."

Layla hugged her baby brother, bouncing up and down. She played until she caught us watching, then released the water baby. Her throat cleared, and her sassy, 'I'm over it' look returned.

"I keep telling them you're not a real witch. Ray only told me about the heart thing to scare me," Layla confessed.

Shit, what did Ray tell her? "Um, how many beers did he have that night?"

"I told you this wasn't real. Layla, you didn't have to lie," the other girl said.

"I swear I'm not lying. My uncle said he tried to rip out his heart. I saw the blood. Mom cleaned it up before I could take a picture. I swear he got hurt! Tell them, Lena! Tell them you ended the love spell!"

My mind blanked. All my guilt and shame from that night rushed forward. No wonder he feared me last week.

I never wanted anything bad to happen.

"It did happen, didn't it?" the third girl asked.

"If you're talking about the night I think you are, Ray fell into my stupid thorn bush and cut up his arm. I think he bit his tongue too. That always bleeds like a bitch. No spell, no drama, no tearing out hearts." I settled for a few truths and snuck in a lie.

"You said *bitch*. I'm pretty sure you're lying, so can we put a love spell on Brandon? We found out he's single," Layla declared.

The three girls swooned at the lifeguard, who was at least eight years older than them.

"Yeah, we can take turns," the redhead said.

"Oh please, teach us the love spell," the other one urged.

"Fuck that. I want boobs." Layla straightened her bikini top over her pre-pubescent chest.

"Layla, how many times do I have to tell you not to curse." Kim swam over with Tully in a pineapple floatable ring made for toddlers. Layla flipped her sunglasses back on, scoffing.

"Mom, I'm with my friends. They curse."

"It doesn't matter. Hi, girls. Why don't you all come with me so Lena can relax and get some laps in? Adult swim time begins now."

"But what about the love…" Layla started. Kim corralled the three tweens and her twins over to the swallow end. I thanked and saluted her. I needed that life raft.

Swimming brought peace to my inner turmoil more times than I counted. I loved the weightlessness, the sun beating down on my shivering skin. Water comforted me. *If I found death and became a witch, I wondered if water would play a part?*

I pushed off the concrete siding of the pool, stretching my legs in the water. I swallowed some air and dunked my whole body underneath the water. My eyes opened, spying on the legs of the other people kicking, staying afloat. A shadow floated over the surface of the water above my head. I jerked my head up as an inflatable lounge chair drifted over me. A book fell off the side, floating until the saturated pages sank.

Swimming toward the left, I came up for air. I grabbed at the book, but it had fallen past my arm's reach. The middle-aged woman had both arms outstretched on the sides of her, and her head laid to the side of the fake pillow. A tiny fly buzzed around her slack mouth.

"Ma'am, hey? You dropped your book?" I spoke. The woman did not flinch at all. "Excuse me, ma'am!" I said louder. The fly went inside her mouth, and I nudged her arm. Her clammy skin moved with my push but fell right back. "Hey, lady!" I touched her again, harder than before, making her sunglasses slide down her pert nose.

Her vacant, bluish eyes stared back. The fly flew back out of her mouth.

"Did Mrs. Remeida fall asleep again?" I heard through a blowhorn. The lifeguard said more, but a ringing so loud blared through my inner ear. I resisted covering my ears in hopes the sound came from something malfunctioning outside. The discordant whirring drowned out everything.

I picked up Mrs. Remeida's hand that had been dangling below the water's surface and placed it on her unmoving chest. Her pulse was gone. No breath escaped her body. Her opened eyes saw no more.

A shrilling scream sliced through the cacophony in my mind. Hiccups and more screaming made it through. The lifeguard tugged me aside, heading for Mrs. Remeida's dead body.

"*Janice!*" The lifeguard yelled into the woman's face. I still heard the screaming in the distance, and another shout followed by splashing joined the chaotic scene.

Someone wearing more clothes than they should in a pool stood in front of me, cradling my face in their hands. The young man, wearing a white collared shirt, snapped his fingers in front of my face and shouted.

"Miss, are you okay? Please stop screaming. I got you." He tried soothing me, but my whole body trembled and shook. My lungs burned from the panic rising in my chest, throughout my bones. I lost my voice while the scared boy rubbed my shoulders, checking over my head every few seconds.

"She's dead. Rich, get that woman out of the pool. We need to inform emergency services, now."

"I'm sorry, they need me," the boy helping me said. He pursed his lips together and jumped out of the pool, gripping the other guy's hand.

"Lena! Lena, what's happening?" Kim shouted. My back fused to the pebbled side of the pool. She wasn't by the steps with the kids anymore. She must be somewhere else close.

"Kim, please stand back. We have a tragedy on our hands. Get the kids out of here," a young boy instructed.

"What about my sister-in-law? She's scared to death!"

"I'll tend to her next. I must continue chest compressions. We can save her."

"Lena, I'll be in the clubhouse. I love you!"

Tears rolled down my shivering cheeks. I barely got a new breath out of my body. I coughed, my palm cupping my mouth. My fingertips felt odd against my skin. All the red veins displayed beneath the raisin-like texture of my skin. I tried closing my hand into a fist, but as if an invisible cage enslaved them, my fingers were spread apart and straightened. Next came the stretching, like my bones were being torn out by a strong magnet attuned to the calcium. I screamed for another reason now.

I hid my right hand in the water, alleviating part of the torture. The weightlessness of the water hindered whatever the fuck was happening. My left-hand laid limp in the water. Nothing special or out of the ordinary took hold of that arm.

Of course, my left hand wasn't affected. I'd only felt the dead woman with my right hand.

"Oh my God!" I screamed again and again.

Chapter Twenty-Two

Four hours later, the cops released me. I retold my story at least twenty times. Mrs. Janice Remeida, had heart issues for the past year, and they suspected she had either a heart attack or stroke, killing her before she knew what happened. The cops and members of the country club kept repeating, "Thank God, she wasn't driving." No, she floated over me. A corpse working on her late summer tan.

My phone ran out of power. I bet Layla never closed the video app, when she returned my phone back to me hours before in another life. A life before I found death.

I sat down in the lobby. The club gave me sweatpants and a shirt, two sizes too big. Nothing felt right through the horrific afternoon. I held my breath, hoping I still sat at the bottom of the pool until the stupid woman floated away.

"Hey, Lena." Ray rose from a nearby black couch. "Kim told me when she got home. Are you okay?"

He reached for me, but I backed away fast enough that he didn't touch me. "Please take me home."

"Are you sure? You can stay at our house. I don't want to leave you alone," Ray said.

"Please, I can't argue right now. Please take me home."

Ray nodded. He took the tote bag the club gave me with a lifetime supply of free shit. Kim must have my beach bag I brought here today. "Do you need anything else? I have your black beach bag in the car."

"No," I muttered.

"Lena don't be stubborn. This was a traumatic event," Ray continued. My body walked through the fog of my brain until I climbed into Ray's truck. He stopped talking and drove me home.

"Can we talk?" Ray asked as we turned down my street.

"No."

"Lena, I know you know I met someone. I know this is the worst time, but I might be moving—"

"Have a nice life. Stop telling your niece shit stories that aren't true."

"Tully?"

"No, not the baby. Think, asshole." I tried the truck's passenger door, but it was still locked. I yanked on the handle until Ray hit the button on his side.

"I will stop by and say goodbye if I do go."

"Go, there is nothing keeping you here."

I slammed the truck door closed. I got halfway to my door and turned back around for my bags. Ray leaned against the truck, holding both. Without glancing up, I lifted my hand out.

"Promise me that you will call Kim or Amy if you aren't doing good? I need to know you're safe."

"Yup, can I have my bags now? Thanks for driving." I spared a glance at Ray. The blinking streetlamp illuminated the concern on his face. I knew him well enough that he wasn't leaving until I walked inside, safe, and warm. "I'll be okay. It's not like I've never seen a dead body before. I just need some sleep."

We stared at each other, waiting for an outcome that

no longer fit us. Ray handed over my bags.

"Thank you, Ray. Good luck in your new life."

"Goodbye, Lena."

I kept walking toward the front door, ignoring my broken heart. Once I shut the front door, Ray's engine started up, and he sped away, leaving an unbearable silence behind. I sat down at my kitchen table like most nights, except tears streamed down my face. I touched death, or rather it found me. *What happened now?*

I pulled out my dead phone and untangled the charger wire from my junk drawer. It took a few minutes for enough charge to restart it, but once the number password unlocked, I wished I hadn't looked. A missed text from Amy informing me about a dead body found at the swim club. *Been there, fucked that up.*

I missed a call from Mom and another from Richard. I swiped the notifications away and dialed the one person I needed.

After two rings, out of breath as always, Arthur picked up, "Lena?"

"I need you."

"I'll be over in twenty minutes."

I sat in the dark, willing my body to move. It was only eight o'clock, but darkness blanketed the kitchen. I walked upstairs and ran a bath. My fingers held no extra tingle where I touched the dead woman anymore. My heart pulsed the same, but agonizing tiredness gripped me like a vise.

I set an alarm for ten minutes. The stench of chlorine radiated off my skin. I wanted it gone. I wanted to be clean. Arthur was right. Death would find me if it was meant to be. I can't believe I sat in a church like my powers would magically appear. I forgot my own rules in the process. No wands, no tricks, just if you got it, you got it.

The warm water soothed my aching body. The bath bomb bobbed up and down at the surface, spreading pink sea salt and lavender. I piled my hair on top of my head in a scrunchie from Kim's last month's extras. I hoped her kids were okay as I sank down further in the tub, right up to my lips. The twins will be fine, but Layla already suspected something was up with me. She's too curious for her own good.

My front door slammed shut. "Lena! Where are you?" Arthur shouted.

"Up here!" It would have helped if the house hadn't gotten darker from the setting sun. I only turned on the bathroom light. *What was still wrong with me?* I thought I'd be better.

By the sound of it, Arthur took the stairs two at a time. He practically flew into my bathroom, looking like a disheveled mess. His searching gaze went wild, and he panted like he had finished a marathon. The flush up his neck worried me, but only for a second.

"Did you run here?"

"No, I didn't. Are you hurt? Where did you get hurt?" His knees slammed down on the bathmat. He ignored my nakedness at first, but quickly his gaze trailed toward my breasts, traveling down my belly to the curls between my legs.

"I didn't get hurt, but something happened."

His eyes squeezed shut, his mouth sucked in over an imaginary lemon, and the shakiest breath left his mouth. "You found a way, didn't you?" He already knew the answer, but we must say it out loud.

"It wasn't easy."

"How did you get close enough?" Shame bombarded me, and I hid behind my tears. Arthur's fingertips lifted my chin. "Tell me, Lena."

"A woman died in the town pool. I held onto her arm at the moment of death or seconds later. It sufficed."

"In daylight?"

"Yes."

He folded his arms over the wet edge of the tub, resting his forehead in the middle. His heavy breathing subsided. I roamed my fingers through his longish hair, soothing him for some odd reason. I thought I invited him here for my comfort. *How did the tables turn the other way?*

"Are you upset with me?" I asked.

Arthur jerked his head back up, his face flushed with tears. "Death found you. It was meant to be." He wiped his fingers under his eyes and sniffled. "I'll give you some privacy."

I almost reached out my hand, hoping he had stayed. I didn't want to be alone. Eyes from nowhere and everywhere heightened my alertness. There weren't any dark corners in the bathroom, every inch could be seen, but I swore someone watched me. The mirror reflected the closed door of the mini closet. Nothing there either. The plastic curtain covering the high window in the tub area concealed any sneaky peaks too. *Where could someone be watching me?*

My bed squeaked from the other room. In his defense, there weren't many options in my bedroom. Before my skin shriveled like prunes, I stepped out of the bath. My naked body held onto the aroma of lavender and shea butter. Like a normal night, my robe waited for me. The oversized, plush terry cloth robe hugged my body like a lover, caressing my most sensitive parts.

I didn't bring clothes into the bathroom, so if Arthur sat on the bed, he was in for a show. My bedside lamp cascaded the room in a soft yellow glow. Arthur leaned back on his palms against my bedspread. The look he shot my way blew every sex dream I had about him to the moon.

"Do you want more privacy?"

I shook my head, walking toward the bed. Even with my robe closed, Arthur's lingering gaze journeyed from my feet up to my exposed neck. "Come on, I can't possibly be sexy wearing a skinned Muppet."

"On the contrary, I thought you were drop-dead gorgeous the moment I saw you a few months ago. Every time I see you, you're more beautiful than the last time. It took every ounce of control I didn't know I had to walk out of your bathroom and not memorize your naked body."

I gulped. "Even after everything today? Did I change? Should I feel weird?" I tugged the plush sash tighter around my waist.

Arthur got up, rising to his full height. His boots added another inch and, with my bare feet, made me a smidge shorter than usual. I expected to be intimidated, shy away from the man who had warned me there was no turning back once a path chose me. Instead, every molecule in my body lurched forward, craving contact like the strongest magnet in the world.

"I'm sorry, Lena. There isn't a set-in-stone right answer to any of your questions. The experience is different for everyone. Quite frankly, only a handful of people ever encounter this milestone. I thought I gave you an impossible task, but you proved me wrong."

"If this doesn't happen often, then how do people become witches?"

"That's just it. They aren't true witches. You will be a real one."

Arthur's chest muffled the sob wrenching from my throat. I wrapped my arms around his neck, sagging against him. The dam on my numbness broke. My tears soaked his flannel shirt in the few minutes he held me, not letting any space between us. He stroked my back and kissed my hair over and over, but no relief came.

"Can I be honest with you?" Arthur asked. He released me, swiping a tear off his cheek.

"Please, I can't handle a lie."

"This is not the end. It's only the beginning."

"What happens now?"

"We wait for a new moon to see what powers will come to you. Flowers are a part of it. I should have started you on a path already, but like I said, I never thought death would find you so soon. We need to make some lists, go shopping, find your spiritual base, um, fuck, there is so much to do. I have a friend who can help us, she…"

I interrupted his anxious rant with a kiss. His last word died upon my lips. A surge, as if my radio plunged into my bathwater, sparked a shock between us. Our joined gasp ripped us apart.

"Arthur," I pleaded.

"It'll be all right. We'll figure it out together." He rested his forehead against mine, our gazes longing for more.

"If I can't kiss you, how is this going to work?" My voice cracked, and a slight tremble rolled up and down my body. Not quite a shiver, but it carried up to my fingertips, caressing the back of Arthur's neck.

"Trial and error." Arthur pried my arms from around his neck, separating us completely. "Lay on the bed as comfortable as you can."

"This just got so sexy."

Arthur knitted his brow together, then rolled his eyes. I grabbed his outstretched hand as I crawled onto my bed. "Hold all your sarcasm until the end, please, or I won't give you a special treat."

"And that is?" I whipped around toward Arthur, still standing at the foot of the bed.

"Kiss me again, and I might tell you." The smirk, the most natural devilish grin I had ever seen, slipped onto his face. The heat burning at my fingertips held no torch to the inferno churning inside me. I fucking liked the killer, flirt version of the dry man I never saw coming.

I inched close to the edge of the bed, near enough that Arthur's fingers caressed the back of my thighs underneath my robe. If I only lifted my chin a few inches up, our lips would meet, and we could try it again. I kept my chin down, unable to meet his gaze.

"Lena?"

"I'm scared."

One of his hands, mere inches from my ass and other parts of me craving his touch, left my curves and lifted my chin. "We can do this together. I'm scared too."

We both leaned in, a soft and firm kiss until Arthur pulled away. "Did you feel it?" he asked.

"No, I'm guessing you did first."

"Kiss me again."

I did, but Arthur's tongue flicked out, asking permission. I sucked it between my lips, catching him between my teeth, and swirled my own tongue back and forth. Arthur's moan weaved the perfect hum in my ears, and fuck, I needed him to do it again. Unbearable heat separated the connection.

I lost the fight. Our lips parted, but his mouth kissed an inviting path down my neck. Each kiss and suck weakened my knees.

All or nothing, I thought. My pink fuzzy robe got me from point A to point B. Now it needed to be crumbled on the bedroom floor. The knot came undone with minor fidgeting, granting Arthur another view of the front of my body. I shrugged the bulky robe off my shoulders, throwing it against the closet door.

"Risky, Lena. Dangerous, too."

"Maybe, I'm making up my own rules. The first one is to forget all your rules."

He chuckled at my boldness.

The back of Arthur's hand caressed the side of my breast. My body leaned forward into his touch, insisting on more. His thumb stroked my puckered nipple until he cupped the full weight of my breast in his entire hand.

"I like that, Arthur."

"Fuck, you tempt me too much."

Arthur arched his head to the side and kissed me harder than before, pushing me down onto the mattress. We fell together, my legs hugging his hips, his handsome face hovering over mine. He traced my lips with his other hand, making a quick way down my chin until he held my taut nipple up for his mouth.

The only zap between us then was his teeth lightly biting my ample flesh. The soft pillows cushioned my head as I moaned. The blinking streetlight created a strobe light of passion in my vision. One second,

Arthur's tongue licked across my nipple. The next, he sucked me in the darkness. He alternated the sweet torment until I gasped, "No more," and he switched to the other breast, beginning again.

My hands combed through his sandy-colored hair until I gripped his shoulders, desperate to pull him off my sensitive breasts. I already spied a love bite on the side of my left breast. I hope it never faded.

"Arthur, please. I can't breathe," I confessed.

"Yes, you can. If our lips don't touch, the rest of your body is mine. All of it."

He yanked his shirt up over his head. Before I saw his bewitching face, my fingers smoothed over the fine soft hair, shielding his muscled pecs. He leaned away, his ass on the back of his calves. Even though he had muscles, his body had a layer of softness, which I wanted pinning me against my mattress.

I held my breath as he unbuckled his belt. When he made love to my breasts, I practically rubbed my pussy raw against the seam of his jeans and his hard dick. I yearned for every piece of him. He undid his top button and stopped.

"Is this too much?" I queried.

"It will always be too little."

Arthur's gaze flicked over my face and coursed down to my pussy. His fingers gripped my hips and pushed me up further to my headboard.

"Arthur." His name morphed into a moan. Those lips that I couldn't kiss more than a few seconds molded over my clit, surprising the absolute fuck out of me. That scandalous tongue traced every inch until his fingers thrust inside me.

"I want to fuck you so bad. Can we? Can we fuck?"

"Please," I moaned.

"Do you have a condom?"

He tore off his jeans and briefs while I fumbled in the drawer of the bedside table. *Please let there be one in here.* I found a condom tucked away in the back of the drawer. Relief slackened Arthur's face.

I wrapped my hand around the tip of his cock, twisting under the head, and dragging my palm down the underside. His moan, that sexy, secret sound I'm convinced only a select few heard, urged me onto my back, legs spread, ready and fucking waiting.

"Lena." My name became his breath as he put on the condom. Then, he crawled on top of me, his hips grinding into mine. His dick dipped inside me. Each slow thrust entered me further.

I squeezed his hands, where he held my hips still. "I need you closer."

Arthur paused above me, the static buzz filtering into my ears. The sound came from all around the room, disparaging my thoughts, dampening my desire. I gripped Arthur close, pushing the incessant reminder away.

I only want to be with him. Ignorant to the change, Arthur steadied his breath, his cock pulsing inside my pussy. I licked his earlobe, nicking the soft flesh smelling faintly of soap. I got a harder thrust that time. His firm ass twitched beneath my fingers.

I loved how we folded together, one piece igniting the other. I waited for the fucking, the hard crash of our bodies slamming into each other, but alas, the look on Arthur's face, as if he had been drugged in the last few minutes, stifled any rough intention. It was too early for love on his part, but mine, I wasn't in the right mind to talk.

The friction building between us, with each slow, maddening thrust, hurdled me further, holding me tight against the wire. He plunged deeper. One of his hands grabbed the back of my neck, and the other lifted my ass for him.

"Lena, fuck, Lena. Kiss me, burn me up, please kiss me."

Our animalistic instincts rushed in. Enough of cautious, inexperienced kisses. I wanted his breath, soul, and heart yearning for me and my love. Our lips would be bruised in the morning by how hard we met in the middle. A few seconds went by, then another, and soon after a minute passed, our lush lips were still locked together with nothing prying us apart.

I thanked anyone responsible for dropping the curse. Kissing Arthur became my new oxygen, the shiny new toy I wanted every waking moment of the day. He already sneaked around my dreams, so I must steal a kiss there, too, if I remembered.

I wished my pillows never lost the intoxicating smell of our frenzied bodies, almost at the peak, working hard for each other to come. He dipped his head, lapping at my nipple. The sight, the distinct angle of his head, and the switch over to shallow thrusts of just the head of his cock, dragged me over the blissful edge.

Heat in waves of pleasure bubbled behind my pelvis. I clawed at Arthur's back. Our mouths fused together. We made it over whatever torment kept breaking our kisses before. We were freed.

I wished the moment, the glorious second, where Arthur realized his rock-hard cock made me come could be captured and replayed any time we fought or disagreed. The smile, the full-teethed, crinkled eyes grin gracing his face made me fall in love.

Arthur groaned into my mouth as our tongues dueled and our lips bruised. His frenzied thrusts stopped shortly after. We both breathed heavily, recovering from the high.

The full weight of Arthur's body crushed me into the soft mattress as if we were fused together, joined impossibly, but not actually. The tips of his fingers tickled my side until they reached my left breast, cupping and toying with their generous size. His nose nuzzled my neck.

"If you don't stop playing with me, I'm going to ask for a round two," I kidded.

Arthur's sex-drunk body shrugged. "That's fine. I don't plan on moving any time soon." He rolled our sweaty, sticky bodies to our sides. "I'm sorry for the mess."

"I like it." I kissed his sweet laughter. "Why can we kiss now?"

"I'm not sure. That's never happened to me before." He drew a warm finger over my plump bottom lip. I puckered my lips, kissing his fingerprint.

"Arthur, what happens next? Am I a real witch now?"

"Can we talk about it tomorrow? Come here."

I scooted closer, and we kissed, soft, loving kisses. Satisfaction almost transformed my closed eyes into sleep. I pulled away with a shaky hand on his chest.

"If we stay in bed, I'm going to fall asleep." I yawned behind my palm.

"All right, let's go out. Let's do something normal."

"How about a movie?"

He looked to the side of the room for a moment, then asked, "Horror or Comedy?"

We both answered, "Horror."

Chapter Twenty-Three

Arthur and I were quiet as we cleaned up and got dressed. While I applied some make-up, Arthur leaned against the doorframe and held up his phone, showing me two seats available dead center for the last showing of a newly released horror movie. I smiled, and he booked it without a second thought.

"We have a half hour. Do you have a big purse?"

"I only own big purses."

"Good, let's stop at the supermarket and get some cheap candy. Cool?" Arthur wandered back into the bedroom.

I blinked at my reflection. Was that another love spell? How had he known I smuggled in stuff to the movie theaters? We fucked, and now we were instantly doing cute couple things.

"Arthur?"

"Yeah, are you okay?" He poked his head back into the bathroom.

"I'm not under a spell, right? Or I didn't accidentally cast one on you?"

The sexy tug of his jawline captured another fragment of my heart. He cradled my face, caressing his thumbs against my heated cheeks. "I promise this isn't a spell." He kissed me. His day-old stubble tickled worse than before. I loved it.

"I believe you. I'm sorry for all the questions."

"It's fine. I'm not mad, but I will be irritated if we miss the movie previews. Chop, chop, Lena," he said. He slapped my ass, and I let out a small yelp. "You're gorgeous. Come on." Arthur tugged my arm toward the door.

"I have one eye done. Give me another minute."

"Then I'll sit on that side of you."

"Ha-ha, I'll be down in a second."

He gave up, throwing his hands in the air. "Can I borrow your phone charger?"

"There is one in the kitchen!" I shouted.

I followed his lumbering footsteps down the stairs two minutes later. Before I reached the last three steps, flickering light shined into the enclosed stairwell, and the sound of crackling flames greeted me. Light from every candle I owned glowed throughout my living room. I swore the room looked dark a moment ago.

"Arthur?" I whispered. The living room was empty. Someone snapped their fingers in the direction of the kitchen, lowering the candle flames down to their wicks. The dark room resembled twinkling stars in a clear night's sky. I gasped at the beauty.

I backed up from the stunning sight into the kitchen, the path visible by more shimmering candles. Arthur stood over the small dinette table with the scorched middle ring. His hand waved over that part, hidden by the pitcher of fake flowers and placemat.

"You will never have to hide your magic again."

As if he had all my decorative candles in front of him on a full sheet birthday cake, he blew a line in front of his face, extinguishing every flame both in the kitchen and the living room. Stunned, I remained immobile with fear and wonder.

We stood in the darkness. Small, stray snakes of smoke wafted throughout the air, illuminated enough to be seen. The stench of the burning wax overpowered my house.

"We're going to be late for the movie. What snacks do you like? I'll run into the store while you stay in the car."

"That's it? We aren't going to talk about your parlor trick?"

"Not tonight. Right now, I want to go out on a date with you. I want to eat chocolate and candy and giggle when you gasp at the first jump scare. Then I want you to laugh your ass off, when I spill popcorn at a scary part I didn't see coming. Can we do that, Lena? Please?"

His phone illuminated the darkness, turning on from the few minutes of charge.

I could beat a dead horse and barrage him with more questions he didn't want to answer, or we could go to the movie and attempt the dating thing. I picked the latter.

"If you email me the tickets, I'll grab popcorn while you run to store and get candy. Deal?"

"Thank you," he said. Arthur kissed my forehead where his lips naturally fell. "Deal."

****

"I met someone. His name is Arthur, and he owns a psychic magic shop," I blurted out.

"You didn't pick him up at a funeral, right?" my therapist asked.

"Well, sort of, but not exactly." Her arched eyebrow judged me worse than my neighbor's cat. "Okay, yes, I met him at a funeral, but I didn't crash it. He brought his mother to my grandmother's funeral a few months ago. We happened to run into each other again."

"The universe works in mysterious ways. You seem excited to talk about him. I said hello, and you pounced. Do you want to talk about him? Is there anything special that you like about him?"

"Hmm, he likes to sneak candy into the movie theater. He likes horror movies, and he's a twin. Um, he's into nature and natural processes for things."

"All right, so he's vegan and potentially smells bad in the summer. Tell me something better. Did you guys kiss yet? Was the movie your first date?"

"We met for coffee once, so I guess our first date was last week. We kissed a lot." Of course, I left out the part about something preventing us from kissing for more than ten seconds until we had sex for the first time.

"Do you have a picture of him?" Doctor Greene asked.

"Actually, no. We haven't been in a *let's take a selfie* moment yet." Another partial truth. There hadn't been an opportunity. *Can witches be photographed?* Maybe I dreamed Arthur and my night together.

"Lena, what are you thinking right now?"

My stomach gurgled. "I was thinking about how I had all these photos of Ray and me from the first day we met. I have nothing with Arthur. I feel like it isn't real until there is some proof."

"Maybe it's a good thing that this new relationship is nothing like your past one? It could be a sign of real potential."

"Like a career path?"

"Ha-ha, no. I feel like you are someone who could never be a housewife. Even if you sell your program, I'm pretty sure you already have another venture up your sleeves."

I drew my knees together, crossing my ankles. It's odd hearing about a normal life path since my world got fucked backward and sideways. I still had not processed any of the events from the other day. The woman dying over me, Arthur and I having sex, the candle trick, or the fact that Arthur chews the loudest out of all the people I had ever known. I hadn't seen him since last week. He had plans to visit a friend upstate before I ambushed his life. I grabbed my phone any time it pinged all week, hoping it was him, sending me something, anything, about us. All I got was a shotty voicemail about crappy reception. On his trip home, he better head straight to my house.

"Hey, if you don't want to talk about him, we can move on?" She touched my knee and offered me an understanding smile.

"Sorry, I don't handle change well. It's all very new."

"Oh please, we lived through a pandemic and lost over a year of socialization. It's okay to be off-kilter. How did your day at the pool go?"

My heartbeat thudded in my mind. I hadn't felt any different since it happened. I still put my panties on one leg at a time and woke up as exhausted as ever. After I orgasmed, nothing special happened. I fell in love with Arthur, but I couldn't suddenly turn silver to gold, change my hair color, or walk on water. I was still me.

Doctor Greene ground her teeth whether she knew it or not. I had to tell her something.

"A woman died at the pool. They think she had a brain aneurysm while reading on a pool float. I found her. She looked like she had fallen asleep, but nope, dead."

Doctor Greene's mouth dropped to the floor. Well, not literally, but her nostrils flared, and she clutched her chest. "Oh my God, that's awful! Did the kids see?"

"Their mom said she fell asleep. I stayed to answer questions while my friend took her kids home. Hopefully, her oldest never learns the truth."

"I bet that could be traumatizing for a young child and for you. Are you all right?"

"Yeah, but it did make me feel my mortality. Arthur came over after I told him what happened. We went to a movie, but he went home after. I slept with the bathroom light on for the first time since I lived in my house."

"Have you had any nightmares about it?"

"Not yet, but I'm sure they will come."

"I know you didn't want to go on daily prescription medication, but if you need something at night, you could get some night melatonin for relaxation. It does not have the adverse side effects of some stronger sleep aids. There are also CBD gummies. You could start with a half and work your way up to two."

"Thank you, Doctor Greene. My problem is not falling asleep. It's not feeling rested after sleeping ten hours a night. I wake up feeling like I haven't slept at all."

"Have you done any presentations in the middle of the night?"

"In the past two weeks, they have all been U.S. potential customers, so no. The latest one was eight o'clock for the west coast."

"We could have the vitamin conversation again?"

"Please, no."

"All right, scratch that, let's go back to something positive. What are some fun things you are looking forward to with your new guy?"

Casting spells, more sex, learning my powers, sex again, and kissing, lots more kissing. I wished I told her all that stuff. I settled for boring. "Hibachi, peddle boating at the lake, getting ice cream before they close for the winter, finding out if he snores."

"I wish all those things for you and more. Great job, Lena. We have come so far from when you first came here. Is there anything else you would like to talk about?"

Our small talk lasted a few more minutes, then I politely left her home. I texted her secretary and sent the co-pay over through my bank account. Doctor Greene's approval of my stretched truth meant something, but how the fuck did I handle the reality? If I lied to her, what was the use of the sessions anymore?

Tears fell into my lap. I thought I wouldn't cry, but fuck it all. I had valid reasons for the sobs raking through my body. I rested my forehead on my steering wheel.

A loud car horn startled me from my misery. The guy in an Oldsmobile beeped again and pointed at my window. I pushed the button, and the string of curses thrown my way staggered my fragile state. "Lady, there are limits to how long you can stink up a parking place. Move or get a parking permit."

I muttered an apology and turned the key in the ignition, but Doctor Greene rushed down her front steps toward us, waving a blue door hanger in her hand. "Beat it, Nick. Pick on someone else. Here is her parking pass."

She handed me the door hanger and opened my door after, presumably, Nick drove off, flipping us the bird. "Lena, please don't ever leave a session and cry in your car. Come on, I'll make you some tea."

"I wasn't crying. I'm fine, really, it's allergies," I blabbered.

Doctor Greene flipped down my overhead visor, revealing the mirror. Red splotches streaked down my cheeks, and fresh tears pooled in my eyes. "Stop lying, hun. Come back in."

****

Two cups of tea later, Doctor Greene, aka Marilyn, and I politely smiled at each other for twenty minutes.

"You're off the clock, but you have to give me something to work with here."

"I feel like if I tell the truth, you are going to recommend I admit myself into the nearest psych ward."

"It can't be that weird. We all have our own superstitions. My great-aunt, God rest her soul, would roll over in her grave if I bought myself anything with an elephant or an owl. She always said it was bad luck."

"It's more complicated than buying trinkets. I need to spend more time with Arthur before I can figure it out."

Marilyn placed her butterfly teacup back on the matching saucer. She poured more tea for herself, and I turned down seconds. "If he asks you for any money, ghost him."

"Well, the universe has other plans. We kept seeing each other unexpectedly, then I met his twin sister by accident. When we're together, the world falls away. I'm overwhelmed by how much I'm attracted to him."

"When I met my college boyfriend, I hyperventilated on a train for two hours every other weekend down to the Jersey Shore. I was worried I made up the sparks, the pure magic I felt when I was with him. Love can do crazy things to a person's mind."

"Like rip your heart out through your mouth."

Marilyn pursed her lips into a tight line. "I hope you're speaking in the figurative sense."

I sipped my tea, watching the leaves swirl in the reddish-brown liquid. I already said too much. I appreciated her offer to talk, but time was up.

"I will never judge someone's belief system. However, if he is causing you bodily harm, I need to know. You loved Ray for a long time, and it's okay you broke up with him. You deserve to have a healthy relationship with another person. You must be careful. Don't let anyone take advantage of you because you don't want to be alone."

"Thank you. I'm not being hurt in any way. He's more nervous than me when we hang out."

I finished my tea and placed the porcelain cup back on the saucer. With a deep breath, I peered down at the empty cup where the damp tea residue lay. Crooked lines stared back, much like ones I had seen before.

"Are you reading your fortune?" Marilyn asked.

"Guilty. I always thought it was a trick, but it means a lot to some people if they believe."

"What does mine say?"

She slurped the rest of her tea and handed over the cup. I crooked my finger through the handle, inspecting the tea leaves. Smudges covered the bottom with curved edges like birds flying in the distance.

"I see birds. Are you planning a trip far away?"

"Get out of here. Oh my God, I swear I just planned a trip this morning. My best friend is working in London, and I'm finally going to visit her. If you don't believe me, check this out!"

She pushed out her chair and ran over to her desk,

nestled in a small alcove in the corner of her living room. Papers scattered over the surface while she found what she looked for.

"Aha, here it is. Look at the time stamp."

The date and time were printed on the bottom of the sheet, and yup, it was today.

"Sometimes, I get lucky," I commented.

"Are you a witch?"

"I don't know. I've always been able to create things with my hands. I used to write blindly for hours. I never looked down, yet it worked. I saw my *abuela* rise out of her coffin and wave goodbye. For years though, I haven't felt anything odd about my life. Certain sounds bother me, but that doesn't make me a witch. I still don't know if I'm at the end of the journey or the start. Arthur said he would help me when he gets back in town."

"The new guy is a witch?"

Ugh, Marilyn better not have any other sessions today. I nodded.

"Do you think he's dangerous?"

"No, I think he's a good witch. He plays with fire, but I've never seen him hurt anyone with it. I still don't know if it's a magic trick he learned. We had our movie date, and then he left town. I need him to get his hot ass back here."

"He hasn't bought you anything with an owl or an elephant on it?"

I peered over at her.

She shrugged. "It's all I know. Look, Lena, I'm not someone who knows a lot about this stuff. I thought my aunt's house was haunted, but that's as far as I go. Do you know anyone to talk to besides Arthur?"

"He has a crazy twin sister. I can try talking to her.

They don't get along, but she might be my best bet."

"Please be careful. I'm not saying that as your therapist, but as your friend. I know there are things you can't explain in this world. If you tapped into something fantastical, find someone you trust to help."

"I will. Thank you, Marilyn. I feel better now."

"Truly?"

"Yes. Promise me, you will buy me something very British, like spotted dick pudding. I swear it's real."

Her nose wrinkled to her eyes. "Whatever you say."

Chapter Twenty-Four

I had three more days until Arthur came back to town. He sent me a text last night reminding me. I wished I was more prepared or even knew what that meant. I searched the internet for anything, but all I found were social media groups of fans of witchcraft.

I did a demonstration first thing in the morning for a company in New York City, took feedback notes, and headed out after lunch.

Before I contacted Idalia, I had two other options thirty minutes away in New Jersey. The first place I drove by wound up not being a magic shop at all. They had magic in their title, but it was a make-up shop. My hope of finding another actual witch deflated.

The occult shop a half hour away looked the part. An all-seeing eye on top of a pyramid decal decorated the window, and neon lights spelling psychic readings shined purple above it. The dented bell, hanging over the doorframe, rang when I entered the shop. The sharp, metal against metal, tinging sound irritated my blossoming headache. Strong incense flooded my nostrils. Aside from the bad stuff, beautiful stones rested in ornate dishes and baskets along two wooden display cases. Mini signs placed on small easels explained the purposes of the rocks.

My gaze drifted to the protection ones as if I searched for the word specifically. I stopped in front of the single moonstone the store owner had left. The white speckled stone reflected the light back, calling toward me.

"I can set any stone you'd like into some jewelry. You can touch them if you'd like. They don't bite." A young girl, perhaps a little under twenty years old, appeared by my side. She offered me a small basket. "You can place the stones you like in here."

"Thank you, but I'm okay. I would like to talk to Sheri, please. I bought a session with her online."

"She's upstairs giving a reading. I don't like to disturb her until she is done."

"It's fine. I'll browse."

"Can I interest you in a trio of crystals? Locally sourced."

"No, thank you. I like to see what calls out to me."

A man walked down the floating stairs attached to the left wall. He tipped his hat to the pushy girl upselling me. Oddly enough, the man reminded me of a gentleman caller finishing up with his lady friend, especially when he adjusted the belt on his pants. The displaced image hit the nail on the head when the woman standing at the top of the stairs appeared in a slip dress with a satin robe.

I should have left when the shop girl got up in my face. I took a deep breath and trekked up the stairs.

"She looked at a bunch of the protection crystals."

I glared and scoffed at the shop girl. My clean slate with Sheri evaporated right under my nose.

"Oh, come up now. We must discuss," the woman said.

I pounded my feet up the stairs leading to the raised loft. Pillows and animal furs cluttered the space. A sneezing attack started along with scratching. The woman laid back against the pillows, propping herself up against a wedged mat.

"Is that a sex mat?" I asked.

"It's a multiple-purpose mat. Please be seated. My name is Madame Sheri."

Yup, she used it for sex.

I rolled my eyes, ignoring the charades. A hanging aerial swing hooked into a beam drew my interest. If she pissed me off more than helped, I would demand unlimited cocoon time.

I cleared away the furs and sat cross-legged on the floor. Sheri already shut her eyes and hummed. Her thumbs and forefingers angled together created two distinct eyes watching me. The void of silence I experienced from time to time sucked me in. Her chanting spit me right back out.

"Who has burdened this woman craving protection?" Sheri asked.

I wished I could legally throw stones down at the girl behind the counter, blasting the music from a radio for the shoppers. She sabotaged my reading by swaying the fortune teller.

"Release her from bondage. Take away her nightmares and frights. Let her shine in the light and only read in the dark. She will not join the other side today or tonight."

"Excuse me, I'm not here for a reading about protection. I am in no danger," I interrupted.

Sheri ignored my statement and continued cleansing me for five more minutes. I paid for the full twenty-minute reading, but I eagerly waited for the next set of discussion. If she compartmentalized her readings like the reviews said, we should shift toward money.

"I sense you are a self-starter. You own your own business, but you want to sell it."

I opened my mouth, but Sheri shushed me. "Maybe not now, but you will sell your company to a broker in Manhattan. You do something else with your hands. I just can't see it."

The truth peeked into the reading. Nine out of ten successful businesses sold them to a guy in Manhattan for big bucks, but I wasn't one of them. Sheri began again on another wrong path. I bounced my knees as her next step started about love.

"You have been in love twice. Your right thumb knuckle reveals the first letter of your soul mate's name." Her flailing hands stopped and caressed the crystal ball in front of her. "If you're afraid of magic, why did you put the spell on him?"

She caught my attention. "It was necessary."

"He almost died. I see dirt and flowers and dark ground. A birdhouse fell near him or a bat house."

"I don't have a birdhouse, and I hardly see any bats anymore."

"Maybe you missed it? It doesn't matter now. The new one loves you already."

I kept my face as expressionless as possible. I felt like a brat, playing with Sheri, the fortune teller. She droned on, relying on vague, impersonal insights any woman visibly in her late twenties, early thirties, might react to for the later part of the reading.

"What was the real reason you came to visit me today?" Sheri asked, folding her hands in her lap.

"I need to talk to someone about something that happened. Do you follow any rules in your trade?"

"Rules? I call them commandments."

"Not exactly original."

"It works for me. I have commandments, much like all the fortune tellers I have crossed paths with in my worldly travels. They may call them different things, but yes, they are rules."

I wished she'd drop the mambo jumbo act and talk to me for real.

"What are some of yours?"

She blinked and scratched the side of her head. I knocked her off her pre-scripted sermon. "No murder, raising from the dead, love spells, and no wishing for money. I'm sure most members of the occult have similar guidelines. I feel energy from crystals. This shop infuses my soul with strength." Sheri outstretched her arms, breathing in the air reeking of mixed incense.

"Okay, are you a witch?" I asked.

"That's a personal question. Are you?"

"I might be. Do you know a man named Arthur Prince?"

Faster than humanly possible, Sheri jolted to her feet. My hair fanned out behind me from the whoosh of air she produced.

"I can't help you. Please leave now."

I scrambled to my knees, leaning toward Sheri. "You know him? What happened?"

The alarm signaling twenty minutes had elapsed tinged from the black cat speaker. "Your time is up. I only have ten minutes between clients. Please vacate my haven."

"Not until you tell me about Arthur Prince."

She winced and rubbed her hands together. "Stop saying his name. He's a fraud, that's all. His cheap sister is a phony too. If you want to pretend to be a witch, they are the finest con artists around. They want your money."

"But I've seen things I can't explain."

"So, have I. It doesn't mean shit, lady. Get out!"

"I have her stones!" the young woman called up.

"She can choke on them!"

"What the fuck? I'm not leaving. Are they dangerous? I need some help."

"They steal powers, dumbass. Watch out for the mother. She's the worst." Sobs took over the woman's voice, bending her over.

I called out her name, but she waved me off. Sheri curled into a ball amongst her furs, sliding her cheek against the soft pelt. It seemed cruel to pressure her more.

Dizziness accompanied me down the floating stairs. The lack of handrails disorienting. A pull in the pit of my stomach rushed me toward the shop's front door. I resisted it and paid for the damn protection crystals.

"Would you like the receipt in the bag?" the shop girl asked.

I nodded, grabbing the small black bag. "Do you know whose powers they took?" I whispered.

The young woman checked for Sheri peeking over the loft's edge. Coast clear. She pointed up and mouthed, "Hers."

Chapter Twenty-Five

I almost called Arthur a dozen times on the way home. I searched through every song on my phone library, not satisfied with any of them. I couldn't tell if I was aggravated, scared, or a raving lunatic after my reading with Sheri. I pinched my forearm hard enough my fingernail scraped the skin. I wasn't in a dream. That happened. I should have asked Sheri a different question. I blew it. If she had powers and Arthur took them, did death never find her? Who was the crazy person now? Sheri or Arthur?

A dog barking snapped me out of my haze. My car idled in front of the modest apartment building across from Arthur's. Idalia or her mother might be home. I should've headed home, but I parked the car and headed over.

Eight units loomed in the shadows of the larger complex. Just my luck, someone scribbled Prince horribly over correction tape on the third mailbox. I tried the door, but I needed to be buzzed in. Before I ran back to my car, buzzing sounded over the intercom. The main door unlocked.

I opened the door and spotted Idalia leaning over the top railing, her wide smile shining bright. Her long golden hair cascaded healthily over her olive-green blouse.

"Right on time, Lena! Come on up!" she shouted.

The old stairs creaked under my boots like a warning, "Go back. Go back. Turn around. Save yourself." I ignored the premonition.

Much like her family's psychic shop, Idalia decorated the place in crimson. Typical apartment layout, nothing special, except for an upright piano with a weathered wooden bench overpowering the main living space. If I hadn't known better, I would have guessed it was the same piano as Arthur's.

"Did your family own a piano store?" I asked.

"That's a silly question. Do yours?" Idalia retorted.

It was going to be that type of visit. "Look, Idalia, I know we got off to a rocky start, but I need to talk to you about Arthur."

"He likes you a lot. He fell madly in love with you when he went to your grandmother's wake, but alas, he sensed the pull of another. Artie waited until that flame snuffed out to pounce." Her hands traced a heart in the air, then she blew a kiss in the middle.

"Come on, Idalia. You don't expect me to believe that?"

"It's the truth, and by the way, please call me Dalia. I feel like you're scolding me every time you say my full name."

Maybe I am. I wished I said that. Both times I saw her, she appeared weak, submissive, malleable. She seemed gleeful, energetic, and spunky now. What the fuck happened?

"Sure, Dalia. Can I have a seat?"

"Of course, fuck, where are my manners? Would you like some tea with crushed-up cherry pits? It adds a delightful twist to a lemon tea," she offered.

"I thought cherry pits had arsenic in them?" *Great,*

she planned on killing me today.

"I wouldn't eat a bag of them, but a few shavings on top won't kill you."

"I'll stick with the tea only, please."

"Be right back. If you want to look at embarrassing photos of Artie and me as kids, there are photo albums in the right end table."

"Thanks, I'll take a peek."

I regretted my decision the moment I sat down. A puff of dust wafted around me. I coughed and sneezed into the sleeve of my sweater.

"Are you all right?" Dalia shouted from the kitchen.

"Yes, I'm fine. You don't get a lot of guests, huh?" The dust particles twinkled in the beam of sunlight shining into the room. On second thought, the dust swarmed in place, irritating my eyes.

I hadn't come here to judge her. I needed help. Even now, the comfortable, lived-in couch encouraged my head to fall back against the cushions and close my eyes. I resisted the temptation and selected the heavy middle photo album from the three.

The frayed plastic protecting the satiny cover of the book had grown yellow and sticky. I flipped through the first few pages of a wedding in black and white photos from 1947. The bride and groom smiled wide at each other amongst blurry rice thrown up in the air around them. They stood at the top of the church stairs as the wedding procession flanked them on either side, leading down.

My lips curled in a smile. I thoroughly enjoyed re-doing my grandmother's photo albums for my mother. I wished I had more photos like these ones. The photographer managed a picture at every step, and the couple held hands as they hugged and kissed the bridal party. Their grip looked strong. The connection sweet as hell for the times.

The beautiful photo effect mesmerized me. I followed the photos placed perfectly underneath the cellophane sleeve, and I watched them start their new lives. I flipped and turned each page, imagining the day as if I, too, stood on the stone landing, throwing rice in the air, listening to the man playing the violin in the corner. I almost missed him in the beginning photos. He stepped up from the darkness of the vestibule, notching the wooden instrument into the crook of his neck.

What did he play? Solo violin music always sounded sad. The long strokes of the bow peddling the misery one musical note per picture. At the fifth page, the couple made it to the bottom of the stairs, and the groom arched the bride's back, reveling in one of those first kisses of matrimonial bliss.

Instead of staring at the couple's embrace, the bridal party and guests' gazes glared my way, pointing outward. I gasped, the book falling closed between my knees and tumbling onto the floor.

Wow, I needed help. The photographer must have asked everyone to look their way. I chuckled, picking up the book and sliding it onto the wooden coffee table. A photo from later in the book peeked out, disturbed from the fall. The spine creaked as I opened it to the slippery page. The cellophane's integrity held on by a thread. I placed the photos back into the pronounced outline in the stickiness left by age. The wedding had moved on to waving at the bride and groom entering the old-fashioned car. A lady held up the bride's long, lace train, and a few pictures later they drove off into the blurry street. The bridesmaid reminded me of Babushka, Arthur and Dalia's mother, but she couldn't be that old. The next picture captured a scream in my throat. If I wasn't mistaken, Arthur and Dalia stood alone, posing for the photographer. Dalia wore a pillbox hat, old-fashioned wavy curves in her hair, and the same bridesmaids' dress the other women wore. Arthur wore a suit with his longish hair greased back like the other gentleman in the photos.

"What?" I muttered.

"See something scary?"

I slammed the book closed.

Dalia held two cups of steaming tea with that shit-eating grin again. "Do you want to sit at the dining room table?"

"Sure, I'll put this back where I found it."

She responded with an airy giggle. I tucked the old album back through the trail of dust. Pain in my right hip twisted as I stood up. I rubbed the aching spot while walking over to the antique table without a tablecloth.

"Did you catch our little joke?" Dalia asked. I shrugged and reached for the teacup in front of me. "Wait, I think I switched the cups. Silly me." Dalia switched the identical cups with frothed milk still swirling at the surface. Pointing at my cup first, then hers, she said, "No cherry pits, the slight poison chaser. Drink up, Lena."

I'd rather not and claim I did. I reached for a factory plastic-wrapped biscotti. She hadn't tampered with them yet. My delicate trust for the woman faded more each moment I listened to the riddled questions and answers.

"I loved the second-by-second photos. I feel like I watched them get married. Clever, especially for so long ago. It's a little spooky."

"Scary, you mean. *Spooky* means Spirits in Dutch."

"Okay, my mistake. Scary."

"No skin off my back. Did you catch the posed shot of Artie and me? Babushka's mother kept her bridesmaid dress from her sister's wedding, and I wore it a few Halloweens ago. Artie had rented a suit to be James Bond, and with a little photo editing, viola! It looks like we were there."

If only I had a lie detector test in my back pocket. "Well, it certainly made me look twice. Can we get back to the reason I stopped by?"

"You never said why. I thought you might ask for Artie's hand in marriage. He wants to marry you. Maybe we can do the flipbook thing like my great aunt. How fun that would be?"

Against my better judgment, I took a sip of tea. I needed the caffeine. Suddenly, I felt as wrecked as if I did a three-a.m. presentation to Europe or China. The tea tasted delicious, with or without the cherry pit chaser.

"Are you all right, Lena? You look pale. Is your time of the month soon? I can give you some herbs and a simple spell to boost your strength. Oops, sorry, I'm rattling on here like an idiot asking about your period and planning your secret wedding in Vegas. Please tell me what's bothering you."

The misplaced feeling bothering me since the pool day roared back. My neck twitched, my throat tingled, and my restless legs begged to wiggle back and forth.

"I'm sorry, Dalia. I think I better go. Maybe I'm coming down with something. I don't have the energy for this." I got up from the table, searching for my coat.

"Lena, I'm sorry. I'm usually not so hyper. I never

get guests. Please sit down. I'll be good. I'll let you talk."

"That's the thing. I can't. I have all these questions to ask you, but I'm exhausted. I can barely keep my eyes open." I stood up, bracing my palm against the cherrywood-stained table.

"Please sit back down. I want to help."

I sat down again and pushed my chair in. On the small buffet cabinet sat a picture of two babies in long christening gowns. One of the babies had a headband with a bow, and the boy had a mini bowtie. The woman holding them had classic eighties hair with all the frizz and volume.

"That's our Christening photo. We were baptized Catholic by our grandmother, Babushka's mother. That's her, holding us. Damnit, I'm moving us off course again. I'm sorry," she said.

"It's very sweet. My mother probably has mine somewhere too."

We smiled at each other. For a few moments, we sat in silence, drinking our tea and eating our biscotti. I still felt off, but better without Dalia bulleting stuff faster than my brain processed. I needed answers about Arthur, Sheri, and my gifts.

"How have you been sleeping?" Dalia asked.

"Terribly. I never slept normal hours anyway, but I have been having vivid dreams, waking up every hour and not being able to fall back to sleep."

"This sounds like common stress. I don't feel a supernatural ping at all."

"Every time something off-kilter happens, I'm wiped, exhausted, mentally and physically. I missed an important dinner, and I never had that happen. The client understood, but my business integrity is at stake."

"Dabbling in any form of craft, be it nature-based, or moon-based, or spell-based, or whatever eclectic type you used can be depleting, especially if it's the beginning and you aren't used to the effect. It's like having great sex. You are so high but then fall too low afterward. I can give you a list of herbs to take to boost your overall well-being. Stay away from calming things and load yourself up with zesty things."

"Thanks for the tip." The caffeine from the tea did nothing for my current state. Another yawn shook me all over. My eyes threatened to close in the silence.

"Do you want to lay down, Lena? You're not looking so good."

"I'm all right. How are you looking as spunky and vibrant as you do right now?"

Idalia looked down, her long eyelashes coated with mascara swept over her rosy cheeks. "I met a guy. He isn't someone I thought I would like, but I can't stop thinking about him. It's been too long since I've had a boyfriend."

"That's all? You didn't get a magic elixir in aisle twelve?"

She quirked her head sideways. "I'm not following?"

"Come on, Dalia. You looked like death warmed over. Did you sacrifice a virgin?" I kept a stern face throughout my accusations.

Idalia scoffed, gazing around the room, except in my direction across from her. She fiddled with the plastic bracelets around her wrists and clucked her tongue. "My mother told me that if you can't say something nice, don't say anything at all."

"So did mine. She also taught me not to lie and lead

strangers on."

"Very well. I tried to be nice, and I will tolerate you for Artie's sake." She leaned over to the buffet table, opening the middle drawer. White, letter-sized paper was stacked to the top of the space. Idalia removed the top piece and snagged a pen from the side. "I'm going to give you a remedy to help you regain your strength. Did it start after your meeting with death?" I nodded. "Great, you were completely exposed."

"Did Arthur tell you what happened?"

"Of course. I know everything. I see it all. Have the witches of Ole visited you, yet?"

"If they did, wouldn't you know already?"

"Touché. I guess I'm one of the lucky ones."

"Should I meet them?"

For a moment, the hyper act Idalia performed paused. Snowflakes frosted over her eyeballs, and her lips slipped down into a frown. "No." She blinked, and the pale blue perky stare returned. "I will write the spell down for you."

My eyes watered painfully while she wrote down instructions and underlined certain steps multiple times.

"Do you know what a mangrove tree is?" she asked.

"No, I don't."

"Do you know what a white candle does?"

"Yes, I do." She squinted her eyes. I wasn't born yesterday. Even though I abandoned that part of me years ago, I knew white candles were powerful tools. "What is the tree?"

"A mangrove tree grows in salt water. I have a few spare pieces I haven't used yet." In a few more minutes, she filled the blank page with instructions from top to bottom. "Stay here. I'll be right back."

I barely took a breath until she came back. My limbs weighed a thousand pounds. I tried lifting my hand from the arm of the dining room chair onto the table. *What was she doing to me?*

"Oh good, you can yield to simple powers of persuasion."

"Release me, now!"

Idalia flicked up her hands and rolled up her sleeves. "I don't know what you're talking about. How could I be restraining you? I'm not even touching you?" Her voice rose a few piercing octaves up. The innocent child act did not work on me.

"Idalia, does your brother know I'm here?"

Like magic, my breath whooshed back in a strong exhale. The unsettling scent of coconut eased into my nostrils from Idalia's defiant stance.

"I don't think we are going to get along. What do you think, Lena?"

"I think I've overstayed my welcome. Thank you for offering me poison. I will remember that next time."

"You're quite welcome. Anything to help a friend of my brother's. Once you stop being a bitch, and want help from a seasoned witch, do the healing ritual. It will help you immensely."

She held up the grocery bag with the mangrove stick, a white candle, and the notes. I snatched it out of her hand, careful not to touch her. A vision of her aging until her body wasted away to dusty bones played out in front of me.

"What do you see, crazy lady?" she asked me. Her chuckle stopped when I frowned.

I imagined foresight being the worst gift possible. The sorrow of watching others' future ends destroyed a part of the seer each time. I shook my head, dismissing the thought and mirage.

My right hand balled into a fist tightly over the plastic handle of the bag. "Thank you for the help."

"Anytime."

The second I walked out the door, she slammed the door shut before I took another step into the smelly communal hallway. "Yeah, fuck you too, Dalia."

I stomped back to my car after the most useless ten minutes of my life. I threw the bag with the obnoxious happy face in the backseat of my car. I snatched the satchel of stones from Sheri out of my purse and shoved them inside the bag from Idalia.

If there were bad witches, today I met both the east and west ones.

Chapter Twenty-Six

"I ordered two more photo albums in the maroon color and one in the navy blue. There aren't a lot of pictures from the seventies and eighties before you came along," Mom said.

"You didn't want to wait for the film to develop?" I giggled.

"Lena, it was different back then. It was normal to wait a week to get photos. We never thought much of it. You were stuck if you wanted to get prints."

"If you say so."

"What time is it?"

"Almost noon. Are you staying for lunch?"

"Your father has his hearing aid appointment at one. Thank you for the offer."

"I made Grandmother's chili last night. Do you want some for Dad, so you won't have to cook later?"

Mom cocked her head to the side. "What's wrong? You only cook when you're upset."

My shoulders lifted as a cold shiver skated down my spine in my off-the-shoulder sweater. "It's not weird for a woman living alone to make a comfort meal."

"I'm still calling fib."

"Mom, please. Take care of Dad. He needs you."

"He's sixty years old. He doesn't want a live-in nurse."

"They sell costumes for that if you're interested."

Our laughter filled my kitchen. "Maybe some other time." We packed up our project. I had to do the labels next. "Waiting on someone?"

"What, Mom?"

"Hunny, you have been checking the clock every two minutes since I got here."

"I'm sorry. I'm a little distracted, that's all. This project is time consuming."

"Why do you think I never did it? It will come together. You are doing a great job."

"Thanks, Mom."

My alarm trilled through the kitchen. I sprinted toward the phone before my mother saw the name of the alarm illuminated. Too late.

"Who's Arthur?"

I ground my teeth together, thinking of a lie out of thin air. If I told her the truth, the questions would start, the theatrical excitement blown out of portion like when she first met Ray. Arthur and I slept together once and had possibly two dates. That was early to meet the parents.

Like magic, my doorbell rang. The back of my head thudded hard against the kitchen wall. Arthur was supposed to come over here after he stopped at home. *Why must he be on time?* He needed to be a normal guy making up excuses for his lateness, not be punctual as fuck.

"Is that him?" Mom wiggled her eyebrows. I died a little on the inside.

"Don't get overly excited. Yes, that's my friend, Arthur."

When I hadn't moved to answer the door, my mother clicked her nails against the table. "Are you going to let him in, or should I?"

I couldn't be a powerful witch, because I willed him to go away, but no, his damn baseball cap with the torn brim peeked into the window cutout at the top of the door.

I opened the door a crack. "No solicitors, please. I bought too many scout cookies last year."

He chuckled. I missed the mini laughs I forced out of him. "Very funny. Can I come in?"

I opened the door, and Arthur walked over the threshold. He passed me by without a flash of his baby blues or a kiss. I would've settled for a fist bump, but I got nothing. Arthur walked into the living room, standing almost exactly where my grandmother's urn sat on the viewing table. "We have to talk."

"Can I come out of hiding now?" Mom called from the kitchen.

Arthur's eyes widened. His head jerked toward the hallway leading to the kitchen.

"Your mother's here?" Arthur whispered.

"Didn't you notice the other car in the driveway?"

"I thought it could have been yours."

"You're finally slacking in the stalker department."

Arthur jammed his hands in his pocket and chewed the inside of his mouth. I meant the stupid jab as a joke, like I had done multiple times. His reaction differed from all the times before.

Mom waited another minute, then waltzed into the living room. "Hi, you must be Arthur."

"Hi, I am." He extracted his clenched fist and waved.

"Sorry about being here. If Lena hasn't filled you in yet, we have been researching our family history for the past few months. We started during the pandemic, and we've been chiseling at it ever since. I'll be over from time to time. I will make sure I call before I come over."

"Lena hasn't told me much about it. Sounds like fun." Arthur sucked in his full lips, letting them go with a pop.

The silence choked me. "Mom was about to leave." In a way, I was kicking her out. Guilt knotted my stomach, but I needed Arthur.

"Yes, I'll tell your father about our progress today."

"Great, let me know if he remembers that cousin."

My mom scooted out the door, hanging back for a second, then closed the door behind her.

Arthur waited a painful two more minutes, then said, "We have to talk."

"Should I sit down?" I pointed toward the couch. His blank gaze followed my finger. I had seen him angry, happy, passionate, arrogant, nervous, and perhaps unsure. The hollowness to his blue eyes that usually shined darker looked pale and unfocused, reminding me of Idalia when I first met her. "Um, let's go in the kitchen."

He followed behind me to the dinette. Pictures and notecards cluttered the surface. I threw everything into the empty photo box I used for the unsorted and unlabeled items. Arthur sat down and picked up a picture of my great-great aunt from my father's side.

"Who is this?" he asked.

"Virginia Whatlen. She was my great-great grandfather's sister."

"She's staring at me."

I walked over to him. Virginia's odd pose struck me funny as well. She leaned against the outside siding of a church holding pamphlets. Parts of her blurred, but her eyes looked right into the soul. I owned the only photo of her.

"She likes you," I kidded.

"She's a witch. Is she on your father's side?"

"Do you see a mole on her face?"

He rolled his eyes. "That's your indicator. She's a witch because she can barely be photographed."

"Cool your jets. She died almost a century ago. Cameras were shit back then. She probably moved. I have no idea how my family managed to get this photo of her. Virginia was a recluse, except she went to church daily. She even lived in the manse of an old church in the Dominican Republic."

"That makes sense. She probably fought her powers. Did she ever marry?"

"I think so." I flipped through the journal containing my research. Virginia's page had a few notes pulled from baptism records. "She had three kids with a man named Samuel."

"Is there anyone left of that line?"

"I don't know. My father doesn't talk to that part of his family anymore."

"I see," Arthur commented. He scratched the scruff under his chin. His facial hair was the longest I had seen it. I guess he had no time for shaving at his friend's house.

"How was Rhode Island?"

"Tiring. Sorry I didn't call or text you more. By the time I hit my friend's awful futon, I was exhausted."

"It's fine. We're not boyfriend and girlfriend or anything. You don't owe me an explanation." *Wow, that sounded bitchy.* "I mean that you already had plans to go away before the other night. I'm not faulting you for going."

"Thank you. I promise you it was business." He pulled in his chair, resting his forearms on the table. Arthur felt miles away from me, especially with his vacant stare and the fact that he hadn't smiled once since he got here. He faked the tight-lipped grin for my mother.

"You're not telling me something. I've seen you nervous. You pant like you've run a marathon. What is this mood?"

Arthur inhaled a shaky breath, exhaling out his nose. "Before we sleep together again, I want to know if you're going to keep your powers or give them up."

I bit my tongue hard enough that blood seeped from in between my taste buds. The overwhelming dread I told Doctor Greene about churned tight in the pit of my stomach.

"Please know this has nothing to do with you. It's about me. I couldn't protect my ex from her powers leaving her. I tried so hard. God help me, I tried. I don't want that to happen with you."

Arthur wiped his runny nose on his sleeve like a child. His eyes grew red and watery, and a single tear streamed down his face.

"Did you think she was your true love?" I asked.

"Yes, for a while. It was easy to love her."

"But you were wrong."

"Yeah, I was wrong."

A part of me wanted to reach over and caress his hand, stilling his fidgeting fingers. Another part cursed him for running away after we fucked. We got intimate too fast and fucked up our chances of a normal relationship.

"Our relationship will never be normal," Arthur said.

I laughed, missing him reading my mind. He hadn't done it in a while.

"Do you know other ways to enhance our powers besides fucking?"

"You seem pissed."

"What do you expect me to say? You were there when I needed you. Thank you. Just because we had sex, I don't expect us to be joined at the hip or fated soul mates. You are the only one guiding me, so I still need your help. No sex, no problem."

"Am I an idiot?" Arthur removed his hat, combing his fingers through the hair matted to his forehead.

"Yes. Relax, Arthur. It's okay."

I got up and kissed his cheek. Before my lips left his heated skin, he turned his head, fusing our lips together. When I gasped, he pulled me into his lap, clutching my chin, holding me in place for his kiss.

Betraying everything I wanted, I pushed him away. "We're doing great. Our celibacy lasted a whole two minutes."

Arthur laid his forehead on the bare skin left exposed by my sweater. I roamed my hand over his longish hair at the base of his neck. He murmured something I missed and lifted me off his lap.

"What are the other ways to learn my powers?"

Arthur's gaze flicked up to mine while his head still hung down. A storm brewed behind his darkened cerulean eyes as he grinned.

"Spells."

Chapter Twenty-Seven

"Those shoes aren't good enough."

Arthur acted as if I came down my stairs dressed like a hiking model, complete with pink high heels and fake plastic supplies. I wore the work boots I used in the garden all the time. He went out to his car and returned with some dirty sneakers with a popular label from years ago.

"I'm not wearing someone else's dirty shoes." I folded my arms over my chest and cocked out my hip.

"Do you like to go bowling?"

I rolled my eyes and sat down on the couch. For the past twenty minutes, every time I protested, he had a counter-argument. *Fuck destiny. He pissed me off.*

"Are these shoes Idalia's?"

He nodded, undoing the tied laces. "She showed me the spot we're going to a few years ago.

"I've been to the Buttermilk Park a million times. What is so special about it today?"

"It's not exactly the park, but the untouched forest surrounding the picnic areas. We need to gather natural ingredients, not pulled or destroyed by our own hands."

"Basically, don't pick the mushrooms?"

"If a mushroom has separated from the cluster it grew with and lays on the ground alone, yes, you can pick the mushroom."

"Can you give me a list of stuff to find?"

"I love a good scavenger hunt as much as the next guy, but this time no can do. You must find what picks you first."

****

We reached the park after a huge party wrapped up. Arthur scoffed and made sure we hiked away from where they dirtied the campsite. By the time Arthur replied no to the first fifty items I picked up, I scampered away. My frustration level peaked. I found the fucking objects on my own. That should be enough.

In my haste in Idalia's boots that didn't quite fit, I fell to the ground with a hard thud. The leaves scattered over the path padded my fall. I scurried up when a long colorless snakeskin deflated under my palm. I half expected it to be warm, but that's silly.

"Arthur! Come quick!" I shouted.

I sat up on my knees, inspecting the shedding. My handprint smushed part of it together, however most of it still held onto the shape of the snake.

"That's exactly what we need! Did you see the snake?" Arthur asked.

Genuine fear hauled me up, despite the pain radiating out of my palm and knee. "If I see a snake, I'm turning around and going home."

Arthur picked up a long stick, poking around the patch of leaves. He yelled and jumped back. "Ahh, there it is!"

I jumped behind him. His laughter disturbed the quiet area. A flock of small sparrows flew high into the sky.

"Not funny."

"It was a little funny. Find more items like this." He picked up the shedding and placed it into a plastic bag.

Instead of barging ahead, I remained by his side. A little way up from the snakeskin, a small clearing caught my attention. The sound of crackling flames sounded in my ears, but the fire had long since burned out. The black patch of leaves and splintered wood screamed their pain. I bet a group of kids had lit a small fire, smoked a bowl of weed, snuffed it out, and left. I pointed at the area.

"Lena, we need pure ingredients, not tarnished ingredients."

I walked around the site, but I turned back when Arthur's knees cracked. He bent down and lifted a pinch of ash into a small plastic bag.

"Hypocrite?"

"It's not for the spell we are doing. Don't worry about it."

All my thoughts switched toward the ash. Arthur had no idea the extent of my overthinking. I had one leg ready to run back to the car any second.

Once I found the snakeskin, other things popped up easily. I collected a few bags' worth of stuff. I had tree bark peelings, fallen flower petals, broken twigs, leaves, and the snakeskin. Arthur had more, and my stomach flipped from his findings. A dead salamander, a cicada shedding, pine needles, a rotten crabapple, fur from a dead squirrel's tail, and a dried-out prickled spore from a plant.

"Are you a good or bad witch?" I asked.

"Irrelevant."

"What's up with you? You have been hot and cold since you came back."

"I'm impatient when I'm tired."

"Oh, is that all?"

A snapped twig straightened Arthur's spine. He

snatched me around my waist, squeezing my boobs against his chest. Arthur's gaze scanned around the trees. Another crack further away from us reverberated off the trees.

"It's probably an animal," I said.

"Lena, shh."

I hadn't felt any fear until he hissed out the order through gritted teeth. I heard nothing. I never thought absolute silence could quicken my breath so fast.

"It must have been a deer. Stay here," Arthur commanded.

Arthur released me. Without looking back, he marched through the trees, touching each bark. I inspected the thicket around me but saw nothing except the trees.

I crouched down, itching under the tight ankle band of my sock. I shrieked as tons of ants exited a mini anthill next to me. I stood back up, brushing off my hands. There were no ants on me. However, the sensation took over. I kicked out my legs and wiggled out my arms.

"What are you doing?"

I screamed, flailing my fist through the air. Arthur stood close enough that he received a swift punch to the arm.

"Ow, what the fuck?"

"You scared the shit out of me!" I clutched my heaving chest.

"Come on, you must have heard me."

My sensitive eardrums picked up nothing. "Arthur, I want to go home."

"We need a few more things."

I held up my mushy bag of dead things. "I think I have enough."

"Ha-ha, funny. This isn't like trick-or-treating. You can't give up when shit gets weird. We need more unique items. The more unusual the item, the spell's success rate goes up. It's simple." Arthur's snippy tone still bothered me.

"Hey, I wanted no part in all this crap. My mother chose to forfeit her powers, and so can I. There is no room for yet another witch coming-of-age story. I've read it, seen it, and the sequel ruined it."

The ground thudded under my boots like thunder erupting from every cloud. A ticking sound surrounded me as soon as Arthur faded from view. My feet propelled me down a steep incline covered in dried leaves. Spinning vertigo distorted the trees on either side.

"Lena, come back!"

I turned left, off the trail, and headed for the stone staircase leading toward an old brick fireplace. Twenty odd, steep steps carved out of natural rock and quartz glistened in the remaining sunshine. I wondered what stood here long ago. A castle, a prison, a soothsayer's cottage?

"They removed a house about a hundred years ago. The townspeople accused the woman living here of being a witch, but without any real evidence, the court dismissed the case."

"Back up, mister. There were no witch trials down here. Traitors from the American Revolution were tried in this county, no witches."

Arthur shrugged. "Fine, don't believe me. Search the internet later. If I'm wrong or remembering incorrectly, I will teach you another part of my craft."

"I thought you were going to teach me everything you knew out of the kindness of your heart?"

"Everything has a price. Let's head back to the car. We have one more stop to make, or do you want to sulk more?"

"You're impossible," I grumbled.

I spotted the car faster than expected. Arthur took a shortcut through a dense thicket of trees. He stepped onto the parking lot, while a split second later, a boney hand curled around my face in the corner of my gaze. I thrashed, digging my long nails into the taut, cold skin.

Arthur's voice bounced off the forest, a shout morphing into a whisper. My imprisoner's other hand snaked around my waist, yanking me down onto the forest floor. Pain engulfed the back of my head, threatening my consciousness. A woman's laughter rose like the crescendo of an orchestra finally hitting the climax of the symphony. Crows interrupted the glee, drowning out the merriment.

"What are you doing?"

I opened my eyes and stared into Arthur's judgmental gaze.

"The tree didn't whack you that hard."

I scrambled to my hands and knees too fast. My body lurched sideways into a thorny rose bush with two distinct branches forking out from the rest of the plant. "Ouch, that fucking hurt!" I yelled. Thorns pricked my right hand as I caught my balance. "You didn't see anyone? Were you laughing?"

Arthur cocked his head at a forty-five-degree angle and pointed at the offending plant. "I will laugh at a lot of things, but I saw you fall. You hit the ground hard. Why would I laugh?"

"I'm losing my mind. Let's get the fuck out of here."

He stretched out his large hand, pulling me up with

one thrust upward. "What did you think happened?"

A silhouette teased my peripheral vision, disappearing as fast as it manifested. I stuck to Arthur's left side, his sweat reeking like vinegar until he unlocked the car and tucked me inside.

The skeletal hands marked my body. They clutched my stomach, flittered over my breasts, and caressed my face. My stomach rumbled from the unseen pressure until Arthur pulled over. I retched all the contents of my stomach until dry heaves burned my throat.

Arthur tested the temperature of my forehead with the back of his palm and wiggled his fingers. "You're clammy. Do you want to stay in the car?"

"Don't leave me alone. Please, don't leave me here."

Arthur wrinkled his brow and licked his full lips. "Okay, we stick together. We're almost at my friend's shop."

"What else do we need?"

"You can't do a spell in a metallic mixing bowl. The material itself isn't relevant, but it needs to be created by another member of the craft. A factory machine shuffling a bowl around conveyor belts is not enough. I believe we need the essence of talent, blood, sweat, and tears of a creator for a working spell. Some other witches disagree, like Dalia, but I strongly believe it."

"It makes sense, I guess. What about silicone bowls?"

"Factory made."

The car grew quiet without my insistence on talking non-stop. At every red light, he glanced my way. I looked dead ahead.

We reached the shop soon after, a hole in the wall in the main drag of a neighboring town bordering the

Hudson River. The parking lot across the street overlooked the river and the cross-county bridge. Small waves hiccupped against the rocky shore, splashing higher each time. A small family of ducks waded through the water.

"Are you ready, Lena?"

"No," I answered. The peaceful scene distracted me. *Will I ever be at peace?*

Arthur held my car door open, his face shining in the sunlight. Rich, blonde highlights stuck out in his hair, illuminated by the setting sun. I stepped outside his car, stretching my arms up to the sky, working out the stiffness in my back. Arthur's hands caressed my shoulders, massaging his thumbs over the top of my shoulder blades and breastbone.

His touch felt good, warm, inviting, but as I leaned my back against his chest, he cleared his throat and arched away.

"We must hurry. Her shop closes soon." *He's such a buzzkill when he wants to be.*

A young woman with long brown hair styled into two braids hanging past her tiny bare midriff stopped flipping the Closed sign over. Her mundane expression morphed into happiness as soon as she glimpsed Arthur waving through the streaky glass.

"Oh my God, if it isn't you! Artie!" She threw open her shop door, throwing herself into his arms. Arthur pulled her up into the air for a moment, her legs bending up at the knees. He placed her back down on the store's stoop. Her hands remained locked around his neck. "You should have called! I would have been devastated if I missed you."

"I'm terrible at formalities. Dalia and Babushka

send their love."

"I miss them too! Artie, please call me sometime. I miss our sessions together." She stepped closer into Arthur's personal space. Her nipples visible through her thin cotton top brushed against his shirt. As if the woman sensed my growing rage, her hazel gaze flipped toward me. "You brought a lady friend. That's not nice, teasing me so."

"I'm Lena. We're just friends. And you are?" I walked up, fighting the urge to wedge myself between them. I had zero claim to Arthur, but back up, lady.

"Vanessa McClare. I own Pots for Knots. I take it this is an emergency."

"Slightly time-sensitive. Can we come in?" Arthur asked. Even with an old friend or lover, he asked permission to enter her shop. He stuck to his rules.

Vanessa ushered us inside. "Rosewater lemonade? It's spell-free and mighty tasty."

"Yes, please," Arthur answered.

Vanessa smiled and even kept it up while bowing her head slightly in my direction. *If she marked me, I'm going to be pissed.*

"Look around. See if anything sparks your fancy," Arthur instructed.

The shop held an eclectic array of goods, showcasing Vanessa's talent tenfold. Large, threaded dreamcatchers with the most gorgeous array of colors I had ever seen dangled from the ceiling, sparkling silver jewelry with birthstones nestled in the knots, and on the back wall sat clay pots. The pots were impressive, all shapes and sizes, and energies wafted off them.

"I made them all. I outsource the dreamcatchers, but my friend gets almost all the money. Let me guess, you are a Leo."

"Yes, how did you know?"

She shrugged much like Arthur does when he wished not to answer questions. "You headed right for the Tiger eye bowl. It never felt finished, you know. I struggled with putting it out on the sales floor. It must have been waiting for you." A shimmering zap of energy traveled through my fingertips as Vanessa handed the pot over. The medium-sized bowl did not look like something with potential witchcraft ability. "What's the matter?"

"This might sound cliché, but shouldn't I use a cauldron instead?"

From our rocky start, I expected a jab, but she smiled and said, "Leave the cauldrons for Halloween. Real magic needs to be nurtured, loved, cherished, and appreciated. Cauldrons have no tie to the mystical world. Besides, I made this one during a happy time. The energy is positively charged."

"Are you messing up my rules, Vanessa?" Arthur added from across the room. He had been fiddling with the gemstones since we came in.

"I would never do that. I want Lena to have the best, and this bowl chose her."

"Sold," I declared.

Vanessa squealed, rubbing the side of my arm. I must check the area later.

"What's your favorite scent?"

"It's basic, but plain, ole Lavender. A lot of incenses give me headaches."

"*Perfect*. I find the beauty of witchcraft is modeling it to you. What works for me may turn you away and vice versa. It's a personal journey, and I'm so happy to start you off."

She took the fragile bowl from my quivering hands. I dove them down into my pockets. This was real now. I chuckled under my breath. Vanessa hoovered the bowl over her head, almost touching the largest dream catcher in the room. She faced toward the far wall of the shop, standing in the lasting sunbeam shining through the high window. I hadn't noticed until then, she had no lights on in the store. Pure natural sunlight illuminated the beautiful space.

I doubted Vanessa traveled in a pink bubble wearing a tulle ballgown, but her good witch glamour drew a small smile on my face. *Such a different experience from the taco shop to now.*

Without turning back, Vanessa asked, "Arthur, do you need any string? I made a fresh batch last week."

"Yes, please," he shouted. I had been solely focused on Vanessa, I forgot about Arthur behind me, selecting his own gems and charms. He joined me, basking in the awe of Vanessa, bestowing a blessing on the bowl. Arthur's basket held a few odds and ends. A polished, large blue rock vibrated toward me.

"What's that stone?"

"You're learning. This is a Larimar stone from the Dominican Republic." Arthur held up the exquisite rock.

The color swirls reminded me of the Caribbean Ocean. My toes sifting through the sand, the paradise coming into the focus.

"Lena?" Arthur elbowed my shoulder. "It got you, didn't it?"

"What are you talking about?" My vision disappeared like sand art ruined by a wave.

"I don't know the scope of your abilities, but I do

know you were not standing here in this shop. Were you running in a field, dusting off rock fragments in a cavernous quarry, or were you standing on the cleanest beach you have ever seen, staring at water so clear, you saw the fish and turtles dance around the coral?"

"How do you always know?"

"It's a trick," Vanessa added. She wrapped the tiger eye bowl in rose-colored tulle. My *cauldron* overflowed with small things. "He hides the truth between the lies."

"Nessa, come on. Don't share all my secrets." Arthur rolled his shoulders back. He smoothed his eyebrow using his middle finger.

"It's my job to warn the next girl about your charms. I'm ready when you are, Lena." Vanessa fluffed out the tulle and wrapped a red and black ribbon around the bunched top.

"Where did you get that ribbon?"

"One of my best friends gave me this beautiful gift basket filled with goodies a few months ago. She had ordered it online. I hoard pretty things, hoping my customers get an exclusive shopping experience."

"You're not going to believe me, but I made that ribbon. I help with my friend's gift basket business. I made twenty of those special bows. How weird you got one?"

Her smile faltered but came back wider. "Nothing is a coincidence. It found its way home. You must use a little extra magic with each ribbon."

I shrugged. Arthur joined me at the counter, placing his supplies on the counter like each item was a priceless, one-of-a-kind heirloom.

"Lena has no idea the extent of her reach," Arthur remarked.

"Then, teach her," Vanessa said.

"I will."

As we walked out of her shop, Vanessa stood next to me right before the threshold. "I'm going to touch your back. Is that okay?"

I nodded. Her soft fingers grazed the small muscle knot that hurt me late in the day. She rubbed a warming serum, accompanied by a thick salve smelling of lavender, around the spot. Pain sliced through the spot, then faded into nothing at all.

"All your demons rest on your back. You don't have to be stressed. Arthur is one of the good ones. You will be okay."

Vanessa leaned over and kissed the side corner of my lips. I puckered back, the reflex shocking me. I wished I found her shop instead of Sheri's the other day. I would definitely visit Vanessa again.

Chapter Twenty-Eight

We got back to my house around five o'clock. I felt like a stranger in my own home. Arthur moved around the kitchen like he knew every nook and cranny.

He laid out wax paper over the counter and the table. I leaned my shoulder against the doorframe, watching him extract each object from his bag.

"Are you going to wash your hands?" I asked.

"Yeah, do you have any latex gloves?"

"I think I do. Wouldn't wearing gloves break the connection?"

"I don't want to dirty up your house. I can wear them for the setup, then take them off when we get started."

Arthur never waited for my response. I held in multiple gags as he extracted his items from the bags. If I cooked in my kitchen again, it would be a miracle.

I copied him as best as I understood. All his items signified transformation, and mine were once beautiful. I wondered if that meant anything.

"What are we going to try to do?" I asked.

"Here's the thing. I know what I'm capable of, but I have no idea about you. You gave a dying flower a rebirth, and now it sheds petals like a fairytale while still blooming bright. Maybe think up a spell to help revitalize the items you found."

"I have to make up the spell, too?"

"You can go on the internet and check out a spell,

but that's someone else's. One spell for them might not work for you."

The side of my head throbbed. Migraines were supposed to be a thing of the past. I did not need a sharp, hot poker thrust inside my forehead.

I kicked my shoes off and went upstairs. I needed aspirin, but that's not where I wound up.

My grandmother's vanity welcomed me as it did several times before. I pulled out the notebook I bought for my sessions with Doctor Greene, and like all the other times, my hand found the pen. Letters formed words I didn't understand for half a page. Arthur wanted a spell. He fucking got one.

"I've never seen anyone do that before." Arthur stood in the bedroom doorway. His refreshing grin perked me up.

"I don't think. I write."

He stepped inside the room we had sex in last week, and I might not have changed the sheets yet. White dust from the gloves covered his hands as he trailed his fingers over my unmade bed. I hoped he regretted taking sex off the table.

"Can I see your writing?" He sat down on my side of the bed.

I handed him the notebook. Thank God, he removed the latex gloves. His pretty eyes read over the prose.

"I have no idea what it says. I once tried researching certain words I repeat unconsciously. No matches came up."

"Maybe you're a Druid? They had no written language, but someone somewhere had to write something down. It could be the language of the angels? I think it has more symbols than actual words."

"Your guess is as good as mine."

"Let's use it as a spell and see what happens."

I followed Arthur down my stairs, pondering the writing. It seemed pointless to mention I never tried saying the odd words out loud. One time I got so scared I threw up before uttering a single word.

"Arthur, do you have a spellbook?"

"My sister and I share one. It's the only twin thing we do together."

He pulled out a worn, black leatherbound notebook with a long, frayed ribbon sticking out of the middle.

"Where do you hide that, the cookie jar?"

"Idalia had it the day you came over."

"You have an answer for everything."

"Most of the time. I can be a real smartass."

"What spell was she trying to do?"

He squinted his left eye and looked up. "My sister and I haven't spoken much since the party. She gets moody, leaves me alone to run the shop for a while, then we meet up at our mom's house for dinner, and it's like nothing ever happened. We've been this way ever since we left for college."

"She seemed better the last time I saw her."

"When did you see her?"

"While you were out of town. She looked healthy."

"Ah, no wonder she hasn't come around."

I shrugged. "She told me she's dating someone new, and he makes her very happy." I dropped my voice down like her lower octave and swished my hair back, mocking her.

Arthur bit down on his bottom lip, closing his eyes. "Excuse me for a moment. Can I make a call outside?"

"Sure."

He came back inside a minute later and continued his preparation. I expected some explanation to his weird reaction, but he said nothing. He pulled out more wax paper and carefully moved each of his items from the counter to the table. He decided against the squirrel fur, dropping it back into the paper bag.

"Do you want to go first?" I asked Arthur.

"Okay, here it goes."

Arthur flipped to a page toward the middle of the book. The lines looked like a poem, decorated in script letters. Either he or his sister taped a used match next to the words.

"It's been a while since I've done any spells. Bear with me," Arthur confessed.

"This is my first spell ever. I'm in no place to judge."

Arthur swallowed his spit, licked his lips, and rubbed a shaky hand over his mouth. He took another few minutes prepping himself.

He mumbled audible words in another language. The singsong-like purr of his voice charmed me. Arthur reminded me of a priest who spoke and sang the liturgy of the Eucharist part of a mass. I half expected a bell chime when Arthur stood up and bowed low enough to rest his forehead on the inked pages.

Arthur sat back down, picked up the candle, and placed it in front of him. With his bare hands, he pinched and released each item he found. With a finger following along the handwriting, Arthur rubbed the end of the fresh wick. Any minute now, I expected a surge of fire bursting from his fingertips.

After five minutes, Arthur banged the bottom of his fist against the table.

"Come on, stupid spell! Don't embarrass me!" Arthur shouted.

"Did you use the right ingredients and spell?" I remarked.

"Yes, that's the first thing I checked." He sat back down and inhaled three large breaths. Arthur exhaled over the candle. Nothing happened.

"Can I give my turn a shot?"

I grimaced as Arthur bit down on his right pointer finger. I wanted to scrub my hands for the next week, and I never touched his stuff. Arthur flicked his other hand my way. He rose from the chair and scrubbed his hands clean, sighing over and over.

I sat in the same spot I did for the love spell. I tried mustering the confidence from that night, the determination. Words hid on my tongue. I placed my items inside the bowl from Vanessa. The faint scent of lavender still clung to the air around it.

"It helps if you say the spell out loud," Arthur said.

"This may shock you, but I never said any of this out loud."

"Try, Lena. That's all we can do."

The words blurred on the page until I closed my eyes shut and opened them again. Kim and Amy popped into my mind. The day we declared ourselves witches. My braces hurt my teeth as we mumbled my Latin homework backward because back then, witches communicated in strange tongues. Amy underlined a makeshift spell and we burned cut pieces of our hair together in an emptied blush compact. We thought the spell to be friends forever worked because the mirror cracked under the flames.

"Lena?"

"Yeah?"

"Look."

The flower petals brightened back to crimson red. I stared at the other items, weary of the snakeskin, but nothing else turned.

"That's it?"

"Try saying the spell. You spaced out for a minute but didn't say anything."

I placed my finger under the first illegible word. As if clamps held my mouth closed, nothing squeaked past. I shook my head back and forth, clearing the air. Again, I spoke nothing.

Arthur gasped when I skidded my chair back and left the kitchen. I walked into the small bathroom between the kitchen and the living room, washing my hands under the hot water. Swift pain radiated off my searing flesh. Steam wafted up from the water. I couldn't stand the agony for more than a few seconds.

I dried off my hands. Arthur stood in the bathroom doorway. His forearms braced on the doorjamb.

"Are you all right?" Arthur asked. I shook my head. "Can I hug you?" I grabbed him around his waist, and he curled his arms around me, resting his chin lightly on the top of my head. Comfort unlike anything I felt before unfurled in my chest. Arthur's beating heart drummed in my ear.

"My powers are leaving me," I said.

"My powers never fully arrived," Arthur countered. His thumbs kneaded the knots in my shoulder. I gripped his waist harder. "Let's clean up."

Arthur's hands fell off my body, but I wasn't ready to give him up yet. "Do you still want sex off the table?"

"I can't rely on sex to light a candle." Buzzkill

Arthur came back. I lifted off his chest, craning my neck backward. His thumbs brushed over my cheeks. He swooped down for a kiss, a short one, making me lift on my tiptoes for more. My feet thudded back to the floor.

I side-stepped him out of the bathroom. I got nowhere. Arthur grabbed my hand, spinning me back into his embrace, and claimed my mouth for the kiss I'd wanted since he returned.

Chapter Twenty-Nine

Another magical ability Arthur possessed was maneuvering me over to the couch, unzipping my jeans, stretching them past my hips, and caressing his hand between my legs, all without skipping a beat in our kiss. The whimper leaving my mouth was pure torment. I refused to come with his fingers massaging my clit over my panties.

I broke our impassioned kiss, missing the pressure of his mouth instantly, and kicked my jeans off my feet. I lifted the hem of my shirt upward until Arthur's hands stopped me.

"Leave your shirt on. Take off your panties."

He might not light candles on command, but I hooked my fingers under the band of panties, dragging them down my legs. The second I stood back up, Arthur reclaimed my mouth, tonguing the seam of my lips, coaxing them open. I closed my eyes, lost in the prospect of what will happen next. His hand found my pussy again with no barrier stinting his fingers.

He slipped two fingers over my clit, swirling in tiny, maddening circles. I parted my legs further, smoothing my hand down his forearm to his wrist, insisting on more than his light touch.

"More, Lena? Tell me."

"Yes, touch me. Please," I moaned.

Arthur flipped me around, my back to his front. I

loved feeling the hard length of his dick against my bare, heated ass.

I bent down, almost touching the carpet in front of the couch, gyrating against the seam of his jeans.

"Fuck," he groaned. His fingers gripped my waist, pinching the taut skin. My gasp, mixed with pain and pleasure, made me move my body faster.

"No, this is your turn," Arthur said behind me. He released his punishing grip on my hips and nudged me forward onto the couch. I turned back around as Arthur kneeled on the carpet, dragging a hand over the fly of his jeans. His eyebrows arched down, and a shiver coursed through his body. If I wasn't allowed to touch him, the rest of his night might be very uncomfortable.

I wanted more kisses, but Arthur spread my legs apart, exposing my wet pussy. Without breaking my gaze, he leaned forward, testing a barely-there lick on my clit. My legs inched further apart, and my back arched against the couch. I earned a sturdy lick from my wet center up past my clit. My eyes closed halfway, but I thrust them open. I trailed my own fingers over my clit where Arthur's tongue just licked.

"I don't know what's hotter. When you stare at me before I go down on you or you taking care of yourself while I watch."

"Let's try the first one."

Arthur was done playing. His tongue ravished my pussy on the couch my ex-boyfriend slept on one night a week for a year. The faint whiff of Ray's sweat clinging to the fibers of the upholstery made me gasp for a different reason. My hips jerked off the couch, as if burned from Ray's scent.

"Please." The only word escaping my throat was the

wrong one. Arthur clamped his palm and forearm over my midsection, restraining me. Instead of pushing him off me, I fisted his wrist, angling his hand toward my clit. He rubbed his fingertips back and forth along the sensitive ridge and licked up and down my entire pussy. I hooked my knee over the arm of the couch, fully exposed for Arthur.

What have I done?

Arthur edged me closer to my release, and I fucked everything up. I angled my head into the back cushions of the couch. Lust from drowning in the scent of Ray's skin poured into me as well.

"Use it, Lena. Allow yourself to come." Arthur's hot breath and lips grazing the warmed skin with his speaking mouth almost did the trick. The kisses with one lick only starting from my ass up to my clit and one powerful suck and nip spiraled me down the cliff.

His fingers thrust into my opening, dragging out the pleasure radiating from my very soul. My scream caught in my throat. I held my breath until the peak of the heat morphed into small spasms inside my body.

When he pulled his fingers free, I found my breath again. It rushed out, shaky at first. Arthur trailed his wet mouth against my inner thigh still hoisted over the couch.

"Arthur," I moaned.

"I'm getting you a new couch tomorrow."

I nodded, understanding why. Arthur gained the upper hand through means I guessed were part of his gift, his powers. He wiped his hand over his mouth and shuffled toward the bathroom.

Shame peeked through me when I returned to a seated position. The embarrassment grew until Arthur came back into my living room. He shrugged off his open button-down, leaving him in his jeans and sleeveless tank top.

"I'm going to go clean up. I'll be right back," I said.

When I passed Arthur, his fingers turned my cheek toward him, and he gave me one hell of a deep kiss. *His wicked tongue will haunt me forever.*

"It's okay. In the beginning, we all do what we must to get there."

"Honesty time. Are you reading my thoughts?"

"Nine out of the ten times. It just happens that I'm correct most of the time with you."

"I'll remember that."

Like a chuckle at a funeral during the worst time ever, I laughed. Half his face stayed in the shadows, but the half in the light smiled, growing brighter and lighter with the pull of his lips.

I pinched his muscular bicep as I passed him by. He sat back on the couch, staring after me like the world made sense for him now. Meanwhile, my thoughts chased themselves through a labyrinth of consequences. I stood against the closed bathroom door, willing the energy coursing through me to slow down. Inside me ached from the orgasm. The thought of Arthur's sinful mouth fluttered my muscles again. I braced my hand against the hand towel rack and shut my eyes.

Behind my eyelids, the vanity lights left small circles in my vision. Each ring held a precious thing. The images flowed crystal clear in the darkness. Amy, Kim, and I walking in the forest, writing at my vanity, my mother smoothing my hair back for a kiss on the forehead, and then my grandmother adorned in an old shawl she wore outstretched her hands for me. I reached my hands up, straining for her touch, her comfort, any piece of her for that stolen moment.

The pointed edge of the vanity stabbed me in the side, collapsing my vision as I opened my eyes. I closed them again, but I only saw darkness. I pounded my hand on the porcelain counter. Fleeting pain numbed my palm. I rubbed it, feeling and smelling the cold cream my grandmother used to rub into my skin at night during the winter she stayed with me.

I hardly understood anything that happened between Arthur and me today. Minus the assassin tree branch, I felt no fear. Even now, standing in the fading effects of my vision, I wanted more.

A rugged moan drew me back into the living room. I peeked around the wall at the room, illuminated by the now burning fire. Arthur's firm hand jerked off his cock as he gazed into the fire he must have started. His mouth was slack, his eyes hooded, and his top teeth bit down onto his full bottom lip. I begged every sexy siren who ever graced the silver screen for the confidence as I sauntered over to him. My return tore his gaze away from the crackling blaze.

"It's too much. I need it." Arthur's raspy, sex voice made me wet all over again. His hips rose with each fist circling down his cock. My arousal roared back, and my heart drummed in my chest.

I straddled his outstretched right leg, stroking my fingers along the stubble of his jaw. "I want to help you come."

"Take off your top. Let me see your tits."

I threw off my top shirt and pulled down my tank top. My heaving breast muffled Arthur's opened mouth groan. He squeezed the soft flesh together with both of his hands, smothering himself in my cleavage. I took over teasing the velvety tip of his leaking cock with my fingertips, the head angled toward his taut stomach.

"No sex, please," Arthur grunted. His gritted teeth bit down on my aching nipple.

"I promise."

Arthur nudged his pants further down his thighs, almost to his knees. We were so close to fucking. If his dick couldn't breach my pussy tonight, I damn well made him squirm under the weight of his decision. I slipped my tank top over my head. My breast popped out of Arthur's mouth, and he whimpered for it back, leaning forward with puckered lips.

"No sex, no problem," I stated. Arthur tugged off his undershirt, and his hands wandered toward my bared pussy, but I derailed his quest by returning his sweaty palm to my breast. My thighs straddled Arthur's waist. He allowed me to climb up on him, but he clamped his fingers hard against my waist.

"Lena, please."

I leaned over his rigid body, corkscrewing my hand under the head of his cock. The back of his head thudded against the wooden frame of the couch. A few more strokes would catapult him over the blissful ledge. I wanted more of a connection if even possible. I sucked the soft, fleshy part of his earlobe, and I tilted his dick up toward his pelvis, rubbing my wet slit against his hard length. A shiver undulated through Arthur's entire body.

"We are going to burn alive if we keep this up."

"Let the fire have us."

Arthur kissed me hard enough to hold my breath until I screamed or cried. Arthur helped me find the easiest rhythm, keeping my clit pressed against him as I rubbed back and forth, slicker each time. He alternated staring at his hand groping my bouncing breasts and peering down at our joined bodies. I wanted nothing more for him to angle his cock up, so I could fuck him thoroughly and for real.

"Oh, Lena."

His hot, sloppy kiss claimed me. The heat that forced us apart the last time burst between our bodies, lifting my weight onto my sore knees. Arthur's hand found my hip and thrust me down onto his cock. For a moment, I thought he hadn't meant to do it. We wasted so much time messing around without fucking. I started lifting back up, but Arthur's lips left mine, and his gaze seared into my soul.

"Please stay with me. Lena," he stammered. "I need you bare. I need to feel you."

"I'm on the pill. Make love to me," I kissed him again, nipping his bottom lip with my teeth.

Arthur's back fell against the couch, bringing my hips down hard onto his lap. He aided my thrusts, helping me fuck him. We never lost the connection. We stayed joined until the pleasure coursed through us. Our bodies writhed together, gripping, pulling, diminishing the loneliness. I collapsed on his chest as my orgasm seized me.

The crackling fire made me turn my cheek toward the orange flames. I caressed my hand over Arthur's short chest hair. Unlike the coarse stubble on his face, the hair over his chest and stomach was soft. His skin smelled like ash after a bonfire.

Blue and orange flames crackled underneath the wood in the fireplace, rising higher and engulfing each piece of wood nestled on the wrought iron holder.

"Did you light the fire?"

"Yes. Do you like me rubbing your back?"

I nodded. His slow movements over my unruly hair soothed me so much I barely noticed it. Everything felt right.

"Arthur?"

"Yeah?"

"Will you stay with me this time?"

"Of course."

Chapter Thirty

Arthur slept on his stomach in the most peculiar way. He held the pillow in a vise grip under his cheek and bent his leg at the knee. His uncomfortable stance kept me awake, along with his soft snoring. We had started out cuddling but separated soon after.

I gasped when my phone buzzed on the nightstand.

—*Do you want to have dinner tomorrow night?*— Kim texted.

Did the spell affect her? The love spell started the next morning. *How long before I heard from Amy?*

—*Sure, text me in the morning.*—

—*Woohoo! Girls' Night!*—

"It's the middle of the night. Who's texting you?" Arthur grumbled without opening his eyes.

"My best friend. She wants to have dinner tomorrow night."

"Is she an insomniac?"

"No. I think my spell worked."

Arthur's eyes opened wide. "You did more than just regenerate the flower, didn't you?"

"Memories of my best friends and I hanging out flashed in my mind. So far, only one of them has reached out. It could still be a coincidence."

"Nothing is a coincidence."

"Who knows? A little sex, and it all could have worked out."

Arthur laughed and slid me back into his cocoon. I fell asleep soon in his arms. With Arthur's breath warming my neck, his hand curling around my waist right above my pajama pant, a nightmare choked me.

I never remembered how dreams started. Suddenly, I drove along the coast, admiring gigantic mansions bathed in shadows. I had no idea what coast I drove on. Two silhouettes forming the shapes of women stood next to the curb. Their outstretched hands beckoned me. I pulled over to the left shoulder on the sudden one-way road. I swore it had two sides with a jarring yellow line in the middle seconds ago, but the dream had a mind of its own.

The stench of decay flooded the car as the two women shuffled into the backseat. The sound of stretched plastic assaulted my ears. Even in the dream, I had an auditory sensitivity.

"Where to, ladies?"

"We don't know. Take us home." One voice, dubbed over twice, echoed from the backseat. Their mouths, hidden partially in the darkness, never moved.

"Where is home?" I asked.

"You tell us?"

I drove for hours, hoping a house felt right. The gas meter remained full the entire time.

"Are we close?" I asked.

"Yes. You can find it, not us."

My house came up on the right. The green Cape Cod style home with black shudders flapping back and forth. The flickering streetlight was fixed. Idalia stood under the light wearing her signature long black dress. Her hair blew in the wind, just like it played with the shudders. Her usual gaunt face hidden.

I stopped my car shy of the light. Idalia trailed a threatening red nail longer than her actual finger up the hood of the car. A white scratch trailed in her wake.

"Ladies, we are getting a third passenger." The two silhouettes in the backseat grunted in response.

Idalia opened the door, rotting coconut wafting off her. She crunched into the passenger seat. My real car did not have plastic seat covers. *Whose car had I been driving?*

"Idalia," I whispered.

"Here it is," she said like the ladies in the backseat without moving her lips.

"What?"

An object pulsed in her hand. Her fingers barely contained it until, one by one, her fingers released their hold. I screamed in silence, gaping at the human heart beating in her lap.

"We have ours for you, too."

My back jerked against the driver's side door, the furthest I was able to retreat from the horror show in my car. I glanced at the two women in my backseat. Amy and Kim's faces stared at me. Both women held their hearts in their hands. I screamed again and again, clawing at the driver's side door, trying desperately to leave. One heartbeat filled the car, then a second, a third, and the fourth, mine beating the hardest.

"*Lena!*" Arthur called my name.

A sharp sting blossomed on my cheek, and then I fell out of the car and kept on falling.

"*Lena, wake up!*" Arthur caressed my cheeks in his warm hands. His beautiful face hovered over mine in the daylight.

"Did you slap me?"

"Are you kidding me? You wouldn't wake up. I tapped you on the cheek. I was going to throw water on you next."

Sunshine covered every corner of my bedroom. Nothing rested in darkness. I panted for air, resting my crossed arms over my raised knees. The drenched sheet reeked of my sweat.

"Bad dream?" Arthur asked.

"I dreamed your sister and my two best friends gave me their hearts."

Arthur's eyes widened. "I was afraid this would happen. Lena, it's perfectly normal to be fearful about the spell. Trust me, that was the Brujah's magic, not yours. She wanted to teach you a lesson for messing with love and people's lives. I promise your friends are safe."

"What about your sister?"

"I think she's meddling where she doesn't belong."

"Did you tell her about Ray?"

"Yes, I did. She stopped into the shop the next day."

The acid in my empty stomach gurgled. "She wouldn't do anything to hurt me, right? Like, you never gave her any of my hair, or I don't know."

Arthur fell back on the pillow that used to be Ray's. "My sister is weird, but she means you no harm. It could be a coincidence that she was in the dream too."

"Why does she always smell like rotten coconuts?"

"Mom says that too. It's a protection thing."

"Oh, that explains everything." I served up sarcasm for breakfast, but Arthur stared at his phone.

"Shit, I have to go. The shop opens at ten." He leaped from my bed and got dressed fast.

"See you tonight?"

"I think I have plans with Carter. I have stuff for

him, but I don't know how long I'm going to be."

"Okay, let me know."

Arthur placed one knee on the bed and kissed me. *Where did the sex dreams go?*

****

Fear nibbled at the edges of my thoughts. Kim always finagled one night a week for herself. It wasn't weird for her to make reservations at a fancy place she would never bring her kids.

I walked into the small bistro with limited seating and gasped as Kim and Amy clinked glasses and turned toward me.

"Is this an intervention? I promise I will do better in the future."

I expected fake laughs all around, but nope. My two best friends glanced at each other like they did a million times back in school, sighing.

"We have decided to let bygones be bygones. There is no reason for the three of us not to be friends again," Kim said.

"I can't believe we let it go on this long. This must have sucked for you, Lena," Amy remarked.

"We're sorry," they both said in unison. If I wasn't already freaked out, the alarm bells started ringing right about now.

"What brought this on?" I asked.

"It was the strangest thing. I woke up today and called Kim. After you told me about the pool incident, I kept thinking about how we used to hang out there and the kissing contest the summer we all got boobs," Amy confessed.

"If I hadn't gotten sick Independence Day weekend, Edward would have kissed me first," Kim lamented.

My gaze ping-ponged between my two oldest friends. It felt like old times before the split happened.

"Do you still have that spirit board in your attic? I think your grandmother stashed it up there," Amy said.

"I have the metal disc somewhere in my house. Layla tried to make a necklace out of it." Kim waved her hand in the air, dismissing the actions of her almost teenage daughter.

"Lena? Are you okay? Is this too abrupt for you? I told you we should have waited." Amy slapped Kim on the top of her hand playfully.

"It's going to take a little getting used to on my part. I hoped we could all be friends again years ago, but I'll take it now."

Kim scrolled through the pictures of Layla and the twins, and Amy warned her about Layla's rebellious streak.

"Oh, I know. She's just like me," Kim had said.

Was I the reason why they had the sudden change of heart? Mushrooms, dead flowers, tree bark shavings, and one dried-up snakeskin brought harmony to my world? It seemed too natural for them, picking up where they left off, leaning in toward each other while they laughed.

My phone buzzed in my pocket.

Richard texted. —*The buyers have a new bid for you I think you're going to love.*—

The offer was ten thousand more dollars than the last time.

"Holy shit, ladies! I sold my first computer program!"

Chapter Thirty-One

The short-lived euphoria crashed down somewhere around Spring Street. Like an eighties' song stuck in your head, Ray's whimpering and muffled screams played on repeat. Spells had consequences. I saw it firsthand. Just like that, my morale boost crashed and burned.

I hoped Amy and Kim would one day bury the hatchet. However, it would be years from now when they joked about who stole the other's tennis balls off their walkers, not from a spell. The memories of us years ago drifted into my mind so carelessly. *How could I cast a spell on them?* I only meant to revitalize the flower petals, not rearrange my whole life.

I waited at the longest traffic light at the corner of Spring Street and Middletown Road. The light turned green, and at the first beep of a disgruntled driver behind me, I opened my door and spewed the red reunion dinner all over the bright yellow lines.

"Are you all right?" the driver in the car next to me asked.

I looped my hand around the air, begging him to drive on.

"Put your hazards on."

I did what he suggested after he drove off. The stench of vomit lingered in my car the rest of the drive home. I took a bath after I threw up properly in the toilet for ten minutes straight.

The edge of the tub, not quite warm yet from the hot water, cooled off my sweaty neck. How could I put someone in danger again? Kim had children, for fuck's sake. *I'm a selfish fuck.*

My phone buzzed on the small wicker table next to the tub. Richard Flanagan was calling. I dunk my head under the bathwater. The ringer found me under the water, booming through the molecules.

I scrambled to my phone, improvising my best nonchalant front. "Hello, Ms. Martin speaking."

"Hey, Miss Lena, I'm so happy to catch you. Sorry to call after hours, but I wanted to review this new bid. It's my buddy's company. You're exactly what he's looking for."

After a hundred uh-huhs, the deal seemed too good to be true.

"I felt terrible for passing on your deal. I have had so many lucky breaks in my life. I wanted to pay it forward. If you don't accept Niguel's offer, I understand."

"Can I have the night to think about it?"

"Yes, of course! I think he's on a plane right now. I sent the damn guy the proposal two weeks ago, and he only read it yesterday. Take your time. I'll send you over his notes."

"Thank you, Richard. I will review it in the morning."

"Great! I told you I wouldn't leave you hanging! Have a good night!"

"You, too."

How do I know if it's real? I swallowed the rising bile coating the back of my throat. Big, steady breaths. I built a great program, and it had nothing to do with witchcraft. The group text from Amy and Kim came through with our picture from dinner. We all smiled wide. Fine wrinkles appeared around our eyes. It happened. Kim and Amy were friends again.

I got out of the tub and put on my robe. Sure enough, Richard forwarded me the email and at least some of my nerves calmed down. Niguel Madden IV sent his email to Richard early yesterday morning, a few hours before Arthur showed up at my house. The offer was real and witchcraft-free. I sold my program fair and square.

"Thank God!" I shouted.

I wanted to sit down on my couch and not move a muscle. That way, everything would stay perfect.

The peace lasted five minutes. Arthur called, then when I hadn't answered, he texted. If I kept my powers, he would be my boyfriend. If not, we would be friends who had fucked. I hated those odds. He called again, and a needle-like pain pricked my sternum. I rubbed the tiny spot.

In the back of my memory, the items Idalia gave me took center stage. They were supposed to cleanse my home and protect me from evil. *Where the fuck had I put them?*

I found the grocery bag in my kitchen, amongst the junk on the desk. Mail and other crap buried it. I barely remembered bringing the items into the house. They should be in my car, forgotten in the trunk.

The bag felt lighter than air as I nudged it out from under the pile. All the items on the desk fell forward, creating an avalanche hurdling toward me. I let it fall at my feet. Flames unfurled from the grocery bag, escaping out the top. I dropped it onto the clutter, gasping at the impending disaster.

Almost as if the flame extinguished itself, the bag flew to the ground like a feather plucked loose from a bird. As soon as the remaining plastic hit the top of the pile, I scooped it up and threw it in the sink, turning on the water full blast.

Arthur would never hurt me. He manipulated fire, but never anything like that. The only person who might wish harm on me shared his last name, Idalia.

I called Arthur, ignoring whatever he said in the text messages.

"Hey babe, sorry about this," Arthur answered.

"Where is your sister?"

"She's right here. I texted you."

"I didn't read it. What is she doing?"

"Inventory. We got a late shipment in. Is everything okay?"

"No, what are her powers?"

"Um, she can see people's pasts and read palms well. Why? What's happening?"

"Someone tried to set me on fire. Dalia's protection shit backfired. I picked up the bag she gave me, and poof. I had a makeshift fire ball in my hand. It could have burned down my whole damn house!"

"Oh my God! Are you okay?"

"No, I'm not fucking okay. Your sister tried to kill me!"

"Lena, she would never do anything like that to anybody. Is the fire out? Did you call the fire department?"

"I'm drowning the candle and the stick. Arthur, your sister gave me the spell and the items. She did it. It's her!"

"Hold on," Arthur said. I paced my living room, straining to hear them. Idalia's voice pitched high, and he shouted. A door slammed.

"Arthur?"

"She's gone." He sighed into the phone. "She got defensive, but I don't trust her right now. Where are you?"

"Home. Can she manipulate fire?"

"Not that I'm aware of."

"I only had one thing from her. I'm pretty sure I'll be all right unless she's headed here now to finish the job."

"I ordered her to go home. I guess my spell didn't work last night."

"What did you cast a spell for?" I stammered.

"I wished for peace and serenity for Dalia. We were having an okay night, cataloging the new shipment. We laughed, Lena. She and I never laugh anymore." He stuttered a broken sigh, then paused. "I can feel her rebellion. The demon whispering in her ear every minute of every hour holds the trapdoor open for her alone. It's hard to explain. I can't follow her down this path."

"Is it possible she didn't know she did it? I visited her when you were away. She gave me stuff for protection. It had a white candle in it. It should have been safe, right?"

"Anything has the potential to burn. I don't know what to say."

"I'm sorry. I made your night go to shit."

"It's fine. I'm glad you're okay. I'll leave here in a few minutes and come over."

"I feel weird. I don't feel safe at all. Can I come to your place instead?"

"I'm sorry you feel that way. Of course, you can. Are you still fancy from your dinner?"

"No, I'm in my robe."

"Are you naked under there?"

The delayed smile took its time curling onto my face. I wanted his distraction again. "Yeah," I muttered.

"Be at my place in twenty minutes, only if you don't put on more clothes."

"High stakes over there."

"All right, you can put on pants."

"Text me when you're done."

"Will do."

Chapter Thirty-Two

My car still reeked of vomit. I wasn't sure what killed my libido more, smelling my stomach acid or almost catching on fire. Both sucked. Arthur had to forgive me for putting on some clothes under the robe. It was nine o'clock, but it felt much later.

Arthur opened the door in sweatpants and a fake football jersey. The electric current flowed between us. I stepped forward, and Arthur grabbed my hand, pulling me against him.

"I'm so glad you are okay."

I wanted every day in his embrace. His hand caressed my back, and he rested his scruffy chin on top of my head.

"I'm going to make it right," he mumbled. Arthur hugged me tight, then released me.

Mixed emotions ran through my mind. From the beginning, Idalia and I started off on the wrong foot. On second thought, Arthur and I did too.

"Is it possible to go back in time and redo it all?" I asked.

"That's more dangerous than a renegade love spell. Never fuck with time, Lena."

"Now, you're scaring me. I'm kidding around."

"I knew that." He squinted, fake nodding.

Yeah, right. "What do you want to do?" I sat down on the couch in my fluffy pink robe. The faint whiff of coconut erased Arthur's soap smell. "Was Idalia here recently?"

"She just left." He cleared his throat, swallowing the lump in his throat. "She said she didn't do it."

"You believe me, right?"

Arthur got down on his knees in front of me. Out of pure reflex, my back straightened, and my knees clenched together.

"I will never doubt anything you experience. Lena, you are a powerful witch, and I trust you wholeheartedly. The only thing I have to question is who did it. Dalia swore on our father's grave it wasn't her."

"Then who?"

He shrugged. "Maybe it was no one. Fuck, it could have been me. I'm the one with the pyro habit. The weird thing is that when you called, we were imputing a new shipment of candles into the database. My weaknesses have always been stronger than my strengths. I don't think it was me, but I'm not sure."

"Are you fucking kidding me? Come on, it wasn't you."

"Did you smell her?"

"No, I didn't."

"It couldn't have been her. You would know if it was her." He laid his forehead against my knees, wrapping his hands under me. "Please don't leave. We will figure it out. I want you to feel safe with me."

I threaded my hands through his damp hair. Again, as he tried comforting me, my loving instincts kicked in. A hug wasn't helping now.

Since my grandmother collapsed on my sixteenth birthday, fear chased me every step of my journey. I controlled the stronghold through my twenties. The inevitable consequence of Ray and I's breakup blasted through every wall I erected. I started visiting Doctor Greene, hoping she would help me without blurting out my best-kept secret.

Arthur toyed with the cloth tie to my robe. He sighed into my neck as he caressed my bare breast under the shirt I regretted throwing on. His teeth and hot breath dragging across the tender flesh at my hairline made me shudder underneath him. I forced my knees apart as far as they went, inviting Arthur in.

"I will keep you safe," Arthur said. He kissed me through the questions begging to be asked. They waited until he fucked me silent.

He pressed my body into the soft, groaning couch. I craned my legs over his hips, but he still had too many clothes on. Thank God he lived alone. After he tore his clothes off and stood naked before me, I licked the tip of his hard cock from where I lay down on the couch. I loved the moan tilting his head forward, watching me as I made his cock disappear in and out of my mouth.

"Take your shorts off. Please," Arthur asked. I shimmied out of them. His warm hand with the scent of his mint soap from his shower lingered on his skin. I engulfed his whole cock in my mouth. "Oh God, stop. I'll come."

I sucked him hard enough that he pinched my nipple, forcing a yelp out of my throat. We were wasting time. I needed him inside me.

He backed out of my mouth, pouncing onto the couch over me. His nose nudged up the other side of my shirt. I pushed my robe off me, but Arthur pulled it back onto my shoulders. "It's too cold. Stay warm. Burn me up." Arthur winced, lifting onto the palms of his hands on the other side of my breasts. "I'm sorry. I…"

I stroked Arthur's softened cock, bringing him close to my pussy. His velvety tip found my wet opening, thrusting barely inside.

How do you get Arthur to stop thinking and slam his eyes shut? I clenched my muscles around him. His eyes rolled back into his head, and his lips fell upon mine. My arms wrapped around his shoulders, pulling his full weight on top of me. I thrust my hips up, forcing his stiffening cock deeper. He kissed me with complete abandonment, flicking his tongue against mine, but he held his hips in one place, letting me fuck his cock from the bottom.

"Arthur?" I mumbled against his opened mouth. I almost scooted back off him until his eyes opened, and he thrust hard, impaling me with his full length. My voice cracked at the heat pulsating between our rubbing stomachs and the knot forming right behind my clit. His finger touched under my chin, a barely there branding between us.

"Lena," he said. His body melted into mine, thrust after thrust, deep into my soul. I sounded like an asthma attack, gasping and moaning each time Arthur's pelvis smashed against mine. My pussy spasmed, the wave of pleasure melting my body into the couch. I came apart, the sole of my foot jamming into the arm of the couch. "Oh, fuck, Lena."

Arthur's strong bicep rested against my cheek as he gripped the other arm of the couch above my head, fucking my spent, swollen pussy until he came, shouting above me with his head thrown back.

Like my alarm chirping at the worst times, reminding me of a task forgotten, a fire alarm blasted through our post-orgasm high. Arthur's body shook above me, and then I smelled it. The tell-tale, something burning, stench. He froze above me.

"Arthur, something is on fire," I mumbled.

"*Fuck!*"

Arthur scrambled off me, his eyes widening. He threw on his sweatpants mid-dash toward the kitchen. I yanked up my shorts and jerked my shirt down over my breasts. I ran after him, hoping he forgot about the dinner he made before I came, and it accidentally burned because, well, sex distracted him.

I turned the corner and skidded into Arthur's back. He held up his arm as if we stopped short at a red light. Three white candles burned higher than any natural height I had ever seen from a simple, corded wick. The flames flickered and danced in the shadows on the far wall. Without any help from us, they extinguished themselves.

"Did you light them before I came?" I asked. I already knew the answer. His dismissal only confirmed the truth.

"Can we go to your place?"

"Yeah." I took a shaky breath, rubbing my hand against Arthur's shoulder. He felt tighter than a thick rubber band ball. All the tension plaguing him daily returned.

I walked back into the living room and sat down on the desecrated couch. I hadn't smelled Idalia's signature scent since I walked in. I didn't smell it now. Every part of me thought it had to be her.

She would never hurt her brother, right?

A cabinet opened, then a thud, followed by a rolling sound, proceeded. Arthur shouted in another language.

279

I slipped on my shoes and peeked around the wall. Arthur held a small, purple crystal ball in his hand. He flicked on the chandelier over his dining room table.

"I know who's doing this. It's not my sister." He held the crystal ball up to the closest bulb. The middle swirled like a faraway galaxy, churning forever in its prison. "She's watching us."

"Who?"

Tick Tock, Tick Tock, Tick Tock. The metronome on the top of the piano flicked its dial back and forth. Usually, the sound came deep within my mind, buzzing, never clear, not happening in front of me.

"Did you do that?" I asked.

"No, let's get out of here. I'll cleanse my home later. We need to get back to your place. I'll follow you."

I thought about moving, but my limbs did not comply. Arthur shushed in the direction of the piano, stilling the metal dial on the metronome. "Who's trying to hurt us?"

He held the crystal ball in the palm of his hand. "I knew a witch a while back who asked me to strip her of her powers. Her name is Sheri. She runs a mineral and oils shop a few towns over. She gives psychic readings in her spare time. Sheri joined my mother's coven years ago for help. We did everything to her with her verbal consent. She wanted out, then regretted it." The swirling inside of the glass ball shined bright, illuminating Arthur's gaze. It almost looked like a burst of flames reflected in his eyes. "Why would she be targeting you?"

"Are those her powers?" I covered my mouth with my shaking palm. The cabinet encasing over twenty orbs murmured toward me in an inaudible tongue. "Omg, they are witches' powers!"

"You hear them, don't you?" Arthur asked. The whisperings intensified. A roar swirled around me, circling around my head. I thrust my hands over my ears, backing up toward the door.

Arthur stood in front of me, glancing over at the multicolored crystal balls. "They can't hurt you. Without a witch's body, they are merely whispers in the dark."

"I want to get out of here, now," I commanded. Goosebumps broke out on my arms and skated up my legs.

"Lena, this is very important. Do you know Sheri Wynwood?" At the sound of her name, the purple orb pulsed bright in Arthur's hand.

My fingernails scratched at the dry skin on my forearm. The burn alleviated a fraction of the fear coursing through my body. I shook, standing in front of Arthur, whose frown reared back.

"What happened?" he asked.

"I visited her shop while you were away. Oh my God, it wasn't Dalia. I had stones from Sheri in the bag."

Arthur sighed into his hand, rubbing around his mouth.

"Did you mention me?"

I nodded.

"Okay, it's all right. We need to go digging. Let me get some shoes on."

"Where are we going?"

"The first place you went to looking for death."

Chapter Thirty-Three

I followed Arthur's car to the old cemetery, dominating the old section of town. At least the damn food truck left the dead alone at night. Arthur turned off his headlights as soon as he turned onto the pebbled entrance by the train tracks. I copied his every move, but I was one misstep away from hysterics. My grandmother told me my curiosity might be my downfall. I knew her gifts included foresight. Hopefully, she was off about mine.

I threw on a coat from my backseat over my ridiculous pajamas and robe. I sneezed and coughed when I walked over to Arthur.

"We have to be very quiet," Arthur remarked. He unlocked his trunk and rummaged around for something.

"Why? Everyone's dead."

"I don't want to spend a night in county jail. We will only be a few minutes."

He extracted a large metal shovel from underneath a blanket. "Fuck, no. I am not digging up any dead bodies." I ran my hands through my hair on either side of my head, pacing a few feet back and forth in front of Arthur. *No, I would not find death again.*

"I would never ask you to exhume a body. I'm not that type of witch. We must bury Sheri's powers. This is the only cemetery I know that is hallowed."

"You're losing me."

"Come on, we must do this fast. I have a spot."

"Why is this graveyard hallowed?"

"It means holy. This is a blessed space. We should be safe after burying her powers."

"If she has no powers, how can she hurt us?"

"Oh babe, there are many ways to harm another from afar. Disposing of her powers under blessed earth will stint her rage. Her intentions will be muted, forgotten from her mind. It's the only way I know how to stop her."

"I don't understand any of this."

"I will explain it all later. We need to go."

Arthur held the reusable bag from a grocery store in one hand and gripped my fingers tight in the other. We passed my *abuela* and grandmother's graves first. He paused for a moment as if an unseen pull distracted him. Before I said anything, he tugged me back along to his mission.

I switched on the light on my phone, but Arthur covered the beam. "We can't get caught. Your eyes will adjust in a second."

A whiff of smoked meat gagged me, followed by the scent of wet, sweaty shoes caked with mud and dirt, and who knew what else. I imagined decay reeked like that. Rotten and dirty.

We made our way to a tree overlooking a set of fresh graves. The branches lurched in the wind growing stronger as we got closer. I knew where we were. My old friend's brother's resting place resided to the left of us.

"They keep getting closer to my tree. I don't know how to stop them."

"Arthur, remember I told you I wound up crashing a funeral? Remember how I said something stopped me from touching the coffin?"

Arthur squatted down in the dirt using the tree for balance. "Is that the grave?"

"Yeah, I was here."

He patted the tree's bark, resting his forehead on it. "Thank you."

I gathered my coat tight around me. The cold air chilled me down to the bone. Arthur's actions ruined me forever.

He dug a hole near the base of the tree, deep enough to cover the crystal ball and then some. I almost shined a light on him. I had a gut feeling there must be more than one set of witches' powers down there. Arthur covered the hole with dirt, patting it down. Nothing looked out of place.

"Do you want to go grab some ice cream?" Arthur kidded, rubbing his dirty hands on his sweatpants.

"No! How can you think of ice cream right now?" I turned back to my car. My footfalls pounded on the gravel, and the chilled air pinched my face. Someone wished harm against me. Arthur and I had been in danger. *What the fuck type of world of witchcraft did I tumble into?*

"Lena, we should be safe now! It's okay!"

I ignored him. My bad attitude flared beyond my sudden bursts of frustration that came and went. Tangible worry ignited the tears flowing down my cheeks and gripped my heart. *Oh, fuck, my heart.*

The avalanche of despair brought thoughts back of Ray, Kim, and Amy. Were they in danger because I was a witch? Meeting for dinner was not worth their lives.

"Lena! Baby, stop!"

I snapped around fast enough Arthur flinched. "If

you extracted my powers, would all the spells go away? Would my friends be safe?"

"Lena, they aren't in any danger. This was a one-off. I've been a witch for over twenty years and never had anything like this happen to me. You're safe."

"Well, I've been an active witch for a few weeks, and I'm scared out of my fucking mind. What the fuck? You didn't tell me any of this was possible! I don't want this life. I thought Ray trying to pull out his heart was fucking bad. That was the tip of the iceberg!"

"That wasn't your magic. I told you that."

"I don't care. The potential is there. Someone can do that to another person. I don't want to be part of it. Oh, and yes, let's fast forward to the present. A woman tried to set me on fire because I mentioned your name. I want my powers gone."

"It's probably too late anyway."

Anger boiled in my blood before, but Arthur's last statement obliterated everything. Red flames flickered in my vision. The illusion made me angrier.

"Once again, Arthur, I'm going to ask you this fucking question. What does that mean?" His breath came out in a hiss. I saw the struggle in him, playing tug of war with the answer. "Arthur, *tell me now!*"

"I'm a selfish prick. I should have handled this better. It's not like I didn't expect you to figure it out. You're smart." He paused for too long.

I stepped closer to him, ready for the next blow.

"It's highly unlikely at this point that your gifts will leave you now, but that had nothing to do with me. When you cast the love spell, even though it was mostly Corrine's magic you tapped into, you forfeited your chance of your powers leaving you. Idalia was wrong.

She thought you hadn't used them that all. I smelled the loved spell shackling you, just as strong as the protection spell on your home."

Tears rolled down my cheeks. I closed my eyes, allowing more salty regret to fall. Arthur hugged me, wrapping my limp hands around his waist. His strong hands rubbed down my back. His heart hammered in his chest. "Lena. It's okay."

I cried harder. "How do I get rid of my powers now?"

"There are options. Painful ones that have proven to work. Let's not talk about such things now."

"I'm afraid for Kim. She can't rip out her heart. Her kids need her."

"That's not going to happen. You used your magic last night, not some shifty Brujah. Your magic is kind, good, healing."

"Is there a test?"

"No, you passed the test already."

"Nothing spectacular has happened since I found death. Maybe I did it wrong." I scrambled for any way out.

"Lena, you found death. It happened. I'm sorry."

Arthur held me crying in the cemetery for a long time. I hadn't stopped shaking. We stayed huddled together until the shivers were from the cold and not from my fears. He walked me to my car, and once I turned the key in the ignition, I pressed the car heater up full blast.

I hoped he'd followed me home. His conscience was not a hundred percent clean either, but I only had him right now.

I made us tea when we got into my house. We sat in

silence. Small talk abandoned us. Every time I glanced over, he gave me a small side smile. When I looked away, his lips returned to their frown.

I processed my fate. It felt wrong. Everything felt out of place. *How did I make this go away?*

The house phone rang at exactly midnight. Impossible dread torched through my body. No one used that number unless someone died. *Oh God, it's happening.*

"Lena?" Arthur asked. We both stared at the old yellow phone with the sticky, spiral cord. I sprinted to the wall.

If I didn't pick up the receiver, the phone would ring until the caller gave up. I had to do it.

"Mom?"

"Lena, everything's fine. Your dad had a tiny accident."

"Please tell me he didn't have a heart attack. Please, Mom!"

"He took a tumble down the basement stairs, but luckily, he landed on Trixie's old bed. He broke his wrist, and he's in surgery right now. He's okay. He's going to be okay."

"Oh my God, I'll be there in ten minutes."

"Lena, calm down. There is nothing you can do. Dad will be fine. I just wanted to let you know. I tried your cell phone, but it's dead."

"Fuck, it's in the car. Dad didn't put a new bulb in the light above the stairs?"

Mom's sigh revealed everything else. A warm hand caressed my back, followed by a firm chest to lay my head against.

"I will call you when he gets into recovery. The

doctor said it would be at least an hour procedure. It was a clean fracture."

"All right, please call me when he wakes up. I don't care how early it is."

"Yes, hun. I will, love you."

"I love you, too." I hung up the phone, resisting the urge to break down and cry.

"Come here," Arthur said. For the first time in forever, Arthur's embrace comforted me. He rubbed my back up and down in the least sexual way possible. "I'm sorry, Lena."

"I'm cursed. This must be a bad omen. This is just like my grandmother. She used her powers and got hurt. I used mine, and now everyone around me is getting hurt."

"Lena, nothing you did yesterday had anything to do with your father. This is a coincidence. You're not cursed. They aren't real."

"Is that a fact or one of your rules?"

Arthur released me and sat down at the table. "Are you going to use that against me every time I say something you don't agree with?"

"Probably. I want you to be right."

"Then, let it be. What happened with a light?"

"My father never changed the bulb."

"Let's go do it now."

Chapter Thirty-Four

I hated moving around my parents' house when they weren't home. Call me superstitious, but their home reminded me of an Egyptian tomb, jam-packed with clutter and treasures. The layers of dust my mother never got a handle on when I moved out tickled my nose.

Arthur shut the door behind us and ushered me first through the dark. The light switch at the bottom of the small staircase leading up to the living room did not turn on the chandelier above us. "She forgot to tell me about the power outage."

"Maybe your father blew a fuse when he tried repairing the light?"

"I doubt it. My mother has been asking him to switch out that lightbulb for weeks."

I flipped the switch at the top of the stairs, the kitchen light, and the hallway light with no luck. We both took out our phones and turned on the flashlights.

"Fuse box?" Arthur asked.

"Basement."

I couldn't tell if Arthur was still irritated. He sat quietly for most of the fifteen-minute drive. If we made an investigation board of our potential relationship, we needed more time.

Arthur followed me past the three identical doors, a closet, my old bedroom, then the basement. I creaked open the basement door.

"Your father didn't hear that noise?"

"All the doors sound like that. It made it impossible to sneak out of the house."

We thudded down the steps. His chuckle and his hand on my shoulder released some of the lingering tension in the air. Couples fight, people dating argue. It was not weird. The caress morphed into a pinch and tug, yanking me back into his arms at the foot of the stairs.

"Lena, we have to get out here." His voice quivered right by my ear.

"Why, what's the matter?"

"I'll explain later. Go upstairs, now. I'll handle the electricity."

"But it's not labeled," I insisted.

"*Lena. Go!*"

Arthur nudged me back up the first two steps. The loud squeak of Trixie's plush cat bed made me yelp when Arthur stepped on it. I muttered a thank you to the damn thing for bracing my father's fall.

I made the mistake of peering over my shoulder. I caught my gaze in the large mirror that used to be in my bedroom. The eyes staring back at me were not my own.

"Arthur," I whispered. "Hurry up with the lights."

I couldn't wrench my gaze away from the piercing red orbs glaring at me with my body. The mirror image's boot rested on the bottom step like mine, our hands gripped the wooden railing, but my trembling mouth hung open while the other smiled.

I wanted to slap that smile right off her face.

"You think this is funny? Fuck you, specter! Go spook someone else." I ran up to the glass, screaming at my adverse reflection. The limbs flailed like mine, my shirt bellowed from my anger, my cheeks sucked in for my scowl. Her smile remained stagnant, and the red eyes swirled into a black hole at the center. White hair emerged from the center of her head, changing the leftover black strains from root to tip.

The dim, low voltage bulbs popped on in the poorly spaced fixtures overhead. In the time I blinked and squinted, my proper mirror image returned. Instead of fear, insurmountable tiredness threatened me. I could collapse against the concrete floor right now.

"I thought I told you to go upstairs. What did you see?" Arthur emerged from behind the utility shelves in the corner by the boiler.

"Was it real?"

"It depends."

"My reflection had red eyes and white, frizzy hair. Is that the witch inside me?"

He shrugged. "It's hard to tell. Lena!"

Arthur lunged forward as I plopped down hard onto the second step of the old basement stairs. I couldn't stand on my feet anymore. I wanted nothing more than endless sleep for the next thousand years.

"I don't want to do this anymore," I confessed.

Arthur kneeled on the first step and kissed me on the forehead. He smoothed a strand of my hair away from my face.

"The beginning is always scary. I told you it's touch and feel as you go. Tough it out. We're going to be fine."

My hair, black as night minus the white streak, swished back and forth with my reply. "No, I'm done. I've seen things I can't explain in the two places I thought would always be safe spaces. I don't want to feel eyes watching me when I fall asleep. I don't want to light a candle with my mind and fear my cousin in Tulsa is going to break a leg. Take my damn powers away from me. I don't want them."

"Lena, I…" I cut him off with a kiss. I prayed to God it wasn't goodbye, but fear fueled my actions.

"Thank you for turning the lights back on. Can you change the bulb in the fixture at the top of the stairs?"

"Yes, but only if you talk to me."

"I promise we can talk in the car."

Arthur fixed the light, I left fresh water for Trixie, and we left. I faked falling asleep as soon as we got in the car. We never spoke a word until my hand jiggled the front doorknob of my house.

"I can do it on the next full moon. Is that too soon?" Arthur asked. He stood a distance behind me. His breath was gone from the back of my neck.

"When will that be?"

"Two weeks. I need to check my calendar. Would you be ready in time?"

"I'm ready now." I turned around. I tilted my gaze up toward Arthur. He looked wrecked. He stared at the dirt patch where flowers had been at my grandmother's funeral. His Adam's apple moved up and down with each swallow for courage. "Arthur?"

"I'm not strong enough to do it now. I will need more strength. Idalia will want to know. She could help. We can make this as big or as small as you want."

The cold night air caught up to me at the mention of his sister. I crossed my arms over my chest with the ringing in my ears turned at full blast.

"Can we talk about this inside?" I motioned.

Arthur took a single step forward but never reached the threshold. "I shouldn't. We aren't meant to be together."

"Fuck you, Arthur."

I slammed the door in Arthur's face as he shouted my name. I wished I had caught his fingers in the doorjamb. He knew he hurt me. The desperation in his cracking voice still calling my name, and his fist pounding on the door confirmed it.

A flicker of light drew my attention to the thin entryway table. My favorite candle, a fried marshmallow smell, illuminated the side of the room where I stayed huddled behind the door.

"I won't leave you in the dark!" Arthur cried.

I grabbed the bewitched candle and blew the magic out.

****

A little after three in the morning, I knocked on Arthur's car window. He never left. Arthur startled awake, grabbing the steering wheel and blinking a lot. When he saw me, I waved. The window fogged up from his breath hid his face.

A second later, Arthur unlocked the door and trailed a few steps behind me back into the house. I handed him the tea I made him with a potholder around it and a cookie. He chewed and drank as we walked up to my bedroom.

Did we break up? Were we even together?

Arthur placed the hot cup on my vanity, sitting down on the chair. His elbows rested on the tops of his knees, his shoulders hunching over. Like other times, I threaded my fingers through his hair, offering consolation.

I loved him. In the short time we'd known each other, I yearned for the days with him. He changed my existence, the part with witches and fire, forever, even if I said goodbye.

"I wanted it to be you. I still feel like we belong together." Arthur's hands wrapped around my hips, dragging me toward him. He laid his cheek on my stomach. "I can see a life with you."

"Who said we don't belong together?" I tightened my grip in his hair, lifting his face up. "You're not giving us a chance."

He looked away from my imploring gaze. His hands left me. A wave of coldness, like a draft from an opened window, flowed through the split ends of my hair.

"Do you feel that?" I asked.

"I never stop when I'm around you." Arthur rose from the cushioned chair. The damn stuttering streetlight flashed over him.

"From everything I've been through since the pool, can my powers still be extracted?"

"I have to ask Babushka." I barely heard his mumble.

"What can I say to make this better? I would still love you if I wasn't a witch," I confessed.

"I can't say," he started. I waited for the rest of the damning sentence, but he never finished it.

I left him to his tumultuous thoughts and slipped under the warm covers. I did the kind part. I got him out of the car and brought him inside. He needed to decide.

When he came to bed, his breath smelled like sugary raspberries. It was the only tea I had left. My mother and I drank all my chai. When his warmed fingers stroked my cheek, urging me to turn his way, I faced him in the darkness.

"Lena."

I closed the small distance between us, brushing my lips over his own. We fell into the embrace, clawing at our clothes, willing them to disappear. I guess being a witch hadn't meant changing outfits at the snap of a finger, burning candles until our lost loves returned, or riding a broom around the neighborhood. No spell ignited the passion between Arthur and me. He thought he'd found his place with me. Now where the fuck were we supposed to go from here?

Arthur's sweet kisses trailed from my neck to my breasts down to my pussy. He licked me long enough until my wetness welcomed his cock. I held onto his shoulders as he thrust, my thighs squeezing the life out of his hips. He pried them off, then curled his fingers under my knees, speeding up his pace. My head fell back against the pillows, moaning and gasping for air. Deep, coarse groans forced their way out of his slack mouth.

I roamed my hands over his short, soft chest hair until I reached his neck. He allowed me to pull him forward, our lips just out of reach. He furrowed his brow, grunted, and collapsed back on top of me. Arthur's chest slid against mine. His hair teased my aching nipples sending tiny shocks down to my twitching pelvis. A short wave of pleasure flickered, teasing me for the grand finale.

I came with Arthur's tongue fucking my mouth in time with the thrust of his cock. My back and hips stiffened. Arthur held up my body by my ass, using his cock a fraction faster while I rode my wave. I collapsed back on the bed, desperate for Arthur's orgasm.

He flipped over his edge as well. As his hips slowed down, I gripped the sweaty skin of his back, drowning in his scent.

We stayed joined together as long as possible. He extracted himself from my encasing limbs gently, planting short pecks on each bit of exposed skin. I cried until he returned from the bathroom. At some point in the night, I got up too but scurried back to our cocoon fast.

High with the fresh orgasm, I stifled the urge brewing a knot in the center of my chest to bring something back together. Arthur's knuckles kneaded the same space over his sternum. He hadn't tried lighting anything on fire, either. We were two songbirds stuck in their cages. Fear was an almost palpable presence holding us down. I silently screamed into my pillow.

If he turned his back on me after he took my gifts, I never wanted to speak with him again. If he hadn't seen that passion, the invisible blaze, shooting through us as we made love, then he was truly a fool.

Chapter Thirty-Five

"You will have to go back to the moon festival. Maybe we can siphon energy off the crowds. I watched the last time you went. You're interesting to watch. I laughed when you walked around in circles holding up your phone for a service bar. I lost sight of you for a while. You stayed too long at the book swap, and I got distracted by the strip tease in the next section. By the time the girl stripped down to the tassels on her boobs, you had passed me."

"I started getting a headache from all the incense and walked down to the beach." I thought someone had watched me. The sun had disappeared from between the trees, and the moon rose in its place. The entire forest watched me, not just Arthur. I had felt everything until the woman dressed like a gypsy joined me.

"Right, you're allergic to sage."

I barely kept my eyes opened. Arthur spoke more, but I'll remember it all in the morning. When he left, he whispered in my ear and kissed me on my cheek. I fell back asleep until my alarm buzzed from the nightstand.

As soon as I woke up, I headed to the hospital. I smuggled in a breakfast sandwich for my father and a muffin for my mother. The hospital asked me what I had brought, and I told them the truth. As soon as Dad ate, he resumed his morphine drip and passed back out. The doctor reviewed the aftercare and stressed the need for physical therapy for the next few weeks. My mother clutched her shirt over her chest.

"The doctor doesn't have a ring on his finger," Mom pointed out.

"You can't be serious right now."

"Doctors make good money, and he has a great bedside manner."

"Thanks, Mom, but no thanks. I started seeing someone."

"The gypsy?"

"He's more of a psychic, fortune teller."

She lifted one hand up, lowered the other, and then flipped flopped her palms. "Doctor or gypsy? There is no contest, Lena."

"Mom, there is a real crisis happening. Please don't stick your nose in my love life."

"What else am I supposed to do? I'm going to be waiting on your father hand and foot for the next few weeks. I can dream about matching you up with someone, can't I?"

"No, Mom. I need more coffee."

"Put your mask back on. You must wear it outside of the rooms. The cafeteria is on the second floor."

"Be right back."

Hospitals gave me the creeps. The antiseptic smell churned my stomach. I should have taken Arthur's offer for company.

The second-floor elevator opened to the chapel within the hospital. The aroma of stale processed food wafted throughout the hallway. Instead of heading left, I went straight ahead, opening the heavy, wooden chapel doors.

A woman kneeled in the first pew, ignorant to my

presence. I sat down in the opposite, parallel spot. Floral perfume fermented past its expiration date drifted throughout the small space.

"Don't let the path go," a woman's voice muttered.

I snapped my head to the left, but the woman there blessed herself and continued her silent prayers. The person who said it sat down on my right. Our shoulders brushed from the proximity. The stench of burning logs replaced the floral aroma. I sensed her movement more than watched.

I stared at the altar, adorned with embroidered cloths. A shrouded cross hung above the altar with sturdy metal wires. The woman by my side pulled one of the bibles out of the wooden notch in front of us, flipping through the pages one by one.

"Are you dead?" I asked.

"No, but they tried to kill me once." Against my better judgment, I faced the woman next to me. She sat staring at the altar as well. Her boney fingers traced every line of printed text without looking down. The pages flipped over so fast they might have ripped apart in her hand. Her voice rang young, but her hands were old and spotted. A black shroud covered her face, and a black lace dress billowed around her body.

"What do you want?" I asked.

"They will steal your essence, child. Let the beast find another meal."

"Who are they?"

"You already know."

"I'm getting rid of it. They can have it."

She lifted the veil, and to my surprise, the woman had no holes for eyes. Wrinkled skin stretched over the vacant eye sockets. Her chapped lips had the reddest, cheapest lipstick smeared beyond the edges of her lips.

I bit the side of my hand, muffling my scream.

"Stop that whining. You control your fate. We can help you only if you let us in."

"Georgina Monroe, stay right there." A nurse stood in front of us with pumpkins on her scrubs and googly eyes on a headband. "I'm sorry, Miss. She got loose."

The woman with no eyes inched closer and grabbed onto my hand. "The beast is here! Slay the beast!"

"Please don't mind her. She has dementia and anophthalmia. It's a difficult combination. Ms. Monroe, leave this lady alone to her prayers."

"She needs more help than God can give. Don't let them take your gifts. Keep them safe."

My strangled voice squeaked, so I nodded at the woman without sight. The nurse waved me off and took Ms. Monroe's hand, leading her out of the chapel.

The universe tried convincing me for the umpteenth time that I needed my powers, my gifts, and to embrace the witch resting inside me. My mind was made up. I did not want that life.

****

As soon as I got home, I packed up every candle, spice, and notebook I owned. I resisted the urge to throw out the taco seasoning. At that point, I knew I had reached my limit.

I called Kim and asked about that week's baskets. She only had two new orders. Layla helped her finish them up. The twins had to be put down, so we talked a few minutes more before saying goodbye. Everything seemed okay with her.

I accidentally woke up Amy from an impromptu nap. She thanked me for waking her ass up.

"I can't believe Kim is a mom. She looks great," Amy commented.

"I post pictures of her all the time. You always liked those posts?"

"I know, but it's not the same as seeing someone in the flesh. I feel so silly for letting a stupid grudge get between us for this long."

"Tell me again, what changed?"

"Every time you mention her, a little part of me cries. At the moon festival, the fortune teller turned over a card and told me to rely on friendships and fix the ones that are broken. When Kim called me the other day, I knew my fortune came true."

"I'm so happy for you." The unease tightening my muscles still had not lifted. I was the final push for Amy and Kim, without a doubt. They seemed okay for now. Hopefully, it stayed that way. "What are you up to?"

"Work until six, then nothing. You?"

"I could really use the company if you don't mind driving over here."

"I never mind."

I checked on Ray last. My finger hesitated over his name on my phone. I checked his social media, and luckily, he had posted something new about an hour ago. He held up what looked like a cartoon hammer, oversized and inflatable, in front of a slender sign stretching taller than him. I had forgotten about the carnival that happened every year in the fall.

I wondered who took the picture. Perhaps one of his students or the new girl. He looked happy and most importantly, alive.

Chapter Thirty-Six

"There is no turning back once they are gone. You will have no powers and forfeit your birthright." Arthur's words repeated themselves in my every waking thought.

"How's the new guy?" Doctor Greene asked.

"He might be leaving soon."

"Another trip upstate?"

"No, it's complicated. We might have to stop seeing each other."

"I'm sorry. This seems sudden. Did something happen?"

"We want different things." I stared out of Doctor Greene's window at the Hudson River view. Cars buzzed down below on River Road, honking their impatience. I wondered what percentage of people were gifted and never knew it. Did someone steal their powers when their time was up?

"Lena? I'm feeling distant from you. This is not how these sessions should be working. What are you expecting to get out of them?"

"This is the most normal thing I do every week. I don't want to stop."

"Okay, let's talk about your gardening. You haven't mentioned your garden in a few weeks. Did you cut down the perennials and redo your tulip patch?"

"No, I barely touched my garden. I did save two frozen roses from my neighbor's yard. They are safe inside my house."

The click of her pen boomed through the pastel office. I probably shouldn't have used the word *safe*. Maybe that triggered her.

"I don't have a green thumb, but people tell me after the summer you should winterize your garden. Now that you don't have to do the middle-of-the-night sales calls, you might need something to occupy your days."

I nodded. "I started writing again. That's something, right?"

"Yes, oh, I'm so proud of you. Writing is so cathartic."

Not when you are in a daze, pouring your subconscious soul into ink and paper. Another thing that might go away when Arthur stripped my gifts.

"Do you think it's going to be more of a journal or a story, or hey! People self-publish poetry books all the time."

"It's not exactly prose. One day I will let you read some of it. Can I ask you a question?"

"Of course, Lena."

"Have you ever given up something you always had but never really used? I don't mean like an air fryer or an old coat. An important piece of you, that you didn't realize you needed until it was too late."

"My grandmother used to tell me stories from her life. I never wrote any of them down. She died before I realized how much I lost. I miss her a lot." Tears streamed down her face. "Excuse me a minute."

Doctor Greene entered the small ensuite half bath attached to her office. Her answer wasn't exactly what I meant, but I got it.

A part of me believed I was doing the right thing,

but another part sat boldly on my shoulder, tempting me otherwise. I laid my forehead against the glass of the window. Nausea rippled inside me as I stared at the ground below. My decision tore me apart.

"I'm sorry about that. I usually don't get that emotional." Doctor Greene cleared her throat and sat back down in her high-back, leather chair.

"No worries. I apologize for being distant. I have a lot of decisions to make. Once again, I'm at a crossroads."

"I must be honest with you. I thought from our last session this one would be easier. We really connected last week. Now, I don't know if it helped or hurt our working relationship."

"It didn't hurt it. I'm not feeling well, today. I'll do better next week."

"Well, I'm going to give you some homework. Write a list of five things about yourself that make you happy. Try to make them solely about you. It can be a personality trait, a skill, an attribute your friends like about you. You decide but work on it for next week. Maybe we can work on getting you out of this funk with self-love exercises. How does that sound?"

I might be a different person next week, but what the hell, I agreed.

"Thank you, Doctor Greene."

"You're very welcome. I'll see you next Thursday."

I started these weekly sessions because I suffered depression. There were days when I stayed in bed until I had a demo and then went back to bed immediately. Ray had noticed the shift when my grandmother moved out. He offered to adopt me a kitten because I had always spoke about how much I loved my cat from high school.

I turned him down. After Arthur stripped me of my powers, what will remain? Will the depression come back?

"Lena?"

"What?" I sounded curt, but I hadn't meant it.

"You were zoned out."

"I'm crazy tired. I need some blacked-out shades and food festival coma sleep."

"Over the weekend, the local college is having a food truck promotional event. Check it out. I heard a truck is making a sandwich with fifteen different lunch meats and cheeses. It will stop your heart, but the taste might be worth it."

"I'll think about it. Bye, Doctor Greene."

****

Arthur and I arrived separately at the moon festival. I left my session with Doctor Greene, and Idalia handled the shop for Arthur. While I drove around for a parking space, the full moon festival already felt different than the new moon one.

"A full moon works best for this type of thing. We both will be at our strongest." Arthur's words infiltrated all my thoughts. I will never forget any of them.

He stood where he said he would, leaning beneath a swaying willow tree. I parted the dangling branches, but he wasn't alone. His friend, Carter, smoked a rolled cigarette and spoke in a language I didn't understand. Arthur answered him in the same tongue, and Carter hit the side of the tree bark with his fist.

"Hey, what's going on?" I interrupted.

Arthur's weak smile destroyed me. Carter never looked my way.

"Lena, you're right on time," Arthur said. He

checked his watch, then frowned at Carter. "Dude, you can't go in without a ticket."

"Watch me." Carter dropped the roach to the ground, smushed the tip of his boot on it, and fisted a path through the branches.

"Hot head!" Arthur screamed. "Are you ready?"

"Not after that spectacle. What the fuck happened? What language was that?"

"Don't worry about him. We were speaking Armenian. I rent the psychic shop from his aunt, so they have been teaching me."

"You sound fluent to me. How many languages do you speak?"

"About five."

"Shit, I barely understand Spanish and took it all through high school."

"When you're in my line of work, languages come up."

"Why was Carter mad?"

Arthur walked toward me and placed his hands on my cheeks. "He's jealous."

"Ha-ha, of what?"

"Usual shit. Money, cars, video games, getting laid. His envy isn't healthy."

"You told him about us?"

He shrugged, then stretched his arms up over his head, grabbing onto a lower branch. "Anything I say is going to come out fucked. Forget Carter. We need to get supplies and go back to your place before the full moon is the highest in the sky."

"All right, you got the tickets?" Arthur nodded. I turned to go, but he stayed under the tree. "Arthur?"

"Are you sure you want to go through with this?"

Arthur asked.

"I'm positive. Why did we come all the way down here? We could have visited Vanessa's again."

"She would have talked you out of today."

"That makes me feel great!"

The stress build-up killed me already. My hair had a freshly turned white strand every day. More strands turned in the past two days. Before the end of the year, I would be a tense skunk.

I walked ahead, joining the crowd dressed in black and various costumes. Arthur caught up, placing a hat on my head. I looked up at the woven brim.

"This is your last night as a witch. You should dress like one at least once."

I left the black hat on and checked it out with the camera on my phone. The cute witch's hat had a subtle conical point at the knitted top. It wasn't made from the cheap, threadbare shit like a little girl's Halloween costume. Effort went into it. I liked how it hugged my head.

The crowd grew behind us, wrapping around the campgrounds and back along the road. My crisis morphed into nervousness. I chewed at my thumbnail, ignoring my confidence affirmations.

"If it makes you feel any better, my ex, Stevie, got panicky before any spell. Fear held her back from going too far."

"Except the night she almost drowned."

"Yes, but I knew nothing then. I didn't know I could have helped her."

"Like you're doing for me?"

"Yes, Lena. You're safe with me."

He held my hand for the last few minutes in the line.

Even though our uncertain future hung in the balance, my stomach fluttered. I rested the side of my head against the sleeve of his light jacket.

Different ladies than last time checked our tickets and handed us bracelets. There were no runes this time blessing our passage. There were no girls with flower petals in the beginning section. The booths were jammed with potential buyers, grabbing at everything sparkling or twinkly. Laughing, crying, chanting, drumming, and a metal spoon beating against a skillet almost like a heartbeat overstimulated me. I bumped into a naked man dipped in red latex paint except for a skimpy thong and devil horns. I muttered an apology, but his all-black gaze pierced my soul. He held up his fingers, making a V over his mouth, fluttering the tip of his tattooed tongue.

"Back off, asshole. She apologized," Arthur shouted.

"Drain, witch, drain!" the Satan said. He grabbed his forked tail and wagged it in my face before scurrying off, skipping through the mob of people.

"Prick, they ruin it for everybody."

"What did he say?"

"Ignore him. We have to go." Arthur tugged my hand, but I stood my ground. My heartbeat raced in my head, my legs became jelly, and fear made my spine straight as a pole. "Lena?"

"Your sister told me that phrase at the party. What the fuck does it mean?"

"Nothing, it means shit." Arthur looked down at the ground, already littered with pieces of trash.

"You're lying."

"Fuck, fine, he can sense you're at your end. He's being a dick about it. Carter knows too. He's jealous because he has no magical ability. I can't give him your powers. No one has that kind of force."

I backed away from Arthur, checking over my shoulder. The booths to my right burned incense, igniting a sneezing fit. Arthur caressed my back, but I flinched away. "Do you need me to get what you want? Can I go sit by the beach?"

"As long as you don't go for a midnight swim."

"I won't."

"I'll call you soon."

Sobs stuck in the back of my throat the entire walk toward the beach. When I reached the edge of the water, tears streamed down my cheeks. My make-up burned my tear ducts as I wiped away the salty mess. I loved the new moon faire. The full moon faire felt wrong the moment I parked my car.

"Can I sit with you?" Carter appeared out of nowhere. He held his hands up in surrender. "I'm sorry about before." The end of each word curled into his accent I hadn't noticed before.

"Apology accepted. Sure, join me."

"Thanks. Where is Artie?"

"Shopping for my demise."

"He's such a twat. Did he tell you it might not work?"

A firecracker shot into the sky, disappearing into the surrounding trees.

"No, what the fuck does that mean?"

"I may be a card-carrying trickster, but I'm honest. He tried this before on an ex-girlfriend. Something went wrong, and she went crazy. She ran into the ocean as if she could swim to the other side. I swam after her and saved her. Stevie was a frail thing in the time he spent with her. She would eat and make feasts, but her mouth would shut. A curse befell her, and to save her life, her powers were lifted but plunged her into madness."

"Arthur won't let that happen to me."

"What makes you think that? Because you two fucked? He wanted to marry Stevie, and yet it still went haywire." Carter shook his head back and forth. He threw a stone, which did the most skips on the calm water I had ever seen.

I buried my head in my hands. I wanted to scream and rake my jagged nails down my cheeks until I begged for mercy.

"I'm not trying to upset you," Carter said. He placed a hand on my shoulder.

"No, just a friendly warning, right?"

"He was convinced you were the one for him, his match. Now, he's torn like before."

"Carter, please stop talking."

"Be careful, Lena." Carter stood in front of me and lifted the brim of my hat. He kissed my forehead along my hairline.

He kept walking along the beach, producing stones out of thin air, skipping them across the lake.

I felt more lost than ever. I texted Arthur, and he answered right away. I found him with two bags full of stuff, reeking of oregano.

He was ready, not like me.

Chapter Thirty-Seven

I made it home in a flash. The time with Amy took
forever. Now, the distance vanished. I talked it out, over
and over, until my subconscious pleaded for mercy. My
powers would be gone tonight.

Arthur followed me into my house. The contents of
the shopping bags clinked and clanged in the plastic.

"Where is the large stock pot?"

I pointed to the counter by the refrigerator. Arthur
blew into it and slid it onto my stove's back burner.

"The forest findings?"

I kept the bag out on the small porch. I combined his
and mine. There was no way I was keeping it in the
house. I glided open the deck door. The bag reeked
strong enough that I gagged twice.

"The oils will dilute the smell."

I sat down at my kitchen table, watching Arthur set
up. His precise, methodical placement of things into the
stock pot calmed my nerves. At least he looked like he
knew what he was doing.

"Shit, I almost forgot. Can you fill your tub upstairs
with water?"

"Hot or cold water?"

"Hot water. It will cool down by the time you lay in
it."

"If I accidentally drown, I'm haunting your ass."

He stopped his fidgeting. "Your head only needs to

be submerged for a few seconds. You will be under less time than it takes to swim up from jumping off a diving board." His voice wavered as his eyes looked up at the ceiling.

"Do I need to be naked?"

"It's not necessary."

Arthur turned his back to me. The objects pinged against the metal of the pot. I left the room, reeking of sour yeast, and itched the inside of my ear.

"The less you know, the better." Arthur's bedside manner sucked.

I slipped off my flats in their usual spot at the bottom of the stairs. My body weighed a thousand pounds as I sulked up the stairs to my bedroom. I had showered the past few days and not used my separate tub. The usual water stains and grime ringed the porcelain. Arthur must wait for a clean tub.

I got down on my knees and scrubbed the tub until it shined. I did it again and repeated the process until Arthur called my name. I pitched back when Arthur's reflection in the clear water caught me off guard.

"Sorry, Lena." His knees cracked as he joined me on the floor. "I have to ask you a serious question."

"Am I going to have a heart attack before the end of the night? The answer is yes."

"Please, stop joking around. I need to know if you have ever had any suicidal thoughts. It's very important that I know the truth."

"No, I never had any."

Arthur exhaled hard. "Thank you for letting me know. Once the tub is filled halfway, please come back downstairs."

I nodded. Arthur took my hand in his and kissed the

top. We hardly discussed the fact that after tonight, Arthur and I would no longer be together. He called it, pushing me away after the first time. I hadn't listened.

My reflection in the clear water blurred. Since the whole thing started, my reflection never felt like mine. I turned off the water.

I rejoined Arthur in the kitchen. He sat at my dinette, stringing stones onto a wool string. The smooth stones had different-sized holes in the middle of them, almost like the deep-end buoys in the town pool.

"What are those?"

"They have many names. I will be protected from you in case anything weird happens."

"How about handcuffs? Why don't you knock me unconscious?"

Arthur rolled his eyes. "I'm going to miss you." He frowned and extracted more items from the bags. The next item was a small crystal ball mounted on top of a wooden nest. The smooth twigs lacked any varnish or paint. It looked like a wild dinosaur egg if I hadn't known better.

"Another for your collection?"

"We can discuss later. Lena, are you willingly allowing me to strip you of your powers? We can also stop now and hit up another movie, or you let me help you as best as I can." I expected anger in Arthur's gaze, but only sadness dulled his tired eyes.

I bit my bottom lip hard and said, "I give my consent to Arthur Prince. Please extract my gifts."

"Very well. I'm not going to record this session. You requested privacy, and I respected that. Please sanitize the tops of your fingers, so we can begin. Part of the extraction spell is in Armenian, another section in

Latin, and the end part will be in English. It's the only way I know how."

I poured a generous amount of rubbing alcohol into the small plastic basin. Arthur clutched his chest for a moment, rubbing his hand over his heart, and took slow, calculated breaths. His nervousness made me squirm in the chair. I hoped one of us knew what the fuck we were doing.

"Sanitized. What next?"

"We begin."

Wind coursed through the kitchen, taking the lights with it. I gasped at my near-dark kitchen. Arthur snapped his fingers, and the small white tealight behind the line of stones lit up. Shadows formed over his face, elongating his eyes, widening his mouth, curving his nose down. Another person gazed back at me from Arthur's seat. I blinked, and he returned to normal. The mirage erased.

"Pasqualena Concetta Martinez has come to this table for freedom. Fear overpowered her. Damage is too great. Grant me the power to help this child release her torment."

My teeth chattered behind my closed lips. My legs bounced up and down. I took small breaths, panting like I'd run a marathon. Arthur stretched out his hand toward me but stayed behind the line of stones. His head flopped forward, and soft murmuring spilled from his mouth.

"Arthur?"

"Shh, you won't understand this part."

The whispers became louder, the chants burrowing a hole in my body. As if I swallowed a stone, my throat grew tight and dry. I gagged, but the fullness in my throat remained.

Arthur shouted, jerking his head upright. The candle flame transformed his blue eyes into black orbs, with no distinction for iris or sclera.

"By the moon, the sun, the crashing waves, the burdened earth, the stubborn beasts, the weightlessness of limbo and purity strangled by sin, fill me enough to burn through the wall and bring her peace. Slice the skin, extract the past, smear the dirt upon the crystal."

I barely noticed the pocketknife on the napkin to the right of me. I cocked my head to the side. "What do I have to do?"

"Make a small cut into each finger. Your powers need an outlet. The fingers are the best way to drain."

Drain, witch, drain. Idalia told me that, and the man dressed like the devil. They knew before I knew my fate. I picked up the sharp serrated knife. The second I breached my skin, the house phone rang.

"Ignore it. Keep going."

"It's my mother. She is the only one who uses that phone."

"Lena, we don't have a lot of time. It's already ten-thirty."

"Why is my mother calling me this late?" I jolted from the chair, picking up the phone from the wall.

"Lena, fuck, you ruined the circle!"

"Mom, is everything all right?"

"Yes, sweetie! I wanted to let you know the albums came! I talked to your uncle about this project, and he thinks it's amazing."

"That's great, Mom. Is there anything else?"

"I'll be over tomorrow unless you have plans with Arthur. He seemed so nice."

He played nice until you called. Arthur held his

forehead in his hands, the flames dancing from his panting.

"Let's do it tomorrow afternoon."

"I'll see you then. Love you, sweetheart."

"Love you too, Mom." I hung up the phone and peeked behind me. "Did that fuck up everything?"

"No, but no more interruptions, please. Sit down." He fluttered his hands and his arms out, getting back into the moment.

I slinked back to the chair and picked up the knife. "Should I redo the first cut?" The nick into the skin didn't even bleed.

"Yes, hold on." He closed his eyes, thumped his hand against his chest, and said, "Now." The deeper slit in my skin pooled with blood. I winced from discomfort. My middle finger hurt worse than the others.

"One hand at a time. Behold her offering. Curl underneath and feast beyond the bone." Arthur held his hands out, palms up. I copied him. Blood dripped down my fingers. Arthur yanked the space between his right hand back to his chest, pulling my messy hand forward to the protection line.

My hand hovering over the table grew heavy. I saw nothing pushing down on it, but my palm descended onto the crystal ball. Blood smeared over the surface. The impenetrable mist hiding the center of the sphere twirled like the storm clouds waiting for the crack of thunder.

When the weight on me lifted seconds later, the copper stench of fresh blood pierced the room, stronger than the adapted smell of the burning pot.

"Pasquelena, do you wish to continue?"

"Yes," I said. My breathless voice came out raspy. Sudden tiredness drooped my eyelids almost closed. I yawned. The light of the candle flickered as all the wax turned liquid.

We repeated the same thing on the other side. The pain in my fingers pulsed and throbbed. I resisted the urge to suck on my fingers like they were mere papercuts instead of self-inflicted slits.

"Please, Moon, lend me your strength to banish these thoughts away. Pasquelena will not partake in any magic from this day forward. Her forfeited gifts will remain encased until needed by another." Arthur placed his thumb in the middle of his chest, over his mouth, then his head. "We need to finish in the tub."

My arms and legs shook, unsteady as I rose from the chair. I felt like collapsing onto the linoleum, a puppet whose strings were cut. "Arthur, help me."

He stared ahead toward the stairs, holding the necklace of stones in front of him, behind me. He whispered again, this time in Latin.

I lifted my shirt over my head and pulled down my jeans. Arthur turned his head for more privacy. If I was his girl, life could be happy, beautiful, and fun. I threw it all away by denying my gifts.

"Step into the water when you're ready."

I held onto the edges of the tub and lowered my trembling body into the cold water. It smarted my skin, almost covering my bent knees. I shivered more than ever. Blood swirled into the water, swimming down to the bottom. My head spun as wooziness took over.

"I don't like this feeling."

"It's almost over. No interrupting."

Arthur spoke in Latin or something other than the first language. The dialect differed entirely. He got to his knees and caressed the side of my hair. That was the first time he touched me since everything got started.

"Arthur," I whispered.

"Breathe, baby. You got this."

The blood looked like eels curling around my submerged limbs. I hardly thought I cut deep, but the crimson poured out the tips of my fingers.

"May the powers invested in you drain into the fount, do not leave one drop."

The light-headedness somersaulted my stomach. I wanted it to stop. I needed relief. My chest rose and fell beneath the water, the stress lost to Arthur. He continued chanting, looking up at the stucco ceiling. As his hands joined above his head, thunder rumbled in the distance. There were no clouds before, only the night sky. It was happening. Something was happening.

I dared closing my eyes, calming my rapid breaths. I panicked worse without my sight. My back slipped down another inch against the back of the tub. My hands jutted out against the sides of the tub, smearing blood above the water. Arthur's heavy palm thrust down, forcing me back into the water. My head slipped under the surface. I inhaled one final breath of air before I sank under.

I tried not to thrash under the gradual increase of Arthur's weight between my breasts. After twenty seconds and his other hand straightening out my knees, I screamed underwater. Arthur's scowl blurred under the bubbles flowing from my open mouth.

The back of my head thumped to the bottom of the tub. I reached for Arthur's hands, clawing at his skin where he held me captive. I should have set an alarm. I should have told my mother. Someone should be here. Amy, Kim, or fucking Idalia could have been a witness.

"*Arthur!*" I screamed underwater. I tasted blood in my closed mouth that wasn't from my bleeding fingers. Tightness weaved through my chest.

Stomach acid burned the back of my throat, but then numbness stripped away all the aches and pains. My terrified body stilled under the water, straightening out as if the sides of the tub vanished. I saw nothing above me, and then I realized my fingers gripped nothing. Arthur no longer held me down.

I wiggled my fingers and each movement got harder as the water thickened. The warm water grew colder by the second. A crackling like warm water poured over cold ice erupted in my ears. The sound lacked the muffled distortion expected underwater. It grew louder as a painful pinching pulled at the skin of my legs.

As if I was buried alive, I jerked and twitched to no avail. No one survived submerged under water that long.

"*Time!*"

Four sets of hands on either side of me lifted my chest from the chilled water. The moment my mouth broke through from the freezing-over surface, I screamed with no sound until my breath came back, blazing through my voice box.

Arthur patted my cheek repeatedly. His fist broke through the ice above my legs, diving down to grab my left leg. A hand from another person thrust their hands in for my other leg. I turned my neck fast enough it cracked through the air. I stared Carter in the face. His round face with thin lips moved back and forth from my gaze to my legs, back up to my mouth.

"We have to get her out of here!" Carter shouted.

The moment I left the water, chills raked through my body bad enough I scrambled to the toilet and vomited pink water until the retching became golden bile. Weakness, as if I had just been born, dictated my actions, sliding me down to the small plushy rug in front of the toilet.

"Lena? Can you hear me?" Arthur whispered.

I heard his hesitant voice, but the shaking stole my voice.

"Dry her off, dammnit! She'll die this way!" Carter shouted. It must have been him, checking my pulse on my wrist.

"She isn't going to die. It just didn't work."

The last part snapped open my eyes. I rose off the floor fast enough. Both Arthur and Carter jumped back from me. "What did you say?"

"Something went wrong. Maybe my rusty pronunciation fucked it up. I don't know. The water should have drained from the tub, not iced over. I couldn't get to you. Oh my God, you're alive. How the fuck are you alive?"

"You let me drown!"

Arthur rushed forward, locking his arms around my back, crushing my face under his neck. "I'm sorry, Lena. I couldn't pull you up. I tried. I've never seen that happen."

"You're lucky to be alive," Carter added.

"What does this mean? Am I still a witch?"

"Yes, your powers wouldn't leave you. They kept you alive instead," Arthur explained.

I stepped back from Arthur's embrace. The front of Arthur and Carter's shirts and jeans were soaked. Carter grabbed a towel from the opened closet and wiped down his clothes.

"Do we try again?" I asked.

Arthur rubbed the terry cloth over my covered arms. "No, we don't. The event has passed. You're mine, forever."

"Who prophesied that nonsense?" Carter twisted the side of his lip up and crinkled his nose.

"Dalia did, several times."

Carter grunted, then a slow, menacing laugh flew out of his mouth. "That bitch will try anything to get a rise out of you. Lena, don't believe that bullshit."

Arthur picked up another dry towel sitting on the bathroom counter. He draped it over my head, rubbing the wet strands like you would for a small child. His breath came out slower.

"What if I want to believe?" I said.

"Then, both of you are fucked," Carter mocked.

Carter threw the towel onto the floor and stomped away. His loud footsteps echoed throughout my home until he slammed the front door shut.

"Oh, Lena. I knew you were the one." Arthur rested his forehead against mine. The first time he did it, it felt weird and right at the same time. Now, the universe brought us together, and I needed to stop fighting it.

Chapter Thirty-Eight

Six months before my grandmother died, she commissioned two boys from the neighborhood to build a deck off the kitchen. I counted the number of times I sat out here on one hand. Rain fell in the backyard, but my must-have addition to the project, a retractable awning off the side of the house, shielded me.

Tonight wasn't Arthur's fault. I was disappointed to a degree. My entire life, I oscillated between wanting and running from this gift. Well, tonight, my gift fought back. It wanted *me*.

The button on my vape pen glowed red. I charged it yesterday, but I kept taking drag after drag. The tingles of the THC running through my legs distracted me from what unfolded tonight. I smoked one last puff too long and sputtered my coughs.

The screen door opened, and Arthur joined me out on the deck. He placed a mug of hot chocolate on the glass table and sipped from his own cup when he sat next to me. He loved me already. I knew that for certain.

"I'm sorry, Lena."

"It's okay."

The enhanced taste of the hot chocolate against my tongue made all my regrets fade away. I passed the dying pen over, and Arthur took a drag.

"It's dying. I'll go get mine." Arthur disappeared back into the house.

My lips curled around the warmed edge of the cup. I felt dry, but my damp hair chilled my scalp. My grandmother's voice rang in my head, "You'll catch a chill in that wet hair. Throw on a hat." I flipped the hood of my hoodie over my hair.

Arthur returned with a smile on his face. "I always envisioned the woman for me would be someone I could smoke a joint with on a back porch."

"I guess that's me."

After we both were high and warmed up from the hot chocolate, Arthur clasped our fingers together. The awkward heave of something unnatural zapped through our hands. I placed my empty mug on the glass table and tugged Arthur up with me. He followed like an obedient, quiet puppy scurrying behind me.

I grabbed the box of coarse-grained salt from my pantry. The neighbor across the street gave it to me as a housewarming welcome, along with some bread in an ornate basket. Many times, I tried using it, but I always placed it back on wooden shelves covered with floral shelf-liners.

Arthur pointed at the box.

I shrugged. "It couldn't hurt," I said.

His tight nod left no room for questions. He confused me how one minute he knew what I needed, but the next time he looked bothered by my decisions and actions.

When our hands parted, our bodies took over. Arthur walked up the stairs behind me, his free hands caressing my hips, keeping us together. At the top of the stairs, he used every bit of his height to advantage. His lips kissed the nape of my exposed neck in my off-the-shoulder sweater as I draped my hand around his head from behind, gripping a tight grasp on his hair.

I broke our embrace, walking slowly into my bedroom. I peeked over my shoulder at the man standing right before the doorjamb. "Aren't you coming?"

"I would be a fool not to come." He passed over the threshold onto my plush carpet. I poured salt around my queen-sized bed. He hesitated before stepping over the spilled protection.

"What?" I asked.

"Old habits."

I kneeled on the bed and scooted up to the pillows. I poured the remainder of the salt behind my headboard, covering every inch around the bed. I threw the empty box toward the small trash can near my closet and missed. It didn't matter because Arthur's lips were on my body again. I gripped the upholstered headboard as he seized the side of my neck with his mouth. He ate my gasp when his thighs wrenched my legs open from behind and nestled his groin against my ass. His long fingers traced lines on the back of my legs, beginning at my heel and ending at the hem of my shorts. There he ground his hardened cock against my ass.

"Arthur," I moaned.

"Shhh, we can't stop now."

We were past all reason and doubt. His ruthless grip on my hips different then the passive caresses he gave me the other times we fucked. I wanted both sides of him right now.

My hips thrust backward. Breathless moans from him, and cries from me echoed throughout the room. Arthur halted our frenzy. The strength in his forearm molded my back to his toned chest.

"Lena, listen to me." *How could I not?* His teeth

nipping my earlobe left me no choice. "Do you hear me?"

I stopped my futile bucking against his hold. "I never stopped."

His chuckle pulsed down his body, reverberating onto mine. The twitch of his cock against my covered sex pinned me. "You're a good witch, aren't you? Tell me you will be a decent, caring witch."

"Yes, I am."

"I don't believe you." Arthur eased off me like a shadow retreating from the light.

I whipped around, shoving off the headboard. He couldn't leave the circle. I needed him in here, inside with me.

Arthur's ass sat on the back of his calves. He lifted his shirt off over his head, clutching the taut skin above his heart. I swore tiny bruises appeared as if invisible thumbs dug into him right before my eyes.

"What's happening?" I tried touching him, but he flinched backward.

"They are trying to stop me. I made it across your threshold, I walked over the salt, I mean you no harm."

"Art, who are they?

One bruise went too far, choking a whimper out of his mouth. A red circle appeared where his liver should be.

"I'll remove every rib to be with her. You can't stop it."

I helplessly mirrored his position on the bed. We reminded me of the candles, those red candles I burned halfway once representing Ray and me. *Maybe I had the wrong couple?*

The bruises on Arthur's body turned into purple

welts, and some of them red, glistening in the pale light. His head fell back, and he shouted at the ceiling.

Fear like I had never known seized my body and stole my breath. Gusts of wind rippled the thick strands of my hair around my face. My heart thudded in my chest, no longer from desire but from dread. I peeled back the mask my hair created, and swift movement above me compelled my gaze upward.

Whomever *they* were, they swirled close to the ceiling, outlining the circle of salt. Tattered, black shrouds covered their bodies, and their long hair, dark like the feathers of a raven, cloaked their faces. Six pairs of blood-red lips widened and stretched into vicious grins.

In any other circumstance, their floating might be beautiful. An unearthly split in time, space, and gravity allowing such a mystical occurrence to be seen by the naked eye. Six beings stopped by the coarse-grained salt. I played the game by Arthur's rules, surrounding us with the simple condiment. His self-made commandments protected us.

A seventh being, the most haggard of them, flew out of the gold-encrusted mirror resting on my vanity. Her hair whiter than the inside of a coconut. Idalia smelled like dried coconut flakes every time I saw her, but her powers couldn't be strong enough for this display of magic. Besides that, the witch's skin looked as if it had been wrinkling for a thousand years.

Soft, warm hands caressed my cheeks, hauling me out of my mind. Arthur's sweet face, with tears twinkling in his eyes, hovered in front of me. The bruises on his body remained, but the bright red ones were snuffed out.

"Lena, promise me, you will never dip your toe in

the river. You won't push further than we are tonight. Please, stay in the light. Be content with the fruits feeding you. I need you to be mine. Never pure, but always good."

I peeked up at the ceiling where the witches flew. They were gone. Arthur and I sat alone on the bed.

"I promise," I said. I meant those two binding words. I avoided the magical part of me every day of my life until desperation forced me back. I was in it now. I was a witch.

We inched our faces closer, and when our lips touched, we fell to the mattress ready for what might stop us next.

Chapter Thirty-Nine

Arthur tore my shorts down my legs, and I yanked
his sweatpants down. His lips only left my skin for
seconds before he kissed and nipped his way until his
mouth found my heaving breasts. He bit my puckered
nipple as I strained against the weight of his body.

Water boiled in a teakettle two homes down,
flooding the air with a sharp whistle mimicking a melody
I had heard before. A woman wailed in agony in a pink
hospital room somewhere. Children murmured prayers
kneeling by the foot of their beds, clutching their
treasured stuffed animals. Metal scraped against a car as
a drunk man misjudged the long meridian separating east
and west.

Arthur bit down on my flushed flesh. "If I make you
moan, will the noises stop?"

"Yes, bring me back."

He clutched the headboard with one hand, arching
his upper body off me. He flashed me a cocksure side
grin right before he held his dick in his hand, thrusting
inside me. I stopped breathing, digging my nails into the
soft skin of his hips. When I placed my feet flush on the
bed, meeting the jerking of his body, Arthur threw his
head back, moaning to the sky.

"I thought you were supposed to make me moan?"

Arthur flipped his face back to me, arching his
eyebrow up. His cock settled deep within my body,

pulsing with each small flinch of his hips. "You are going to be the death of me." He fell flush against my heated chest and lifted my left leg over his shoulder. "I'll fucking make you moan."

His thumb found my clit between our sweat-drenched bodies, rubbing as fast as he could and still thrust inside me. Pleasure, sharp like the blade cutting through my fingertips earlier, pierced by my psyche, my soul, right through my heart. I caressed his shoulder blades, flexing hard with each fast thrust until I fisted his hair above the nape of his neck. A low whimper flew out of Arthur's mouth. He was close to losing the battle waging inside him.

I didn't care about my orgasm. I wanted every bit of him to be obliterated. I wanted his heart flayed open, his soul reborn, the witch struggling to be freed to lash out at me insisting on taking over.

"Arthur, look at me."

His blue eyes iced over just like his sister's. I never asked if it was a good or bad thing. *Dammnit, why didn't I ask?*

Crystalized snowflakes replaced every spec of deep blue. Air sucked into his throat casting forth a hollowed growl above me. "Arthur?"

"I love you, Lena."

Arthur's lips sealed over mine, replacing his lost breath with mine. The headboard smashed into the wall with the strength of our fucking. We screamed our releases. The inferno from the first time we kissed flared strong enough I was surprised actual flames didn't flicker between us. He tore his lips away from mine.

I sucked in fresh air for the first time in minutes. It burned my throat as if I tunneled through a wormhole, clawing my way to the other side.

Arthur buried his head into my shoulder. I wanted his weight on top of me and his twitching cock inside me forever.

The fire alarm downstairs broke the spell. A second later, the alarm in the upstairs hallway sounded. Arthur pushed off me and gritted his teeth.

"Not again. Do you have a fire extinguisher?"

I nodded. We disentangled our bodies in the least sexy way. He pulled on his boxers, and I slipped on my clothes from earlier. Arthur held my hand as we stormed down the stairs looking for fire. The living room was dark. All the candles sat still with their glass and metal lids.

"Where is it?" I shouted.

Arthur pulled me toward the kitchen. Orange light flickered over his face, then I saw it. My table, scorched from the long-ago love spell, raged with flames. The fire, oddly enough, stayed contained to the circle in the center. No smoke flew out of the crackling blaze.

"Are you doing this?" I asked. Arthur nudged me close, my head resting on his chest over his frantically beating heart.

"Maybe."

We watched the flames dancing before us as if we sat outside on a cold night, mesmerized by a simple bonfire. There was nothing normal about this burning table. The ceiling above it did not blacken, no warmth radiated from it, but the roar tore me out of Arthur's embrace, jamming my fingers in my ears.

Arthur wrapped his strong arms around me, running his fingers through my frizzy hair. I got momentary relief from his embrace. Perhaps fear gripped me, or the natural reaction to uncontrolled fire moved my body away from Arthur, further from the table.

"Lena, we have to do something."

I read his lips more than heard him. I barely thought about his love proclamation upstairs. Even though I hadn't said the words, every bit of my being wanted him.

"What?"

"This is another test! We have to protect ourselves." Arthur grabbed my cheeks, and I held onto his wrists. "Our powers," he kissed me, "our love!"

"How?"

A horrible habit from childhood presented a great idea. I bit the cracked, dried skin on the side of my fingernail. After I got a good firm piece between my front teeth, I pulled back, wincing at the sharp pain of my flesh ripping open. Of course, the hole of my torn skin drew down past my nail. Blood pooled where it ended.

I used my other hand and removed the fresh slice from between my teeth. "Does this suffice?"

Arthur stared as if I sprouted another head while I mutilated my body. Each shocked expression, jerking of his neck, wringing of his hands made me believe him more of his innocence with witchcraft. He nodded and popped a piece of gum into his mouth. "Do you have a nail clipper?"

I ran to the bathroom downstairs through the living room. I threw open the medicine cabinet and grabbed the metal clipper. My feet flew through the space back to Arthur.

Wind whipped through the kitchen without the aid of an open window. We were running out of time. Arthur snatched the nail clipper from my opened hand, clipping off two of his longer fingernails.

"We must get closer. Throw the pieces of us into the fire."

"What will it do?"

"We'll fight about it later."

"That's not a good answer!" I shouted. I raised my voice over the howling wind. The gusts intensified while my patience felt thin. My hair flew around my face, my body pushing back. Arthur's hair swished over his forehead over and over.

"We will be bound together, forever. Your witch and mine. It worked. We made it!"

"What if we break up?"

"There will never be an if."

Arthur snatched the piece of my cuticle out of my hand and threw both pieces of us into the flames. The absent heat ignited throughout the room. Thick black smoke bounced off the ceiling, radiating out the center of the table. Arthur and I submitted to the coughing fits, prying our bodies apart.

"*Arthur!*"

My sight abandoned me, and my heart pounded. I flailed my hands in front of me where Arthur stood a second ago. I felt nothing, only smoke. I tried taking a step forward, but the wind catapulted me backward away from the sink and the window.

This energy could not remain in the house. If I learned one thing throughout the past few weeks, it was that I had to release it. The ache in my body tried diverting me, but my will fought it.

"*Lena, help me!*"

Arthur's voice boomed from my right near the sliding door. As if I walked through a thousand pounds of cement weighing down my legs, I barely stepped in the direction of his voice. I shielded my face with my left hand and reached out with my right. An ice, cold hand grabbed my own, propelling me forward.

The front of my body slammed into the thick glass sliding door. Arthur maneuvered my hands onto the door handle.

"*Pull!*" Arthur screamed, or at least that's what I imagined he said.

I fumbled for the lock. It was thrown to the left side. We just needed to slide the door open with all our might.

The full moon shined through the glass, illuminating my simple yard. Beyond the small deck, the seven shrouded figures stood once again. One of them pushed back their hood. White hair flowed wild behind her.

Upstairs, I thought them as foes. Now every fiber of my being whispered to trust them. They were there to help. The white-haired one, resembling Arthur's sister, rushed through the air hovering above the wooden planks until she lowered herself outside the glass. She parted the curtain of her hair. For a second, I saw a beautiful woman with her eyes closed. The wrinkles were gone, her lips full and parted, and her long eyelashes fluttered. As her eyelids pulled up, she morphed into an old hag with her skin hanging off her bones.

I screamed, pulling at the door. Adrenaline and terror infused my last tug enough that the door opened. The smoke, the fire, the magic slammed into the old woman, pushing her back to the grass. She absorbed every piece of the inferno.

Arthur grabbed me around my waist, turning me toward his chest. He bent at the knees, looking at me eye to eye, speaking something in my face. He cupped my cheeks, shaking me slightly, urging me to do something or not to do. I shook my head back and forth.

He kept one of his hands on the side of my face, rose to his tall height, and kissed me. I wanted to drown in the kiss that didn't quite make sense now. I couldn't. I pulled my lips away, looking outside for the woman.

Nothing stared back at me. I spun around toward the outdated kitchen. Nothing was out of place. The ceiling was back to its ugly shade of yellow. The table remained on the side of the kitchen with all four chairs pushed in. The bowl, hiding the burn marks from the love spell, sat in the middle.

One last blood-curdling screech shifted my focus back outside. The stench of coconuts flooded my senses. The white-haired woman stood under the full moon in the middle of the yard. She waved her hand through the air staring at me, and then faded away.

"We did it!" Arthur jumped up and down, happiness bursting out of him. I had no emotion from the last few minutes. Nothing at all.

"Did that just happen?" I asked.

"Yes, baby, all of it. We won. You're mine, and I'm yours. Nothing can break the spell. We are one." He kissed me, breathing through his nose, warming my cold skin. "How are you cold, my love?"

"I don't know."

The worst drop I had ever experienced threatened to close my eyes and make me faint on my feet. Before I crumbled to the floor, Arthur scooped me up into his arms as if I weighed nothing. "I got you. You're mine, Lena."

I used the last of my strength to remain conscious until Arthur placed me gently on my side of the bed. He walked right through the line of salt. I fell asleep staring at the tiny salt particles dispersed into the carpet, hoping we were still protected.

Chapter Forty

Sun beams sneaked through the slits in the blinds, shining across my face. I had forgotten about releasing the looped tassel holding the darkening shades captive against the window frame on the right side of the room. The sun set on that side of my house. I slept the day away.

It was four o'clock in the afternoon. I yawned while the crazy events of last night played back in my mind. Arthur no longer laid beside me. The pillow he used remained crinkled in the middle as if he'd slept there for years instead of hours. His presence lingered as if his arm still caressed my skin. My dented side of the old mattress tempted me into laying back down.

I found my cell phone underneath my pillow. I had no memory of how it got under there. With the little battery life I had left, a mere six percent, I checked my messages. I had nothing new from Arthur, Kim, or Amy. No one had checked in.

"They must be jealous," a voice whispered in my foggy head. My bed sat in the middle of my bedroom. There was no one else here. I dismissed the wayward thought as tiredness.

A spasm from my lower back climbed toward my shoulder blade. I bowed my spine, working out the tight muscles. I had never experienced a surge of energy like that before, but the first night as a witch forever had consequences.

As the pain receded inside my body, I sat up away from the warmth of my bed. The faint aroma of our lovemaking mingled with salt lingered under my nose. I checked the tips of my fingers. The cuts clotted, but once I consciously saw the jagged lines, my stomach gurgled.

The sense of dread remained as I changed my clothes and stripped the dirty sheet off the bed.

Each stair creaked beneath my feet. I hardly noticed the old wood moaning in my daily routine before Arthur came into the picture.

"Arthur?" I cried out. He wasn't in the kitchen or the main living room. I checked the downstairs bathroom, too.

When I inspected outside and saw his car in the driveway, panic bubbled beneath my skin. I ran throughout the yard, the garage, and back through the entire house, including the basement. No trace of Arthur remained in my house.

The mess of last night cluttered every inch of counter space in the kitchen. In one swift jerk of my arm in mid-air, all of Arthur's supplies scattered to the floor. Glass broke, I sneezed at the combination of herbs and spices, and the last of the vinegar trickled across the slanted floor.

I jumped over the pile, not processing how I cleared my countertop with magic and ran back upstairs for my phone.

"The number you have reached has been disconnected."

"The number you have reached has been disconnected."

"Hi, this is Jemma. Thank you for reaching back out

to us. Please leave your name and number so we can get back to you about your car's extended warranty."

Arthur, Idalia, and the number for their shop were gone. Every phone number gone. I searched their shop on the internet with zero results. The truth stabbed me in the gut as I pulled up the group photo from the trash-the-dress party. Idalia had leaned against the counter and held up a peace sign when we toasted to freedom. The original photo had changed. She was gone, and another woman took her place sitting at a table with a crystal ball in front of her. The mystery woman's hands were folded on the black tablecloth, with an uncomfortable side smile frozen on her face.

I slumped down to the floor, lifeless. *What the fuck was happening?*

Amy answered on the first ring. "Hey lady, what's going on."

"I lost my mind."

"Did the date go that bad?"

Fuck, they already got her. "What date?"

"The guy buying your communication program. You said you were meeting him last night for drinks."

I panted into the phone. "Amy, tell me exactly what I told you and when."

"Hold on a second. I'm getting a pedicure."

I considered how long it took a person to hyperventilate. Last night happened. Everything happened. I committed every second with Arthur to my memory. It fucking happened.

"Sorry, hun. I'm back. I had to switch chairs because the jets weren't working."

I thumped the back of my head back and forth against the puckered edge of the mattress.

"You called me last night asking me to text you around nine o'clock for an escape if the date was dull. I texted you, and you said you were good. You were having fun."

"I'll call you back." I didn't wait for her response. In black and white, Amy's text checking in on me stared back from my phone. A missed call from her and an incoming call from yesterday. I never made or picked up any of those calls.

She rang me again, but I was already in my car, driving a town over to Arthur's magic shop. The Open sign pulsed with purple and black LED lights. It used to be red lights. I charged out of my car, up the brick steps, and without knocking, entered the shop.

A woman yelped in front of me. The tray she held flew into the air, along with all the stones and merchandise on it. I jammed my palms over my ears. The stones scattering over the hardwood floors stirred my nearing migraine.

"You scared the shit out of me! Do you have an appointment?" the fortune teller asked. She looked like she wandered off a vintage carnival train car, a sheer scarf shielding the bottom half of her face as well.

I held the frustrated beast back as I took in the room. Instead of the crimson décor, everything matched the purple and black color palette. *Where did all the red go?* My feet took me past the cheap purple beaded curtain toward where Arthur's large television was, but a desk with a three-tiered tray holding essential oils took up the space.

"Miss, if you don't get out of my home, I will call the cops," the rent-a-gypsy said.

"Where are they?"

"Look, I don't keep much money in the cash register. Most people nowadays pay with credit card. There is nothing special here to steal."

I shook my head back and forth, growling my frustration. "Enough of this crap. I'm not here to rob you, and I don't want to see the letter of my true love in the wrinkles of my thumb. I need answers, lady. Where is Arthur Prince?"

The lady stopped backing away. Her delicious fear coursed through the room. I frightened her. *Good job on my part.*

"The name sounds familiar. Do you know him? Is he your counselor?" The skin between her eyebrows cinched in with deep lines across her forehead.

I exhaled and massaged the aching space above my breasts. "I'm sorry, I barged in here. It was a rough night. I'm not on drugs. I need to find Arthur Prince or Idalia Prince."

Recognition sparked behind her gaze. "Oh child, I'm sorry to say, but Idalia Prince is dead. She and a local boy drove off the Sparman bridge last night. The boy was a professor at the college a few minutes down the road from the accident. They weren't wearing seatbelts, and the police felt like they died as soon as their bodies crashed through the windshield." I stared back at her, void of an emotional response.

I fell to my knees. Hysteria bubbled inside of my mind. "What was the name of the boy?"

The woman's hand shook as she jammed her hand into her skirt pocket. She took out her phone and typed. Once she found the story, she tiptoed closer, shining the bright screen in my face.

The photo of Ray's car dangling from the crane

above the water broke me. My choked sob came out as a gasp of breath, then a sonic boom disturbed the air in the house. Glass splintered and cracked the windows, blowing the shards out into the yard.

The woman screamed, dropping her phone. I lunged for it, laying on the floor.

Newly Engaged Couple's Lives Cut Short. I scrolled further down the news website, not exactly absorbing the printed words. The last picture fisted its way down my throat and successfully snatched my heart out of my chest. Ray and Idalia stood in the typical engagement shoot pose. His hand wrapped around her tiny waist while she angled her body and pressed her left hand with the new ring on her finger on his chest.

My aching body curled into the fetal position on the floor. The usual comfort I got from the position obliterated. I was dumbfounded and shattered by the article. *Was it real? How am I lying on the floor of a room that less than a week ago had lush red carpet?*

"If you promise not to hurt me, maybe I can help you? I can take you to Saint Helen's hospital. They have a mental ward there."

I continued reading the article, ignoring the woman's suggestion. "Survived by her father, Arthur Joseph Prince."

Nothing made sense. Arthur and Idalia were twins. Their father died years ago. The journalist must have it wrong. The entire article must be a spell constructed for one purpose only. My final push over the edge into insanity.

I threw the innocent lady's phone across the floor. A thousand-pound invisible creature planted itself on my chest. I barely took a breath, only when my lungs hurt and my eyes watered.

I peeled myself off the floor and attempted to stand. One of the woman's hands stayed behind her back. She had a weapon.

The woman inched closer, but I was already out the door and back in my car by the time she reached the street. "I can help you!"

"No one can help me now," I muttered. I drove to the one place I had left where I felt safe during the daytime. Oddly enough, my mother stood in her driveway waiting for me.

Her happy smile slid away when she saw me. She rushed to the end of the driveway toward my car.

"Lena, your hair? What happened, baby?"

"Mom, I don't know what's happening," I cried. I unbuckled my seatbelt as she opened my car door. She grabbed for my hand. My body felt heavy like a boulder in a shallow lake. I lost the strength needed to stand, breathe, live. I collapsed over my mother's chest, dragging her down to the ground with me.

"*Sean!* I need you! Lena, needs you!" Her shouting trilled through the afternoon air. I covered my ears, cringing in my mother's lap.

My dad ran out of the house, white as a ghost, when he saw us on the ground. He looked at me as if I was a fragile piece of glass. "Should I call 911?"

"No cops. It's witchcraft. I know he did this. His name is Arthur Prince. They escaped. His sister too," I stammered.

"What was the last name?" Dad asked.

"Prince."

My dad cradled his left hand over the right bandaged one in the sling. "Why do I know that name?"

"I knew you were in trouble. Why didn't I go over there? Baby, what's happening?" Mom cried.

"I don't know. I'm so fucking tired. I need to lay down."

"Stay with us! Oh my God, your hair. Look at yourself!"

Mom angled her phone's camera at my face. Under my eyes shined beat red, the roots of my hair frizzed out in white strands, and a cut on my lip I hadn't remembered looked infected. I touched the scab and winced. Raw, unadulterated pain coursed through my body from my head toward my toes.

"Susan, we have do something! What can we do?" Dad yelled.

My mother crouched down, offering me a bottle of water. The flavorless water felt so good down my throat I chugged the whole bottle, crunching the cheap plastic. "I can't let you dehydrate while we figure this out. You must keep drinking."

"Don't worry. We won't let your daughter die."

Static charged the air, snapping between my mother and me. Naturally, she hoisted her body in front of mine, protecting her only child. I peeked from behind her like a small, shy child.

Arthur's mother, Babushka, stood with a lit white candle balanced in her palm. Three perfect rows of women stood behind her mimicking her stance. Someone clapped, and each candle lit itself one by one.

If it was December, these women dressed in black lace, not the sexy kind, but the witch kind, looked like Christmas carolers at the start of their route. Bright eyes and real smiles, and a collective presence thickened the air. My mother and I lifted our arms up, shielding our faces from the wind lashing out from them as if they became one gigantic moth flapping its wings.

"*Stop this now!*" my mother's voice boomed through the air, raspier than any punishment she ever bestowed upon me. The wind stopped as quickly as it started.

Babushka stepped toward us, hunched over on the grass. The short, stout woman wore no smile, her cheeks rosy from makeup only, and her eyelids swollen from tears.

"Sorry for the show. We can't help it. It's all we know," she remarked.

"Please leave my property at once," Mom demanded.

"I don't think you want to do that, Assunta. We need your help. Arthur needs her help."

"Where is he?" A squeaky sound shrieked out of my mouth.

Fresh tears flew down Babushka's cheek. Another woman offered her a handkerchief, and with a hand up, she declined.

"Idalia has him, both of them."

"Who?"

"Oh, my dear. She has Arthur and Ray."

A word about the author...

I'm a marketing analyst by day and a writer by night. I've always wanted to pursue my passion for writing and finally had the guts to do it. I've lived in New York my entire life, and it will always be my home. I live with my husband and my son. https://tootsplusdill.blogspot.com

Printed in the USA
CPSIA information can be obtained
at www.ICGtesting.com
LVHW011618240624
783873LV00012B/747